When They
Took Away the Man
in the Moon

Also by Kate Lehrer

Best Intentions

When They

Took Away the

Man in the Moon

By Kate Lehrer

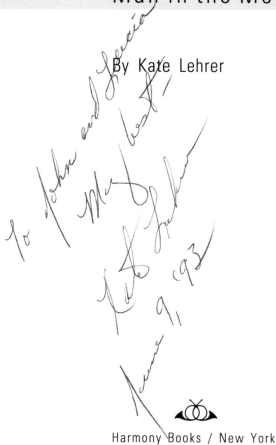

Harmony Books / New York

Published by Harmony Books, a division of Crown Publishers, Inc.,
201 East 50th Street, New York, New York 10022. Member of the Crown
Publishing Group.

Random House, Inc. New York, Toronto, London, Sydney, Auckland

HARMONY and colophon are trademarks of Crown Publishers, Inc.

Manufactured in the United States of America

Library of Congress Cataloging-in-Publication Data

Lehrer, Kate
When they took away the man in the moon / Kate Lehrer.
I. Title.
PS3562.E442W48   1993
813'.54—dc20   92–40764
                                                           CIP

ISBN 0-517-59441-2

10   9   8   7   6   5   4   3   2   1

First Edition

to
Jim

Acknowledgments

I want to express my appreciation to John Deardourff, Barbara Dixon, Albert Hunt, and Bob Squier for their insights into the political consulting world, and to Lewis Nash and Raymond Nasher. I am also grateful to my daughters, Jamie, Lucy, and Amanda, for their constant support and wise suggestions. To John Ferrone, whose invaluable advice kept me going at crucial times; for my agent, Ron Goldfarb, whose enthusiasm and attentiveness never flagged; for my editor, Shaye Areheart, whose perceptiveness, patience, and generous energies made all the difference— my inexpressible gratitude. And, finally, a thank you to those women whose spirit inhabits these pages, including and especially Lily, Mildred, Lucy, Katie, R.A., Polly, and Joan.

When They
Took Away the Man
in the Moon

Prologue

Since Roosevelt died we haven't the heart for the news. We play croquet at the Wellses, and Sheila and I fill a mason jar with lightning bugs until the rain starts. The grown-ups and Sheila hurry to pull the wickets and store away the mallets, but I find a secret place behind a tree. I stand still and feel each raindrop and its slow, spreading wetness on my face and arms. They are magic drops to have always, but I must remember each one and remember the smell of the wet grass and remember the click of the croquet balls or the spell will disappear forever. In my enchanted place, I close my eyes and count up all the numbers I know, then run to set free the fireflies just as the thunder arrives over our heads.

At home, to cheer Mama, Daddy puts "Don't Sit Under the Apple Tree" on the Victrola and says we'll have a party of our own. Mama says some of us have partied enough already. I tell them

1

Sheila doesn't care about Roosevelt, and her parents say good riddance.

"What can you expect from a hick Kentucky town?" Mama asks. "They're all a bunch of damn Republicans." During the Depression Mama worked for the WPA, and she and Roosevelt saved Texas from starving because of the damn Republicans' greedy ways.

"Don't be too hard on them, Sudy. We know a lot of nice people here," Daddy answers and puts his hand on the back of her neck. "You're just homesick for Rollins."

"Then let's move there," I say, calling up aunts and uncles and cousins and picnics and softball and pallets under a million stars. My parents won't fight in Texas, I am sure.

"Your daddy can't leave the farms or the lawsuits, you know that." She sounds out of patience with me.

"We'll make it back," he promises. "It just may take a while."

I poke my toe in a bare spot on the dark red Oriental rug covering the music room floor. Though we are not a musical family, we have a music room because my daddy's aunt Esther left him a parlor grand piano, two violins, and a Victrola. She also left him three farms, two hundred blackberry bushes, and our house, which has enough bedrooms for three aunts and all my cousins to visit at the same time without putting anybody out. We like having family here.

"What color are they?" I want to know.

"What color is what, Miss Reese?" Daddy asks.

"Lawsuits."

Mama laughs louder than Daddy. "At least she's not going to be a genius," she says to Daddy. "You said you didn't want her to be one and she's not."

My mother is always finding reasons why I'm not one. Daddy's brother was a genius and my parents think geniuses come to no good end. That's because they drink themselves to death at an early age.

Daddy kisses me on the cheek and heads for the kitchen.

Mama calls me over to fix my barrettes and pull my hair out of my eyes. When I started first grade, she wanted to cut my hair, but Daddy says she should wait until I'm at least six, that I'm still a little girl even if I do go to school. Because my questions drive Mama crazy, she decided somebody else might as well try to teach me something, so I took a test and started school early.

She fusses with my hair and dress sash until Daddy hands us our drinks and pulls her up to dance though she says no. Then they put me between them and we dance to "A String of Pearls." I am cozy and happy, as I feel the music and Daddy's gray trousers and Mama's soft yellow dress, the starch in it all gone.

My feet stay in time with theirs. My body sways with our laughter. I don't have time to be still and count, but I know this is a magic spell, too. And if I hold this moment in my heart forever and ever, Daddy won't get fussed at and Mama won't be lonely anymore and that minister won't have to come around here all the time to make her feel better.

When Daddy gets bored with the records, he starts singing "Carolina Moon" and waltzes with Mama. The thunder is far away now and can't bother us. My dolls don't mind at all the rain humming with the music. Sometimes when Daddy tells Mama she doesn't love him or Mama yells that he doesn't pay attention to her, my dolls hate it. Then I tell them the stories Daddy and I tell each other. I tell them not to worry when daddies and mamas fight. When they feel better, I put them in their red bunk bed Daddy built.

But tonight none of us have anything to worry about. Now we are all part of a happy story, one we'll make happier and happier. The minutes stop still so that each one fills up the world, and when it is brimming with so much gold joy, it spills over into the next and then the next until we live happily ever after.

"Carolina moon keep shi-ih-ih-ning," Daddy sings to Mama.

"We have a Kentucky moon," I say just to remind him I'm still here.

3

"So it is," he answers and lifts me up. "And we should take a ride to see our Kentucky June moon." He starts singing another song about June-moon-spoon and whirls me around and grabs Mama and we all go round until we collapse on the floor in giggles.

"Come on, Sudy. Let's go take a fine ride. We'll show H.A. the man in the moon."

"There is no moon out, let alone the man in the moon," she answers, not really minding his mistake. "It's raining, re-member?"

Daddy looks disappointed. He puts me down so he can loosen his tie, his starched white shirt as fresh as when he put it on. He and Mama both are proud of his flat stomach and both worry that his hair is thinning in front.

He and I have the same fair skin except he doesn't have freckles. Sheila's mother says we look alike, though it isn't always so good for daughters to look like their fathers, even handsome fathers, and I would have done better to take after my dark, fiery mother. Still, Mrs. Bascom thinks I should feel lucky to belong to such a romantic couple and live in a storybook house. My mama says what is lucky is that my daddy has a banged-up knee and doesn't have to go to war.

"We'll see the moon another night," I promise him. Both my parents laugh.

"Tell you what," he answers, "tonight we'll read a story about the moon."

But we can't find a moon story, so he makes one up about the man in the moon coming down to earth just to make a little girl with golden curls and gray eyes happy, but he must return to his home before the moon is full. The man in the moon explains that though he will disappear for a while, the little girl must not give up hope of seeing him again, for the moon always comes back. And just as the moon has its cycles, we have them in our lives, too. We have sad times, but happy ones always follow. That night the little girl slept soundly because she knew she didn't have to worry about the moon's return, and she thanked the man in the moon for teaching her such a good lesson about hope. So the moon's coming and going has made people all over the world feel better for thousands and thousands of years, more people and more time than we can imagine. My father finishes sooner than I want.

"Is that stuff about the moon true or part of the story?" I ask.

"Mostly true."

"How do you know?"

"Because I'm nosy like you. Now, start dreaming quick. You and I have a big day in Cincinnati tomorrow. After you see the eye doctor, I have a surprise."

As soon as he leaves, I hear my parents' raised voices and I pull the pillow over my head. I wonder if we will see lawsuits in Cincinnati.

✳

"You girls want an ice cream cone?" Bennie asks. He is Sheila's daddy, and Sheila is my best friend. They have come with Daddy and me to Cincinnati. Mama says Bennie is a drunk and is a bad influence on Daddy. This morning before we left, Mama made Daddy promise he'd behave himself and me promise I'd behave myself and mind him. I say I don't want an ice cream cone because I'm going blind.

Daddy is holding my hand. "You aren't going blind. Your eyes are dilated. The doctor told you the drops will wear off in a few hours."

"Come on," Sheila says. "I'll tell you the flavors."

"You can't read," I say. Sheila hates it that I already go to school and she doesn't.

"I can so," she answers. "Chocolate, vanilla, strawberry . . ."

Daddy and Bennie laugh. They're getting ready to have a good time.

"I want to go home."

"Tell you what, we'll skip the ice cream and go straight to the surprise, how's that?" Daddy asks and puts his arms around

5

me. "You'll be able to see before long, Miss Reese, I promise."

"Yes," Sheila agrees, "and the ice cream would spoil your
lunch, anyway."

Daddy and Bennie both laugh again, but I don't know what's
so funny about Sheila.

The zoo is our surprise. I like the bears and the giraffes, but
the monkeys smell bad and the sun hurts my eyes. Daddy keeps
joking with us. He and Bennie make more jokes than Sheila
and I do when we are by ourselves, and theirs don't make any
more sense than ours. Next to telling stories—and he tells the
wildest in the world—my daddy likes to joke. He once traded
my uncle Curtis colored water in a fancy bourbon bottle for a
case of beer.

By the time we have a hot dog, I'm used to being blind.
Daddy is having such a good time that I stop worrying about
Mama getting mad at him for drinking too much. I don't even
bother to pray to God to stop him. I figure we can fool Mama if
we have to.

Daddy pulls me to his lap and starts singing "I Went to the
Animal Fair." Bennie joins him, so does Sheila, and pretty soon
people start smiling at us. I cover my ears and shut my eyes to
hide.

The monkey he got drunk
And fell on the elephant's trunk . . .

At this point Bennie and Daddy decide we should buy peanuts to feed the elephants. I drop my bag of nuts, but no one
notices, they are having such a good time. I pick up the peanuts.
"Wait for me, Daddy," I say, whacking the bag against the iron
pickets as I run to catch up with him. This time the bag breaks.
Before I can cry, Daddy comes back and scoops all the peanuts
into the skirt of my brown and white gingham dress that I hold
out for him. We pretend they aren't peanuts but cocoons ready

to burst into butterflies. "A lapful of butterflies, is that what you want?" He reties the ribbon in my hair and kisses the very tip of my nose.

On the ride home Sheila and I stick our heads out the window and play "Wizard of Oz." Both of us are Dorothy because we really only like to be her. Daddy pulls the car to the side of the road and asks Bennie to drive. We bring our heads back in.

"What's wrong?" Bennie asks.

Daddy shakes his head. He looks the color of Aunt Ruth's old porcelain doll—so white but without the red cheeks. I start to cry. He gets in the back with me and takes my hand. "I'm okay, Miss Reese, just an upset stomach."

Bennie keeps looking back at him. Once he asks, "Want us to stop?" Later, "Want us to find a doctor?" Daddy says no both times.

He pats my hand. "I'm all right," he says, but he's fibbing. Sometimes I think he fibs to Mama, but never to me. I let go of his hand.

"You promised Mama Bennie wouldn't drive," I say. "She said she didn't want me in a car with Bennie driving."

Daddy puts his finger to his lips to shush me, but Bennie has already heard and he is laughing. Sheila is not. I don't care. A little girl shouldn't be in a car with Bennie driving. Daddies are supposed to take care of their children.

Now he closes his eyes, but he's not sleeping.

"You've caught my blindness," I say to him.

He looks at me and starts to answer, but a moan comes out and he grabs for his stomach. Bennie stops at a roadside restaurant and says he's calling home. This time Daddy doesn't say no. He slumps in his seat. I wish I had made him mind Mama today. This is what we get for not minding. I roll his window up in case he has a cold.

Sheila is crying. Bennie tells her everything is going to be all right, to be quiet or she'll upset me, but I'm not upset. I want to hit her for being such a baby.

A drop of sweat comes on Daddy's upper lip. I roll the window down, but the wind sounds too strong. I roll the window back up again. Even the crease in his chin is white. Today every minute takes a long time to get to the next and fills up with witches and scary stories. Not one single minute calms down.

I take his hand again and don't let go until after Mama gets in the car with Bennie to take him to the hospital. She hugs me to her, but she makes me stay at Sheila's even though I tell her I want to go with them and help. I watch them drive away.

The phone rings before breakfast, and I don't like the way Mrs. Bascom sounds this morning. She talks to me, but I don't believe her at all. She and Bennie must have had a fight, for she has lots of tears in her eyes. She tries to baby me like she thinks I'm Sheila or sick. While we eat our oatmeal I tell Sheila horses are ugly animals. She cries. She loves horses.

To make up I promise she can put her doll Betsy on the top of my doll bed. The bed is bright red and has string for a mattress, I tell her. She knows that, she says, she's seen it a hundred times. I have never let her use it before because it is so special, "a special bed, for a special girl," my daddy tells me. I feel something hurting in my throat, the way it does when I want to cry. Anyway, I don't believe Mrs. Bascom.

Sheila wants us to go outside to their goldfish pond and make hollyhock dolls, but I tell her I'm going to play in her room with my butterflies all by myself.

After she leaves, I sit on the windowsill listening to summer. I hear crickets and a piano and the wheels of Sheila's red wagon. I also hear butterflies. I hear a car engine shut down and a car door close and a screen door open. I hear my mother's voice calling up to me. I don't hurry going down the stairs.

✳

Later, much later, after the memorial service, my mother and I stand beside the casket, her arms around me. "Tell him good-bye," she says. "We've got to close the casket."

"No!" I yell and break away. I run upstairs to my bedroom. She follows.

"No! No! No!" I scream as she holds me tight.

"You have to come!" she yells back. "He wants you to."

I hide my head in her skirt, but I let her take my hand and lead me downstairs, both of us crying. Together we lean over the casket. My mother hands me a rose to place in my daddy's hands, cold and white. But they aren't his hands at all. They hadn't made my doll bed. They didn't love me.

Bennie closes the casket, and my mama calls to my daddy, telling him how much she loves him. Bennie holds me and Sheila while Mrs. Bascom tries to comfort my mama, who cries, so hard I am afraid she will die, too.

Remembering the promise from Daddy's story about the moon, I go to her and pat her hand. "Don't cry," I tell her. "We can still live happily ever after. It just may take a while."

In

Over My

Head

I jumped from the boat with my shoes on. That's the only decision I remember making, the one to wear my sneakers. That, and I never wanted to see Ned Sampson again.

"H.A., get back in here!" he shouted, but I'd swum to the front of his boat on my way to shore.

Luckily, we'd anchored close in. By the time he untied his dinghy and began rowing toward me, I was climbing up the dock with the help of two teenage boys. When Ned tried to follow, I pushed him into the water and took pleasure in knowing it was cold and slimy. I regretted not taking the Sony Walkman, then hated having a silly concern at such a dramatic moment.

The boys, sunned and beery, clapped and whistled me on. "Keep him off the dock," I told them and ran toward the waterfront restaurant, already serving drinks before the evening meal.

As I caught my breath, I stood outside the plate-glass windows and watched the diners breezing in, hugging, imagined them throwing out witticisms thought up as they dressed, readying themselves to meet others' expectations. I envied them their small occasions. An hour before—fluffing my hair, dabbing perfume behind my ears and between my breasts, carefully buttoning a credit card and twenty-dollar bill in my blue work-shirt pocket—I had anticipated just such an evening at that same restaurant.

Earlier in the afternoon, I had volunteered to treat us to dinner on shore. "Grilled fish and an old Meursault will cheer us up," I had suggested after Ned came up on deck with an office fax in hand. "Our guy is in trouble," he said, referring to our client Ralph Stone, a big-deal Connecticut real-estate investor, running for the U.S. Senate. He was an important account for the political consulting firm where we worked and, as fate will have it, a first-class bastard. If he did lose, Ned wouldn't take the defeat lightly, and I became uneasy about my duplicity in the matter. I had signed on as a loyal political consultant, but along the way I had begun to suspect that Ralph Stone was a liar.

As Ned and I tacked for shore, we made up bawdy political lyrics, a pastime we particularly enjoyed. But all that happened before the next fax telling us some sleaze sheet had picked up a scandalous story on an opponent of Ralph's. Certain that Stone had spread the rumor himself, I lost my temper, but Ned defended Ralph and assured me our man couldn't be involved— primarily, it appeared, because he was married to a saint, a beautiful young woman who fairly glowed every time she saw Ned. The argument quickly turned into name-calling. I called him "naive"; he called me a "know-it-all cynic." I called him a "tight-ass jerk" and he said he doubted I functioned at all below the waist.

To my relief the money and card were still on me. I remembered his affectionate response to my offer of dinner and began to cry. And cry. Once I'd begun, I couldn't stop. Though I hadn't a clue as to how to get out of this little Maine town by nightfall,

I started walking away from the onlookers, toward the town's center, or so I hoped. My memory was hazy.

Realizing my ridiculous predicament, I sobbed harder. Already the air had cooled. Since I didn't have much time to dry before the sun dropped, I started jogging to warm up.

"Hey, honey, want a ride?" a male voice asked, as a car pulled alongside me. I kept on jogging, but I stopped crying, suddenly acutely aware of its presence.

"It's us, your rescuers. You can be friendly with us."

I looked over. "I'm old enough to be your mother."

"Where you going?"

"Buzz off." Too angry with Ned to be scared, I wasn't even particularly annoyed with them, but I could tell I was going to feel sorry for myself again. I had to fight back new tears. The boys kept coasting.

"Lady, we aren't being fresh. Where you going?" This was the driver, leaning across his friend and trying to affect a soberness.

I stopped to stare. They were drunk, though not too, and I still had a superior, if unrealistic, sense of strength left over from my tomboy girlhood. Reluctantly I decided the risks outweighed my discomfort.

"I'll be fine, I don't need a ride, thank you," I said, but the "thank you" was muffled by the screeching of car brakes and the banging of a door.

"Get the hell away from her!" Ned bellowed and I knew how splotched his face looked before I saw it. Ned Sampson was by far the youngest and the hottest-tempered man I'd ever come close to getting involved with. "H.A., get in this car." He turned to the boys: "Shove off." He didn't look much older than them. Because he isn't, I told myself grimly.

"We're staying put until she tells us different," Trusted Eyes answered. "Hello, Jack," he called to the driver of Ned's taxi. Jack grinned back, and I wondered why he hadn't been around when I needed him. If any of this seemed unusual to him, he wasn't showing it. Probably we weren't the first couple to dock here ready to chop each other up.

"I'm not coming back, Ned. Leave me alone," I hissed, hiding my face from the taxi driver and the two boys.

"What are you going to do? You can't walk around here all night!" He yelled loud enough for all the diners in Maine to hear. Then he made an effort to sound reasonable. "Come back for now. Tomorrow, if you want to go, you can."

I shook my head no even as he took my arm and walked me to the other side of the road, away from our audience. His wet clothes made a sloshing sound as he moved.

"Look, I don't blame you for being pissed," he began in a placating voice. "I shouldn't have lost my temper. You had a right to be upset. I didn't mean it. You know how much I respect your abilities."

"Not from your conversation, I don't." I twisted out of his grasp.

"I admit I was hotheaded, but your opinion of me means a lot. You are probably the best friend I have. I feel as close to you as anyone I know—even women I've dated." He shook my shoulders.

"Well, thank the Lord I never had that last privilege." He let go of me, and I turned my back to him. This whole conversation made me feel absurd. Ned was thirty-three years old and I was forty-four. All right, forty-five.

"Why do you deliberately push me away?"

I pivoted toward him. "I'm too old for you, Ned. This was a fluke to begin with."

"Where do you get off on this older-woman shit?" he asked, hands on hips, his feet in a boxing stance. "It's never mattered before." The taxi driver honked. I noticed that the boys had gotten out and were talking to him.

Ned, in his single-focus way, paid no attention to them at all. His blond hair, almost white now from a summer in the sun, swirled against his neck. He needed a haircut. "I might add," he went on, "you were not seeing an elderly gentleman when I met you."

"A casual acquaintance. Besides, he was almost forty, and I am—"

"I don't give a damn what you are." He jerked my arm. "Get in that car."

"I'm not coming."

He was trembling. "Just who is David?" he asked quietly, accusingly. "It's because of him, isn't it? He beckons; you run. 'Forgive me; see me; come to Texas.'"

"How dare you read my letter!" I yelled, as surprised as I was angry.

"What did you expect, leaving it open like that? I thought at first it was a memo from Ralph."

"Then you read it anyway!"

Just before we left I had received a letter from David Wright, my first love and for years after a sometimes love. Though not anymore. I had torn up the note, but evidently not soon enough.

"Why haven't you told me about him? Obviously he's important in your life."

"He stopped existing for me years ago and for the same reason you will: not worth the trouble."

"You bitch!" He let go of my arm.

The boys came back over to where I was standing by their car, and the one who had been driving opened the back door for me. When I slid in, the plastic seat felt hot and sticky to my legs. Ned came to the window.

"Don't do this. Please, H.A."

The driver, with the grace not to smirk, turned on the ignition and began pulling away, but Ned wouldn't let go and kept running along beside us. "If anything happens to her, I have your license number. I'll kill you."

The boy revved his motor. "Let go, mister."

"Where are you going? Tell me that much."

"Home!" I shouted as we burned off.

We drove in silence for a minute, aimlessly it seemed. The car, dipping along the highway, had the smell of old hamburgers and stale beer. Occasionally I glimpsed a portion of rocky beach collecting the last shafts of the day's sun; not enough to warm the rocks much longer. But the stones, broken into their separate pieces centuries ago, were substantial enough to withstand the cold. Unlike me.

I had done it again. Made a mess.

"Where is home, lady?" the driver finally asked, sufficiently sobered by the past hour.

Once more I saw the disturbed expression on Ned's face as he showed me the fax. "Our guy is in trouble," he had said. "And I might do my best to see that he gets in more," I should have answered. I didn't plan to hurt Ned's career or betray his trust, though I knew better than anyone else that, in politics, events had a way of creating their own momentum.

"Lady, where is home?" he patiently asked once more.

"Home is . . ." I began and pictured my Boston apartment with its spare Scandinavian furniture and book-lined bedroom, designed to satisfy my every need—a quilt Great-Aunt Iris concocted of yellows and reds and greens, a Bang and Olufsen C.D. player, a remote control so I could watch news programs to my heart's content, an honest-to-God Matisse print I loved and couldn't afford. A self-sufficient, contained environment arranged to please me and no one else. I saw myself walking in, putting on Bach, something with a lot of brass, pulling out a good book, taking a warm bath, and fixing a light Scotch—all the things that brought me solace.

"Rollins," I finished. "Home is Rollins, Texas."

Returning

to

Texas

The train crossed the Mississippi River and my heart lifted. Two days and nights of travel in a train compartment no larger than a single bed had given me all the time I needed to nurse my heartaches and guilts.

I had managed to convince Ralph Stone that his campaign would be well-served if I got out in the American heartland to take the pulse of the people. The concerns of the people of this country were the concerns of Ralph's would-be constituents, I argued. Though he had been uneasy about losing me for a few days, he agreed that this trip could be important to him. The best of it was he had no idea where exactly I might be, or even that I was on a train. I marveled at his gullibility and my own exploitation of it. Now I was ready to get on with this interlude.

Soon I would be in Texas, I reassured myself, but sadness stirred in me as I remembered the train ride back to Texas after the death of my father. Then my mother and I had shared an upper berth and unspoken fears of the years to come. Sitting with us during the day was a woman who had brown hair and a peach-colored blouse with little black Scottie dogs on it.

From the way my mother had warmed to the other woman, I could tell our life story was coming next and I wasn't interested. Having asked if I could look around, I wandered toward the dining car and pressed my face against the train door's glass panel. Each table had a white cloth and a red rose. I was glad I couldn't smell the rose, and now I was glad Sheila's mother had packed us a picnic basket. If my mother and I had eaten our meals here, the smell of flowers might have made her sad, too.

I tried to remember what my father had said about sad times and happy times and wished with all my heart that my mother and I hadn't wanted to move back to Texas so much. I hadn't really meant it. My throat tightened and I ran back to my mother.

When we got to Bowling Green, our Pullman car hooked up with another train for the rest of the ride to Texas. My mother stopped talking and put her arm around me. Out the window a couple of workmen were walking up and down the tracks. I noticed two other men rolling a large box.

"That's your daddy," she said, and I hated her for saying it. Hated myself for wishing bad thoughts. Hated him for leaving us.

"I don't see anything," I said.

Now I saw the black, flat land surrounding me, just the way I liked it, a minimalist landscape. In only a few hours I would be in Rollins to mend and to search for something I knew I needed to find.

When they took away the man in the moon, they took part of me with him. I just didn't know what part. Rollins would be the place to look for an answer. Rollins had given me back my childhood thirty-nine years ago. Maybe it would give me back my life now.

I eagerly awaited sight of the Texas prairie, looked forward to the surprise and pleasure on the faces of my mother and aunts, even if this trip wasn't for them.

I was going home for my own sustenance and to escape. Mostly to escape. With a distance of forty-eight hours and two thousand miles, I had become more objective about my quarrel with Ned.

Certainly, I was upset with him and troubled about what was going on between us, but neither circumstance would have driven me away if I hadn't been looking for an excuse to leave. And though I was still furious with him for reading my letter, I could understand his reaction once he had. David had begged for a reconciliation, had spoken of the old love we had for each other as if it had never stopped. While Ned and I definitely were not lovers, we both exhibited the symptoms of said disease, a silly state but one we'd tacitly accepted for the time being.

My quarrel with Ned was incidental; a catalyst, propelling me away from an uncomfortable state of affairs. If Ned complicated my situation, Ralph Stone made it untenable. More and more I regarded him as a destructive and dangerous force, so much so I'd begun to have moral qualms about working on his campaign. At the same time, a resignation amounted to nothing more than a momentary virtuous feeling, for he still could win.

If I really cared, I should try to stop him. Of course, that option posed a serious ethical question of its own. As it was, I had my own investigative sources checking him out more thoroughly—on an informal basis and off the record. Still, any time others got involved, leaks could occur. I'd been willing to take the chance, small as it was, because of my uneasiness about him.

I also had a few questions for myself: Was he really a more compulsive liar than most? Or more inclined to indulge in sleaze? Or did he only appear menacing because his charm allowed him more easily to indulge his vices? Finally, was the keenness of my distrust based more on my sense of disappointment than on any sound actuality? For in the beginning I viewed Ralph only as an omen for good.

On some days childhood still felt possible. The day I sailed alone. The day my mother and I discovered Paris. The day my first candidate won. Other days too numerous to mention, including the hyacinth-scented day that I stood at Ralph Stone's walnut-groomed, double-breasted front door. On impulse I had kissed my thumb, stamped it and sealed it to my other fist.

"What's that all about?" Ned asked; Ned, born age eighty-five and cautious. I thought of him as the Young Stodge.

"In Texas you do it for good luck when you see a white horse." Ned looked puzzled. "I sometimes *imagine* white horses," I explained. He gave me his off-putting formal smile. "When I feel like it," I added.

"Of course," he responded through thin lips on a too skinny face. His hair was a pale blond shade women spend fortunes for.

I certainly wasn't going to explain to him how my luck had picked up again, how I could fairly hear it humming. Boston was a new city; Pelham and Jackson, a new job. I was beginning to enjoy my independence and felt, once more, in control of my life—a good sign though sometimes a dangerous one.

Now I had landed this plum candidate with a fine door befitting his country estate. A successful entrepreneur, Ralph Stone was already regarded as potential presidential material, provided hubris or the world didn't bring him down too soon.

No, I wouldn't explain any of this to Ned Sampson, all of thirty-three and the youngest vice-president of the Pelham and Jackson consulting firm. Twelve years younger and a hundred light-years less experienced than me, he had a way of making me feel I had smeared my mascara. Unfortunately, because he was a sailing buddy of Stone's, he too would be working on this campaign. Even so, he was a mere blip, an inconsequential gnat on my day, on my new life. As with our client—absent human frailty and providential mischief—I planned to stay on a long roll.

The massive doors opened and a properly decked-out butler led us down a wide marble corridor, a kind of deco-gothic concoction. In a dark wood–paneled room smelling faintly of a popular pine-and-rose potpourri, Ralph Stone hunched over a mahogany desk, room-sized itself, and made notes on a yellow legal pad. The scene included dark brown leather chairs, rows of leather-bound books with an untouched look about them, and a vast fireplace burning logs—all props in a fantasy of an Edwardian gentleman's study: "Masterpiece Theatre" incarnate.

Our host scribbled long enough for us to absorb the surroundings, then began a whirlwind of motion. In a series of dance steps, he rose, swept around his desk, clasped both my hands in his, kissed my cheeks, shook Ned's hand, hugged our shoulders, and twisted open a bookcase concealing a built-in bar.

A mass-of-brown-hair health nut, Ralph Stone looked to be in his mid-thirties, though he was close to fifty. He wore a red-striped dress shirt with a tapered fit that only over-forty men who do one hundred sit-ups a day can look good in.

"So how about a drink? I always seal my contracts with a drink." He held up a cut-glass decanter with a brass label attached, put it down, examined another one, and rejected two more before opening an already iced-down bottle of champagne. "Do you object to champagne?" he asked as he handed us flutes. Into his flute he poured Evian water.

"To the Three Musketeers," he said as we raised our glasses, "and many wins." He gestured for us to sit on the brown leather couch and placed a slightly higher straight chair directly opposite it for himself. "I've got myself the most prestigious firm in the country and the best woman in the business." He looked from Ned to me. "Did that sound sexist? I mean about buying a woman. You have to be so careful. What I meant was—"

I interrupted him with assurances, though he had missed the real point, the one about the best woman as opposed to the best person. But I tried to ignore my hurt feelings.

"She's got a reputation for being picky, did you know that, Ned? She's considered uppity. Practically checks your forebears before taking you on. Expects you to be literate. Has a masters in economics." He turned to me. "I even know H.A. stands for Hope Annabella. You're surprised I know that, aren't you? Well, I did a little checking myself. I'm from Texas, too, you know. Spent summers on my family's ranch outside Tyler. Visited the San Jacinto battlefield every day to get inspired. The courage of those men . . ." Here his face took on a prayerful countenance.

"I've always felt it's important to study heroes. Read about them all the time." A pause, then: "I won't disappoint."

"I'm sure you won't," I agreed, though he'd already gotten some facts askew. A spread of land outside Tyler, which is in East Texas, would be called a farm, and the San Jacinto battlefield is nowhere near that.

A large cat came into the room and he scooped it into his free arm. "Beautiful, isn't she?" he asked.

"Beautiful," Ned echoed. I nodded in agreement, but Ralph waited expectantly for more. "Very beautiful," Ned amended. This time, pointedly raising one eyebrow, I added, "Gorgeous," whereupon Ralph Stone skipped to another subject.

"I want to build this campaign on issues that matter. We'll focus on quality of life, and we'll spell out what that means. As I've told you before, I want to tackle some hard ones and make a difference in the public dialogue. I want my participation to *matter*."

He talked on, occasionally flashing us his boyish smile, always watching for a reaction, sometimes pausing long enough for one of us to make a comment. He observed everything— Ned, his glass in hands dangling between his knees, me watching him watch us, the cat licking the dot of black on its paw, himself as he paced and declaimed. He was no fool, this Ralph Stone. He brought us along with his seeming lack of guile. I had worked for a lot of charmers, but this one ranked at the top. So far.

He told us how, as a teenager, he had worked for John Kennedy and how Kennedy had been so impressed with Ralph's political instincts that he took him on a campaign trip to West Virginia. He told how his grandparents had been Methodist missionaries in Africa and what it was like to visit them and how he wanted to recapture their sense of mission, to share their values and love for the country, as well as their love for God.

"We have to show that sense of mission with each other right here at home—with our neighbors as well as those less fortunate," he ended.

He was trying out a campaign speech, in part a comforting call to selflessness; even so, he'd begun to form a vision, part of which was intriguing. And he had the capacity to become one of those rare few: a centrist who could tap into the righteousness of the electorate. Though I knew as much as anyone of failed promises and hopes in this business, I found myself responding, so much did I still want to believe somebody could say something pertinent.

I suspected Ralph of embroidering his stories more than a little, but flourishes were the mark of any good storyteller. And these stories, certainly the rhythms of them, had a worn familiarity, but one of nostalgia, of timelessness. I could still hear my mother, my aunts and uncles on those faraway Sunday afternoons in Texas, telling their stories. Over the years the words changed; but the patterns were the same, working their magic on the hours, forming the daily details into order, and always with flair.

Ned appeared to be enjoying himself, too. He sat on the edge of the sofa, with an almost military bearing, and listened carefully. When he approved of a point or liked a story, he nodded his head, blinked his pale blue eyes rapidly, and took another sip of champagne. But Ralph had to earn Ned's approval. No smile or nod got handed out gratuitously.

Whatever else, the Young Stodge had integrity. I suspected that he was too young and too sheltered to understand how little of it was out there to go around. Not that I didn't believe in Stone, but mine was more the willing suspension of disbelief: I knew a good leading man when I saw one, but I also knew plays ended. From what I'd seen, Ned didn't yet worry about endings, and suddenly I wanted to protect him from that certain knowledge.

When Ned and Ralph began trading campaign slogans, I eased my head back on the couch to listen. The slogans, the issues, were comforting. In this room we were all one breed, not always an admirable one, but a connected one.

A quick knock on the door was followed by a slender woman with brown puppy-friendly eyes and long brown hair caught at the nape of her neck with a gold clasp. She wore jeans and a tobacco-brown cashmere sweatshirt. "Jack Stoddard is on the phone. He is insistent," she said to Ralph, delivering this bit of information in such a way as to brook no discussion.

"Then come keep Ned and H.A. company while I get rid of him." Ralph excused himself and Ned introduced me to Rachel Stone. Though her fluid lines gave her an appearance of height, she could have been no more than five-two, a good five inches shorter than me. Feeling like a gawky adolescent towering over her, I shook her hand.

"My husband tells me you are the best," she said to me as she put her other hand on Ned's arm. "Barring Ned, of course."

"Of course," I answered as she smiled up at Ned.

Then she turned her attention back to me, saying, "I'm a little shaky about all this and need your guidance." She interrupted herself to laugh. "I have no idea what to do as a political wife. I'll need all the help I can get."

"With your charm, you have nothing to worry about," Ned assured her. If first takes were telling, she was perfectly cast for her part. The cat bestirred itself and began rubbing its body against Ned's legs.

"Bumpkin, leave him alone. You know Ned doesn't like you, naughty girl." She pulled the cat over to her. "Ned tolerates this cat only to humor Ralph."

"I tolerate this cat because of you!" he said. Upon the arrival of Rachel, his eyes—of that pale blue color destined to film over in old age and form watery puddles—had lit up. With her he showed flash. "Cats mirror the worst in me, and I'm damned if I'm going to approve such deliberate flaunting." He said this to me, but it was for Rachel's benefit, too. It was my turn to look puzzled.

"Ned thinks cats are cold, unattached creatures," Rachel explained.

"That's because they are," he said. He put his hands in his pockets and walked over to the fire. "But look who's talking, a pretty spring morning and I'm freezing."

"That's because you won't take the vitamins I gave you," Rachel scolded.

"I told you I don't believe in vitamins," he answered cheerfully. He had ceased being the Young Stodge and I felt a little jealous of Rachel. I wanted the same response, wished I were that easygoing. At any rate, Ned could prove more interesting than I'd thought.

I found myself regretting his youth, though I was not much interested in any entanglement; I could not manage hurting or getting hurt anymore. The few men I did see didn't hold my attention for long, nor I theirs.

Not that I had anything against younger men—a few years younger, anyway; the ones who still had an aura of immortality about them. Had I found one to marry back when I believed in husbands, I could have ensured myself against the probability of widowhood. The younger, the healthier—or so my admittedly cockeyed reasoning went.

As we continued to exchange pleasantries, I tried to decipher the reason for Jack Stoddard's phone call. He was one of the largest land developers on the East Coast and a major campaign contributor, so he got to share his thoughts with the candidate and, from the length of Ralph's absence, he obviously had a lot on his mind. For all I knew, his call might not touch on the political, but I doubted that.

Ralph's reentry proved me right: he came in cursing and punching his palm. "Goddamn environmentalists," he said, frowning on us all as if we were the culprits. "After a major sugar daddy of mine. Can't have that. H.A., make a note we're coming out for the environment with a capital *E*. Stuff like that. You got one of those note recorders?" He came to a sudden halt.

"I'll remember."

The punching began again. "I *can* be everybody's friend. I can do a lot of poor bastards some good, but first I've got to get in and that takes money, including my top banana's."

Ralph Stone articulated well the new rationale for greed, its raw form being out of favor these days. Ambition held the day:

money counts as votes, as in buying exposure, as in buying expensive consultants like me to help buy even more expensive television time and travel time and personality-remake time. All this by way of saying money was as corrupting as ever, as Stone inadvertently continued to demonstrate:

"And that means I can't be too particular or too sloppy. Got to walk that in-between line. Isn't that right, H.A.? See? I'm not such a neophyte as you might think."

"Never occurred to me you were," I responded, but I was pretty sure the political lecture had been intended solely for the benefit of his wife, who did not look at him.

Abruptly he switched subjects. "Did you two get acquainted?" he asked me. "Rachel speaks five languages and can read menus in eight."

"That's impressive." I worried that I sounded almost as patronizing as her husband, but she responded good-naturedly.

"I have a good ear. In a minute Ralph will tell you to hum a tune, any tune, and then ask me to play it. Isn't that right, darling?" She put an arm around his waist and laughed. "Maybe that's what I should do at political rallies. I could be the early entertainment—what do you call it?—the warm-up act." They smiled at each other, though she had put him on and he didn't much like it. She looked ready to say something else but instead excused herself from the room. The three of us watched her glide away, the cat cradled in her arms.

Though not a great beauty, she carried herself like one, and with an ease born out of an essential regard for herself. What Rachel Stone had somewhere in her past was a father who adored her, doted on her flourishing, called her the prettiest girl in the world and believed it and caused her to believe it, too. And she would always have that. No matter what might happen later, she had somewhere in her a sense of unconditional love the rest of us spend lifetimes trying to find. I envied a Rachel Stone with all my heart and could spot one a mile away.

With her exit we began to make ours. "You sure we can put together a winning campaign on such short notice?" Ralph addressed his question to me.

"Don't forget the other candidates are in the same position as you, and with less name recognition. Besides, entering a race late tends to be fun. You don't have a lot of time for substitutions or foul balls from the other side." I've found that sports metaphors reassure most men.

"It's just the three of us," he said. "I plan to be my own campaign manager." He took Ned's and my hands in his. "After this election, we'll all take off for Italy. You like Italy? This suit is from there. A Barbera. You've probably heard of the place. I'll treat both of you to the suit of your choice while we're there. We'll row ourselves over. Did you know H.A. sails, too?" He pivoted in front of me. "There! Got you again, didn't I?"

As we were driving away, he yelled, "The Three Musketeers!"

We crested the first hill and Ned asked, "You really sail?"

"Beats me how he knows."

"I could use somebody to crew for me tomorrow. Would you come on such short notice?"

"I'd love to," I said in surrender to the pleasure of mutuality, the pleasure of travel on bounty mains, the pleasure of victories with new best friends, and the pleasure of competition with Rachel Stone.

On this day I had only good in mind for all of us. That was before I contemplated changing Ralph Stone's destiny, a determination that grew from a need in me to perfect the world, if not myself. Some of us are doomed to want to take hold of an injustice or disappointment and shake it by the neck and curse it and, if need be, destroy it. But on that day filled with hyacinths and champagne and bonhomie, I was caught up in making hopeful wishes on imaginary white horses.

That last I had learned from my mother.

Leaving

Kentucky

We had buried my father, and I stopped crying. My mother, so far as I knew, did the same. Still, I constantly asked, "Are you happy, Mama?" and expected reassurance. I took to singing and dancing for her, as I had for my father, but while she watched with a patience I had never known her capable of, I felt invisible.

While others enjoyed the last days of summer, my mother and I packed. We planned to auction our house and farms and move to Texas when she settled the mysterious lawsuits. Nearly every evening she went over the papers my father kept in an old black leather doctor's bag. She studied each page as if deciphering a code while I read my first-grade reader, featuring a perfect family with a newborn baby sister and a first-grade son. I had no problem identifying with the young boy or rereading for the twentieth time a book that had bored me all year.

Then on a cloudy summer morning that whiffed of fall, she smiled a real smile and announced that she knew what to do about all those papers. She had a plan: we would drive to the next county, find a decent lawyer who wasn't in cahoots with Edgeville's S.O.B.'s, and let him look at our mess. "The problem is your daddy thought everybody was as honest as he was. I told him all along not to trust those fools. They've been taking us to the cleaners." We would go this very morning.

After I put on my white socks and white sandals—polished every day by my mother now that we no longer had a housekeeper—and Mother put on her favorite hat, wine-colored with dark green feathers, we piled into the red Plymouth and headed for Lufkin, the adjoining county seat. For the first time in weeks my mother came alive, her expansive gestures and love of good talk returning. "There's a white horse," my mother said, practically swerving off the road as she pointed it out to me. "Make a wish."

We took our time finding a lawyer's office in Lufkin, for we wanted one that looked prosperous—proof of customers and a good reputation—but not too swank—proof of a rip-off. Finally she decided on one just down from the courthouse because we could walk right in.

Our visit was brief. "You sign these, lady," the lawyer said, "and you're sharing everything you own with the bank and half the town of Edgeville." He spoke of power of attorney, ownership of cows, mortgages, and a lot of other words not making much sense to me.

"Those jackasses!" she said, shoving her papers into the case and opening her purse. "How much do I owe you?"

"Not a thing. You've got enough trouble on your hands."

"I'm not the one with trouble. I'll cram this down their throats." She shook the case for emphasis, looking as fierce as I had ever seen her. So long as the look wasn't directed at me, I was comforted. In some undefined way already her temper had become my shield; her anger, my protector. Four times she thanked the lawyer.

"Just don't sign anything," he called after us.

We drove as fast as we dared on our old tires. I could tell how excited she was by the way she kept tapping the steering wheel with her fingers.

"We'll be out of here by the end of the month, and you can finish the summer in Texas. We'll take care of Papa Bear. He needs us now." She was speaking of her father, who might marry someone called the Old Bad Woman. If we moved in with him, my mother and aunts had decided, he wouldn't be lonely and wouldn't marry this person we all hated and thought terrible.

She smiled at me when she said it. "We can live in Rollins for good. Would you like that?" she asked.

She knew the answer, or thought she did, for I would have my cousins to play with and, as the only girl-child, enjoyed the lavish attentions of my aunts. The truth was I still halfway thought my father would come back if I could find a way to make this happen. But all I could say was, "I love you, Mama."

"I love you, too, honey-child." She looked down at me. "Do you think about your daddy much?"

"No," I answered and marked the occasion of my first lie. What else could I say without making her sad?

Outside the bank's entrance, she hugged me tight but then spoke abruptly: "H.A., throw your shoulders back."

Hand in hand, we marched soldier-upright through the heavy bank doors. The lobby with its cool white marble and vaulted ceiling reminded me of the entrance to Mammoth Cave and promised to be just as forbidding as the darkness lurking only feet away from that other stagy entrance. She let go of my hand and strode past the tellers' cages and the trust officers' desks and threw open the door of the president's office. A round man with glasses sliding down his nose and wisps of gray hair brushed straight back sat behind a desk as he filled an ink pen. I had seen him at my father's memorial service. Before he could rise, she slammed the case down on his desk.

"You jackass," she said in a voice loud enough for us and God to hear. "Did you think because I'm a woman you could get away with this?"

"Now, Mrs. Reese, let's be calm. Please sit down," the pompous-voiced man pleaded and went over to close his door. My mother was having none of either.

"Leave that door open. I want everybody in this town to know what you and your friends are—a bunch of damn crooks. How do you have the nerve to show your face in public?" He was still trying to close the door, but she blocked him.

"You and that damn lawyer of mine thought you could take a widow." She got close to his face and shook her fist under his nose. "Well, I'm here to tell you, you can't—not this one. If I have any more trouble out of you or him or anybody else about the sale of my land or the payment of notes, I'll sue the whole rotten bunch of you. I've found a lawyer who says I'd win hands down."

As she moved once more into his office, the whole bank quivered along with her green feathers and black curls. She unfastened the black bag and dumped the papers onto his desk. He had to jump out of the way, for his bottle of ink spilled over the papers and onto the floor. "You can have these. I'm not signing anything."

She marched back to where I had glued myself on arrival, had curled into myself to marvel at the splendid and awesome righteousness of my mother. I reveled in it as she delivered her parting volley to her audience:

"All of you are dealing with a bunch of damn crooks. They steal from widows and children. They're rotten to the bone." With those lines delivered, she grasped my hand. We marched back out. And on to Texas.

Campaign

Jitters

I could use a white horse right now, I thought while staring out the train window. I was close to getting my career in real trouble and wasn't even enjoying the thrill of the risk. Closing my eyes, I remembered exactly when things started going wrong.

Ned kept shifting in his upholstered desk chair while looking at the news copy in front of him as if, any minute, some knowledge would be revealed that had previously been withheld.

"Does Ralph know yet?" he asked. Somehow, miraculously, underneath all those bleached-out freckles he had managed a tan. If his neck weren't so damn skinny, he'd be attractive, I thought, but this morning I was too unsettled by the poll to do more than briefly register Ned Sampson's appearance. Ralph's opponent, Mary Cardigan, was pulling closer.

"Are you kidding? He called me at five this morning with the information." I lowered myself into the chair by his large, nondescript cherry desk. "We're going to have to cancel our boat race on Saturday. He wants a meeting on *his* boat. That makes us a part of his official weekend family sail." I forced a smile.

"Shit!" Ned said and shoved a small bronze paperweight across his desk. "We had a good chance to win. The best we've had all year." For the last six weeks I had crewed for him most weekends, both of us relieved to spend pleasant days together on his sailboat with nothing more required of us.

"So what did you tell him?" Ned asked.

"Not to panic, of course. Some shifting was bound to happen."

"But did you expect *this*?" he asked, holding up the sheets of paper he'd been studying and giving them a laconic shake.

"I should have. He clutters his speeches and obscures his message. He sings, but the tune gets lost in trills."

"Ralph wants people to understand his concerns and the complexity of the solutions."

"Yeah, well . . ." I patted the top of his head.

He grabbed my wrist and jerked it away. "Don't rile me," he said, then smiled, trying to soften his gesture.

"Why not? You've got a temper. Flaunt it."

"Easy for you to say. You don't pay the consequences." He did his blue-eyed blink before asking, "How about dinner tonight instead?"

"I've made plans, but I wish I could. Really." Although we'd had working dinners or pick-up dinners after sailing, this would have been the first purely social one. I felt bad about telling him no, doubly bad that I couldn't tell him why. I added lamely, "It's not a date. It's just that . . ."

"You don't have to explain your private life to me." Possibly he blushed; I couldn't tell for sure.

I got up to go. "Maybe I should try to explain it to somebody who could then explain it to me."

He stood up, too. With a quick gesture I reached over and patted his head again. "For a punk kid you're all right," I said.

On the way home I bought wine, groceries, and flowers for my mysterious evening caller. Sally Cummings, one of the best pollsters in the business, had asked me to see an old neighbor of hers named Gary Boatwright, who was in town for a conference. A former disgruntled employee of Stoddard Development, he had information that might affect Ralph. Not that Boatwright was threatening trouble—he had a terrific job in Florida and wasn't into rocking boats—but she thought I ought to know what he knew.

For the most part, I looked forward to the evening. Silly as it sounded, I liked the idea of showing off my culinary skills, albeit to a stranger delivering a message I'd just as soon not hear. Walking up a steep flight of stairs, my arms loaded down with sacks and flowers, I anticipated the old familiar pleasure of arranging the peonies, broiling the salmon to the exact nth of a second, and whisking up a brown sauce in less than three minutes. Cooking was the only area of my life in which I took unabashed delight, and I had done precious little since coming to Boston.

This wasn't the first time I'd gone into isolation in a new city and a new job. Usually because of some disappointment I had left behind—usually some man—and at those times I needed to dream my life more than live it.

Whenever the magic wore off, for him or me, I had learned to make a quick, clean break, then deny the loss until the dark place in me settled down. I holed up in myself even as I remained the competent, sometimes creative, professional; a good sport; a good listener. These roles I could perform in my sleep.

But when the loss felt too big, too much like a flood sweeping my life away, I packed up and moved on to the next town. In the new surroundings, I always breathed a sigh of relief that I had survived, as if I hadn't known all along I would. The moves had mostly involved a husband or David. After a second marriage, I gave up on husbands, but David had been a harder habit to break.

The problem with Washington, I thought, rubbing the silver as I lay it on the table, was that I stayed on five years too long. Professionally I had thrived, but failed marriages, failed affairs, plagued me. I should have left when David did. I would think of him and replay our scenes, for no other reason than to remind myself why we hadn't worked and why we never would. I'd been determined not to let him upset my life again. He had anyway, though I had to admit there were other disappointments that followed David, but those just blurred together.

Well, you're through with blurs, I told myself and stood back to look at the table: white china set off by a dark green paisley cloth, Christofle silver, plain with a good heft, the same as the crystal. Such a pretty table, I was sorry Ned couldn't see it.

I would invite him some night soon. I could have Sally, too, and a few others. I should ask him to bring someone. Maybe the frizzy-haired, red-lipsticked young woman who had picked him up after work one day. Whatever possessed me to explain to Ned that I didn't have a date tonight? Such a pretty table. I sat down with a light Scotch and a scratchy Nellie Lutcher album to wait for my guest.

Gary Boatwright fidgeted with one thing or another. During cocktails he fingered the miniature book of Flaubert's *The Tale*, which Aunt Ruth gave me ten Christmases ago. In the kitchen he tapped a serving spoon as I finished up the salmon and asparagus. At dinner he played with his knife.

So far we had discussed the relative merits of Northern culture versus Southern culture, food, weather, our friend Sally, and his job as vice-president of an enormously successful construction company. A large-boned black man of medium height, he came across as no-nonsense and more secure than his fidgeting attested to.

"So what is it that I ought to know about?" I asked when I couldn't stand watching his fingers twitch another minute.

Gary didn't hesitate, but got right to the heart of the matter. "Stoddard asked me to do a report on some wetlands they were interested in developing. I didn't say the right things. They got rid of me. I can fill you in on the details, but it's not a little scheme. It's a big one and Sally wanted me to warn you that Stone's connection with that outfit won't do him any good. Among other things, the bastards have a security apparatus that stretches across the country. I'm almost certain they keep tabs on a lot of people, including me—and I don't consider myself paranoid."

He went on to explain how the plan involved massive repercussions for East Coast and Midwest wetlands—up to seventy percent could be affected. This tale took a while to tell and my eyes glazed over when he got into the technical intricacies of the subterfuge. Yet I didn't doubt the seriousness of his message. As he talked, his hands slowly stopped moving. Now they lay quietly in his lap. A cautious man, I thought, but not someone given to intense deliberations.

"The situation is going to explode someday and Stone is going to get caught under the debris if he's not careful. He and Stoddard are best buddies. I'd be real surprised if he weren't a lot more involved with Stoddard than he lets on."

"Do you plan to light the fuse?" I asked.

"I'm too comfortable, and I couldn't prove anything, anyway. But you don't have to get fucked by that bunch to know their oar won't row—not in environmental waters."

I nodded, but if Stone had involved himself, he'd probably covered himself well. For all practical purposes there would be no reprisal. Worse political supporters committed worse crimes all the time with no consequences to the candidate.

Still, under the sweet haze of good food and good wine, a kernel of unease lodged itself in my stomach. I didn't plan to go poking for it, though. In my business, I couldn't afford to get preoccupied with small sources of moral discomfort.

The evening ended mercifully early. After Gary left, I washed the dishes, dried the silver, and wished I could tell somebody how I'd grown sick of candidates who could be shined up as pretty as my expensive silver, only to tarnish a lot faster.

But Ralph wasn't some paltry piece of tinsel. I was letting a past mistake—something that happened long before I knew him—color my relationship with him. Since the last election, I'd not been so proud of myself for helping to put a man I didn't respect or trust in office. As I finally turned out the kitchen light, I decided I wasn't being fair to Ralph.

Yet again I resolved to put mistakes behind me and get on with the present. I would make an effort to meet new people. I would give that dinner party. The kernel stayed in my stomach, though, not growing really, just moving about to make me uneasy, disturbing that dark place.

Pay

As You

Play

Richard was the first son of a bitch I sabotaged in order to pay him back for my paying him in the first place. But both payments came later. In the beginning we had fun—or, at least, I did. Possibly everything, including affairs, was work to Richard.

We met at a buffet supper given by a mutual friend, someone I'd known in Atlanta. He was the attorney general of an industrial, Deep South state with a shot at winning a Senate seat on a liberal platform. Hero of the moment for his successful prosecution, his name recognition, his dark good looks, and an admirable civil rights record, he, nevertheless, did not have the heavy war chest of the incumbent, his opponent in the primary. (Whoever won the Democratic primary always won the election, barring some truly catastrophic discovery.)

The night we met he got my professional interest and advice gratis. Although I supported his candidacy, my gesture wasn't particularly generous, for I was playing the old game of work as a protective device until I settled down again emotionally. By this time I had moved to Washington, ended my second marriage, and had a string of wins as a political consultant. Since work left me little time to learn the city or meet people, I welcomed the occasional social opportunity.

My Georgia and Texas connections helped us through the ordeal of tedious chitchat. My job and my Washington access he determined quickly—part of the appraisal I glossed over at the time. Midway through the cassoulet, he asked how I would suggest he run his campaign. As a testament to his charm, this flattered me when I should have started billing him.

We both agreed that none of my ideas would work if he didn't come up with a ton of money for television spots. He needed the money soon and it had to come from outside the state, probably New York, a place with a good share of affluent liberals. As it turned out, he was way ahead on this last point. He pumped me for information about New York sources.

As another testament to his charm (and, let's admit it, my susceptibility), I agreed to introduce him to a couple of my Wall Street contacts, even help arrange a fund-raiser in Manhattan if possible.

When I dropped him off at his hotel, he cupped my chin in his hand. "I had almost forgotten what a wonderful woman was like," he said. "These days I'm too busy for women at all. May I see you again?" I nodded yes, both relieved and disappointed that he didn't ask me to come in with him. He spent the next few minutes studying my face with an actor's ability to make the gesture seem fresh, not the practiced seduction device that it was.

"I'll call tomorrow," he promised.

He called every day, though I didn't see him for two more weeks. During these calls we told each other little stories about our days, shared whatever political gossip came our way, planned his campaign, and discussed in minute detail the New York fund-raiser I had by now arranged.

For this last favor, he thanked me profusely although I'd made only one phone call. (The ability to make that call impressed him more than anything else I had done so far.) What I didn't explain was that the phone call went to Madge Prothro, a friend from my Dallas days, who had become the executive assistant to a Wall Street robber-baron.

She told her boss that my guy was a good cause and then arranged the rest on her own. Between us we provided money and glitz, tapping into the theatrical world, the public-relations world, the art world, the filthy-rich world. We congratulated each other on our accomplishment for such a swell guy.

"Do I need a hotel room?" he asked when announcing he was coming back through D.C. on his way to New York.

He had made dinner reservations at Jean-Pierre, the least he could do for me, he told me when he arrived at my door with a chilled bottle of Korbel champagne, a small box of Godiva chocolates, and a pleased-with-himself little-boy smile. A dutiful mother, I praised him for his thoughtfulness; a dutiful mistress, I iced the champagne and got out the caviar, *my* contribution.

As I came out of the kitchen carrying a tray with our goodies, he was removing his shoes. Already he had taken off his coat and tie. As I leaned over to place the tray on the coffee table, he said,

"Do you mind if I relax awhile? It's been a long week—in lots of ways."

He put a hand inside my blouse.

"Don't get too relaxed." I said this because our dinner reservation was in forty-five minutes and I didn't want us to move too fast—either way. I had spent two whole weeks thinking about this night and this man and had no intention of allowing the first time to turn into a teenage, three-minute stand-up.

"When I'm Senator," he said, now holding one of my breasts, "we'll have champagne every night."

"A deal," I murmured and broke eye contact, which I hated to do, but I didn't have much choice. More aware of the awkward position of my back than the pressure of his hand, I was still leaning over and holding the tray, which got heavier by the minute. Still, he knew what he was doing.

"When I'm in the Senate . . ." he whispered and then, unfastening my bra, said, "This way?"

"Aren't we rushing—"

"We have all night," he interrupted.

We ended in my kitchen with pasta and leftover chicken, a pattern we continued to repeat. For the first few times I felt flattered by his ardor; I even fixed elegant meals for the two of us, though my schedule had no room for such domestic indulgences.

"What a treat," he would say with a sigh, after which I would glow, happy to have pleased in who knows how many ways.

Before long, however, we moved into another phase. One evening after our usual, much-anticipated bout in bed, he sighed, said, "What a treat," and propped himself up on his elbow. I mumbled something inane back, not really wanting to talk just yet.

"Maybe you could visit me soon. Would you?" He traced my face with his finger.

"Mmmmmm." I slid my hand onto his belly, and he flopped over and sighed again before saying, "I'm having to spend so much time and energy fund-raising, I wasn't sure I had the stamina for the likes of you."

"You have the stamina," I assured him but kept my hands to myself.

"Some days I question the whole enterprise." He paused, then added, "Not us, the campaign."

"I thought prospects were looking up. Your ratings—"

"My ratings don't mean a damn thing if I can't find more money."

I said, "Remember, your New York benefit is next week, and it's already a success. People believe in you." I patted his back.

"Do you believe in me?"

I sat up. "You know I do." He sat up, too, and looked around my high-ceilinged bedroom.

"This is a beautiful place you've got here," he said.

"Yes," I agreed, admiring the heavy moldings and ornate fireplace mantel.

"Expensive."

"Not so much. Adams-Morgan is still affordable."

"Are you kidding? I know the price of real estate in this town."

"More affordable than some other areas," I corrected myself.

He pulled up the sheet and went back to his other subject: "Back home some friends of mine are scraping together a thousand dollars each for me—not rich friends either, just plain, ordinary folks."

"I told you people believe in you."

He turned toward me. "So why haven't you contributed? I thought you wanted me here?"

I started to say something flip about paying for services or getting propositioned in bed, but while Richard told good stories, had good looks, and performed admirably, he did not have a great sense of humor about himself. And none where this campaign was concerned.

I extracted my face from his grip and asked, "What do you figure me for?"

If he caught the edge in my voice, he didn't let on. "A thousand dollars," he replied without hesitation.

On the day of the benefit, I came down with the flu and did not make it to New York. Richard called about three in the morning to tell me how well it had gone, what a fine man his host was, and the amount of money—considerable—we had raised. Since I had the flu, he would not come back through Washington. The last thing in the world he needed was to get sick. I wondered why it bothered me so much that he canceled our plans before I could.

After three days I came out of my misery enough to call Madge. "I understand your party was a huge success," I began.

"Yes, it was."

Responding to her tone, I apologized for not getting to her sooner, explained my fever and sore throat, and, in the process, wondered for the first time why she hadn't called me. "You've had a sick friend here," I said with possibly a trace of accusation.

"That's why I didn't call. I didn't want to make you sicker."

"What do you mean?"

"Your friend is an asshole. He played Mr. Big Shot with me and kiss-assed with my boss. He thought I was the upstairs maid," she said dryly. "Fortunately, my boss knows better and has been given to understand he is never to have anything else in any way to do with that prick."

"I told Richard what you'd done. He knew who made that event happen."

"Don't count on it. Don't count on him either. Turns out he's slept with half the women at the party."

"He's given all that up," I answered, the worst of my flu symptoms returning. "Not just because of me. The campaign . . ." I trailed off, knowing how I sounded, having heard the same kind of reasoning from other women in the same situation.

"Come see me next weekend. We'll forget all about trashy men."

"As soon as I'm well," I promised.

Two weeks later I did make it to New York on business and stayed over an extra day. In the meantime Richard had come back full of good cheer and good sex. Nobody's perfect, I told myself when I thought about Madge, but I did take the precaution of making a reservation for the late seating at *i ricci*. I dismissed the women, however, as part of Madge's sour grapes.

"Why don't you call Alma Parks up and ask her?" Madge suggested. "Ginny Lovell, too. Better yet, have lunch with them. But reserve a large table. They can recommend others."

"He's in the middle of a campaign."

"Nobody ever accused him of laziness."

We had three things in common: we had all slept with Richard— some for longer than others; we were all blondes—some more so than others; we had all given him a thousand dollars. At least we priced out the same, Ginny Lovell observed over our fourth glass of wine.

Richard continued calling every day. My advice got vaguer. He kept me posted on his fund-raising, especially on his prospective contributors and whom he planned to call about giving more benefits. After his initial success, he wanted more New York events.

"I think Joe Blow is interested in helping me out," he would confide. Immediately and without his knowing, I would call Madge with the appropriate name.

"How 'bout that," she'd answer, and somehow, mysteriously, Joe Blow would never materialize. As it happened, Madge always knew someone who knew someone if she didn't know the someone herself.

The parties never materialized. The New York money never materialized. Not a lot came out of Texas or California either. Madge took care of Texas. I don't know who took care of California. Madge and I never discussed what she was doing, or that she was doing anything.

Richard is still attorney general. He plans to run for the Senate again. I know because on two separate occasions five years later, he asked me for a thousand-dollar contribution. Neither time in bed.

Smoke

Screen

For a time, Ralph, Ned, and I did indeed become the Three Musketeers. Ralph liked meetings, some weeks as many as three a day—one early morning, another in the evening, and sometimes one at lunch. Usually we held these at his Hartford campaign headquarters in his private office. Ralph was obsessive. In between the meetings would come the phone calls, and in between the calls, the faxes.

On one trip I decided to drive back to Boston with Ned; I had missed the last commercial flight and Ralph's plane was already in use. To pass the time, I rattled off occupations more nearly suited to the Young Stodge's compulsions. "You could be a monk. Or an assembly-line worker. You could do the same thing in the same way every day."

"Sounds great to me," he agreed good-naturedly. When he talked, he turned to look at me, so I kept my eyes on the road for him. "I always thought I would be a drummer in a rock band," he confessed.

"A drummer?"

"Not a very good one."

"A drummer!" Maybe that helped explain the muscles in his arms, lean and graceful, unexpectedly so, for he looked too svelte in his business clothes to have this hidden toughness.

"What's wrong with that?"

"I'm surprised, that's all."

"Not any more than your being an economist surprised me," he responded.

"I was pretty good," I told him as he accelerated our already-speeding car.

"But you liked politics better?"

"Not then." I turned to check right-lane traffic. Ned needed a little help with his lane switching, his excessive lane switching. We drove the rest of the way listening to his tapes of The Doors and The Talking Heads. Had The Doors not been mesmerizing and the highway not stretched on in one amiable white sheath, I still would not have seen the need to divulge my past.

I also hadn't told Ned the whereabouts of San Jacinto or that Barbera suits and sweaters were available in catalogs as well as department stores or that neither John Kennedy nor missionary grandparents were anywhere to be found in Ralph's background. Partly I needed to respect the confidentiality of my sources, but partly I wanted to shield Ned's idealized view of our candidate. We'd had enough conversations to make me realize that Ned basically believed in Ralph—as did I. Up to a point. Besides, the less confided, the better. Squandered confidences are one of the least remarked ills of our time.

"You've been quieter than usual," Ned said as he let me out at my apartment.

"But never so quiet as you."

"Do you want me to talk more?"

"I want you to get a good night's sleep. Exactly the same as I'm going to do."

✳

From a sound sleep I picked up the phone to hear my mother's voice: "H.A., where did you put the cigarettes?"

"Cigarettes?" Was this part of a dream? I wondered. I burrowed deeper into my pillows but kept the receiver to my ear, just in case.

"That carton of cigarettes you hid when I gave up smoking. I told you to hide them, but Stella says you threw them out. I know perfectly well you would not throw away good cigarettes. If you didn't hide them, you would have given them to her. She says you would not have done that because you know she hates my brand. Which is a damned lie. She smokes them when her own run out. She's always bumming from me. That's why I don't have any in the house now." She stopped talking, but still sorting through confusion, irritation, and sleep, I didn't respond. "H.A.? Are you there? You're sure not in a good mood. What's wrong?"

"I'm trying to wake up. That's all."

"Are you sick or something? It's only midnight."

"It's one in the morning here."

"I'm going strong and you're a lot younger than I am. You've let yourself get run down again. I can tell."

"I'm fine." I had turned on my back and tried to put a little extra oomph in my voice.

"But you can't remember where you put the cigarettes?"

"Mama, that was four years ago. I'm sure you found and smoked them a week after you started back."

"You and Stella! Just because you all can't remember anything, don't think I can't."

"It's easy to forgot something like that." I refrained from pointing out that she forgot a lot these days, but I heard the condescension in my tone. So did my mother.

"Don't get know-it-all with me! You're not too big to spank, young lady."

I sat up in bed, wishing I had a cigarette myself—and I don't smoke. "It's just that—"

"I tried the freezer. Stella said it would be just like you to put them in the freezer."

I burst out laughing. "Why does she think that?"

"She says anybody who keeps her tea and coffee in the freezer would probably keep cigarettes there, too. It is a little peculiar of you, H.A."

"Did you check your underwear drawer, where you usually hide extras from her?"

"I hide them from Ruth. She's worse than Stella when it comes to bumming. I've got a good mind to go over and take hers. See how she likes it. Wake her up, too. Ruth and Ben go to bed with the chickens." Aunt Ruth was my mother's other sister who lived in Rollins. On the whole, my mother got along much better with her sister Ruth than with her sister Stella.

"What if you try going to sleep early for a change yourself? You can get cigarettes in the morning."

"Why don't you try minding your own business?" With that she slammed down the phone.

Staring at the ceiling, I debated whether to call her back, but she surprised me by calling again. "When we talked last Sunday, I forgot to mention that David Wright called here looking for you."

"Oh?"

"He tells me he's an old friend of yours from college, as if I didn't know perfectly well who he is," she said in such a way I wondered just how well she did know. "I told him you lived someplace in the Boston area, but I'd misplaced your address."

So, she knew all too well. My mother might forget where she had put her cigarettes, but nothing was wrong with her uncanny ability to know exactly what was going on with me at any given time.

"I haven't seen him for years," I reassured her.

"That's as it should be."

"What about your cigarettes?"

"I'm going over to borrow one of Stella's."

"In the middle of the night?"

"Why not? I'm over twenty-one."

"Then be careful."

"Don't be such a worrywart."

For the second time tonight, I laughed out loud. "Look at the pot calling the kettle black," I said, lapsing into my mother's idiom.

"*I* take care of myself."

"Aunt Stella says you fill up on sweets."

"Stella's as bossy as you."

I started to do a variation of the pot and kettle again but thought better of it. My mother won the "bossy" title hands down, but it was the label she flared at quickest.

This time we said a proper good night to each other. I hung up and stared at the ceiling, willing away all thought of David Wright. Instead I conjured up a late-afternoon sail with Ned. Those were our best times. I had learned to be as comfortable with our silences as he was. And I loved that boat, a return to the cradle from which I roused myself only long enough to feel the excitement of a swift race or a stinging wind or a whipping rain; and someday I felt I might stay on it forever.

As I was losing consciousness, it occurred to me that the purpose of my mother's phone call all along had been to tell me about David. She had waited until she'd found a way to deliver the message and the warning at the same time.

Skimming

the

Surface

Ned and I might never have conceded that anything was going on between us if we hadn't drunk a pitcher of rum punch one long sunset aboard his boat following a day on the water. We'd been watching some greenish spotted fish neither of us could identify. The sun was still warm, but a breeze and the spray from a speedboat caused me to shiver. Ned reached around my shoulder, giving me a hug—half friendly, half more.

"You need your jacket?" he asked.

"I don't think so. I've got enough rum in me." He laughed and rocked my shoulders. His bony, callused fingers bit a little into my arm, and I became aware of how closely our hips matched up as we continued to stare at the fish and sip our rum drinks.

When the fish disappeared, he said, "I'll bet you were a cute little sailor," a tone and line completely out of character for him. I wondered if this was Ned's idea of flirting or if he was just acknowledging that I was not one of the guys.

"In Rollins, Texas, there wasn't a lot of opportunity to sail. Speedboats and waterskiing were big on the lakes, but sailboats didn't catch on until after I'd left. I learned to sail in Washington."

"So did you water-ski in Rollins?"

"Not much. I was too busy trying to prepare myself for 'life,' whatever I thought that meant."

"And then you married."

"Then I married. I worked at being an economist and worked at being a wife and didn't do well at either. So I gave up both and left Dallas."

"Just like that?"

"No. But I did it." We became silent again. The odor of his overheated body lingered from earlier in the day. A lovely man's smell, one I had missed.

"I worked for the Dallas Federal Reserve and put a lot of effort into a long-term economic forecast of Dallas. In my final report I predicted economic disaster within twenty years and recommended that the financial community diversify its holdings, not depend so much on oil. Nobody could refute my arguments. No one agreed with them either. I received an institutional pat on the head from which I never recovered." I said this last lightly, but at the time I'd been crushed.

The blow had hit both professionally and personally. Until this episode I had not realized how dependent I was on the illusions of others. Then I discovered an unsettling truth: if nobody else thought I was wonderful, my image of myself collapsed.

"You quit over that?" he asked in such a way that I couldn't tell whether he considered the incident large or small.

"I stayed on for a while, but I put all my energy into volunteer work for politicians I deemed worthy." I laughed. "The field for my candidates wasn't too crowded."

"And a consultant was born."

"Something like that," I answered. "In a way giving up economics was really the last leave-taking in a series of leave-takings that began in college—back when I was looking for absolutes.

"First I gave up on philosophy because I couldn't find a satisfactory system—one I could live by. I was really after *sureness*, something I could believe with my whole heart. Next I concentrated on my old love, mathematics, guaranteed to bring order out of chaos. That lasted until I found Gödel, who proved to me once and for all that neither mathematics nor ideas could be tested against themselves."

I looked at Ned to see if he could possibly still be paying attention. "I'm sorry," I said. "I guess I can't resist a captive audience. I haven't thought about any of this in years."

He moved closer to me. "Don't stop."

"Well, by then I had driven myself crazy trying to fill up the hole, not seeing that the hole itself was impossible to prove. Enter economics, which allowed me to play with patterns, still in a neat and tidy way, but without expectations of cosmic revelation. After that phase, though, I haven't much bothered with being neat and tidy—intellectually or otherwise. As you can see, your need for order just has different symptoms than mine."

"I suspected as much," he said, shifting his weight. He kept holding me, neither of us looking at the other. In a while, he asked, "And the marriage?"

"I finally realized a marriage doesn't guarantee sureness either," I said. "In Atlanta I tried again, but after that I gave it up for good."

"I didn't mean to pry," he said.

I laughed. "You're the unpryingest man I know. You never even asked what a hot-shot political consultant like me was doing fleeing Washington."

"You've got a reputation for being independent and quirky. I just assumed—we all assumed—you were ready to try something new." He was quiet for a few moments. "You bore easily, I've observed."

Without meaning to, I sighed. He looked at me sharply. "Are you bored with me? The boat and all?"

My God, you are a baby, I wanted to say. But stranger words popped out: "You are the only man whose elbows I've ever noticed," I told him.

He looked dumbfounded, as if he'd suddenly found himself in the presence of a madwoman. Oh, damn that rum, I thought, making a mental note to avoid it, but he started laughing. I did, too. We began shadow-boxing with our elbows until another fit of laughter overtook us. Then we stared into the water again, searching for those green fish, anything to stay close without acknowledging the need.

Eventually he turned his face to me. I noticed how chapped his lips were and touched them with my fingertips. He wrapped me in both his arms, and we started staring at the fish again, or rather, at the place where the fish had been.

He pushed my hair behind my ears. "Do fish feel?" I asked. "I mean, do they like each other? Do they miss their babies? Do they nest, in a manner of speaking?"

"I don't fish," he replied, but he took his time getting out the words.

Why not kiss him? I thought as our fingers laced together. He's young and healthy and can take care of you in your old age. Except you are not planning an old age with him or anyone else, I reminded myself as his breath came whisper-gentle on my neck.

At most you would be having a lark with a young man whose stack-heap of memories haven't grown to overwhelm him, a refreshing change, I amended as he caressed the small of my back, curving my body into his. Except you are going to lead a life of equilibrium, of abstinence and equilibrium. And Ned Sampson would be about the millionth attempt at the right equation.

I stretched and yawned with appropriate casualness. "I need to get home. The rum, I'm afraid." I shook his elbow. "Come on. Let's leave the fishes be."

Keeping

Secrets

Ralph stared at the puddles of notebook paper on the floor, abandoned by his daughter Annie, who now cruised his desk, touching her right index finger to every object. During an earlier photo session Annie had announced her intentions of "working" with her father, whereupon Rachel had taken their son Scott to buy a baseball mitt.

For the past twenty minutes at Stone's campaign headquarters Ned, Ralph, and I had watched Annie while talking in code about Mary Cardigan, the one competitor who made Ralph anxious. Once more we tried to persuade him that excess worry was premature.

"But there's got to be something on her," he said. Then abruptly: "Annie, stay out of the desk." From where he sat he couldn't see her, but he could hear the scraping of wood. She closed the drawer some but not all the way and looked at me defiantly. I met her gaze but figured this to be a Stone problem, not mine. At the moment my chief concern was to keep Ralph from shooting himself in the foot. Obsessed with Mary Cardigan, he was more intent on tearing her down than with building himself up. Usually we could cajole him, but today he resisted.

"I don't know why we've never brought up her divorce," Ralph continued petulantly.

"That was twenty-five years ago, and her husband left her with three children to support," I reminded him again.

"Divorce doesn't play so well anymore," Ned added. "Too many people have been through one."

The little girl quietly began to examine the objects in the drawer that she hadn't quite closed. She soon produced a key and without hesitation walked over to the file cabinet to fit it in the lock. She hummed to herself, bobbing her brown curly head from side to side, as if she were carrying on a conversation with a friend.

My straying glance gave her away. When her father turned to look, he was not charmed. "Annie, didn't I tell you to stay out of those drawers? What do you think you're doing?" he snapped as he got up and snatched the key away from her. Why all the fuss? I wondered. As upset as Ralph was, he still appeared to be restraining himself. Was he so orderly or so furtive? I looked at Ned, who shrugged his shoulders, but were we acknowledging the same excess?

"It goes there," she was able to say before her face broke into a thousand pieces. She began to sob loudly. Ralph stood over her, patted her shoulder awkwardly, but the little girl jerked away from him and, sobbing more loudly, cradled her head into her folded arms on the desk.

Before Ralph could decide between scolding again or consoling, I gathered her papers from the floor and stooped down next to her. "These are really nice S's," I whispered. "I had a terrible time learning to make an S. What's your hardest letter?"

"F's," she stammered into the desk, though she didn't stop

crying. Ralph looked at me gratefully and sat back down to resume talking to Ned.

"Oh, *F*'s. I'd forgotten about them. I'm not sure I ever got
them right. Did you know there are two ways to write *F*? Here,
show me which way you do it."

Annie stopped crying, and when I touched her hand, she took
mine and curled up next to me on the couch to show off her
handwriting. Ralph grinned at us as if nothing had happened. She
was his charming child again, his precious Annie.

In a few minutes he said, "What if she likes little girls?"

"Who?" Annie asked, looking at her father with interest,
having also forgotten the entire incident.

"An enemy of Daddy's, honey," he answered.

She looked at me. "Enemies don't like little girls."

"No they don't," I said.

"Or maybe little boys," Ralph said, getting up to stretch.

"Do you know something we don't?" Ned asked.

"Maybe."

"Count me out," I said. "Count Pelham and Jackson out."

"I'm just saying there might be . . . you know . . . I've heard
stories."

"I mean it," I said, staring Ralph Stone down.

"Oh, hell, H.A., I didn't." He sat down next to Annie and
took her in his arms. "Ask Annie here. She'll tell you I don't mean
half of what I say, do I, sweetheart?"

She patted his face. "Mama says you go off half-cocked."

Ralph and Ned both laughed as Ralph reached across Annie
for my arm.

"I'm just worried, that's all. I really want this, H.A., but Ned
can vouch for me. He knows I think a lot meaner than I act. He's
watched me in boat races, and the Lord and Ned know I play
fair, but I want to win any race I'm in. I want to win this election."

"What's this about races?" Rachel asked as she entered the
office.

Ned's face lit up as usual when he saw her, but I was pleased to note that I was gaining on her, wattage wise, even if she was closer to his age, ten years closer.

"Look at my glove, Daddy," Scott said as he followed his mother into the room.

"Hey, look at this!" Ralph shoved the small mitt on and raised his hand for a catch. "I was just explaining to H.A. that my bark is a lot worse than my bite."

"Of course, darling," she said.

Watching him there, handsome husband, good father, concerned citizen, I hoped to hell she was right, but the kernel was rolling inside me, ever so gently.

Seducing

David

By the time I had rented a car in Dallas for the drive to Rollins, I felt ready to cope again. I was even glad I hadn't reached my mother when I called from the train station. This way she would be more surprised. I congratulated myself on not letting her know any sooner. If Ned tried calling, she could truthfully tell him that I wasn't there and wasn't expected. I anticipated her surprise and pleasure at seeing me.

Ned had been much mistaken about one thing: our quarrel was not about David. Not about David at all, I told myself again. Except that the whole of my adult life seemed to begin and continue to connect through David, despite all my efforts.

difficulties and his guilt about taking their money for school. I confided my fear that I would never find anything I really believed in or wanted to do. Our intimacy came too rapidly, but the pleasure of confession was heady.

Yet all along I assumed nothing as wonderful as David would last for me. When I was with him, every moment felt special, but I had tried to capture magic before, and one way or another it always escaped.

✳

After eighty push-ups, David stood by his Thunderbird smoking a cigarette. "I read some of your Tillich this week, but I'm not sure how I feel about him."

So pleased that he'd made the effort, I didn't bother to tell him that I hadn't been interested in Tillich in over two months. "I have a hard time with him, too," I admitted, warming to the subject. Theology was easier to talk about than sex. "I mean, I can understand Kierkegaard's 'fear and trembling' and 'sickness-unto-death.' I can understand all that. But I have a devil of a time with Tillich's idea of grace and his unconditional . . . well, it's another way to say nothing, I think."

"Mmmmm."

"I want grace," I went on, "I want to know grace, but leaps of faith leave me cold. Do you know what I mean?"

"Mmmmm."

"Are you listening? I don't think you're listening. You don't care about any of this. You think you know everything. Well, you don't! I don't. I'm not sure there *is* anything to know. Nothing works!"

He put his arm around me. "You come to this conclusion every few weeks. I think you must run out of steam about once a month."

"Don't patronize me," I said, shrugging off his arm.

"Listen, you read philosophy like a self-help manual." He stabbed the air with his right hand as he lectured. "You've been an existentialist, a Platonist, a nihilist, an empiricist—and who

was it last month? Heidegger? I don't think you understood half
of what you were telling me about him; I certainly didn't. And
you're getting worse. The closer you get to graduation, the more
desperate you've gotten to find a system."

"I won't bore you anymore," I said, close to tears.

"You don't bore me, but to tell the truth, maintaining an
intense level of excitement is hard."

"So I've noticed."

I walked away from the car. David followed down the dirt
lane, but there was no place for us to sit, so we stood staring at
the dark flat fields lighted only by a half moon.

"Are you going to marry me?" he asked, but I didn't answer.
Though he proposed and I declined often enough, marriage
mostly seemed something other people did. I sometimes thought
he kept proposing because he knew he could get away with it.

After a pointed silence, he asked another question: "Have
you started your job interviews?"

"What job interviews?" As he well knew, I was considering
graduate school.

He took a deep breath before plunging ahead. "Your mother
and I think more school will encourage your worst tendencies.
We think the real world will be good for you."

"What's going on, David? You and my mother?"

"She hates to see you flailing around. I do, too. Besides," he
went on, taking my arm and steering me back toward the car,
"maybe you'd be better off forgetting about cosmic problems and
concentrating on something more immediate, like what you're
going to do next year. Like marrying me. Or getting a job. With
both of us working we could save a lot of money."

"We've been over my future a hundred times. Everyone has
been over my future a hundred times."

"Why don't you marry me?" he interrupted.

"Did that option come up in the conversation with my
mother?"

"I'm working up to it. First she has to see how responsible
I am."

"Parachuting out of airplanes is responsible?"

He pressed me to him. "You're evading."

When I shook my head and said, "Never mind," he opened the front car door for me. No more titillation tonight, I realized.

As I climbed into the car, my eyes smarted with disappointment. Was my life to be one of contemplation or action? I asked myself. Quickly I came to a decision. I grabbed his arms and pulled him down on me. His head bumped the steering wheel.

"Damn it, H.A." He rubbed his head.

"David, do you want to have sex with me or not?"

"Of course I want to. I just did."

"No. Real sex. I want us to have sexual intercourse *now*."

He kissed my forehead before he began disentangling his body from mine. "Maybe, honey," he said, "you should try push-ups, too."

Unquiet

Times

Clutching the phone in my mother's kitchen only minutes after my arrival in Rollins, I listened to the high, distraught pitch of Aunt Stella's voice and struggled to grasp the words—"stroke," "partially paralyzed," "intensive care," "prognosis." Where had I been? Thirty-six hours now. Everyone was looking for me.

And I should turn on my mother's answering machine. I had all kinds of messages—if they weren't erased. Somebody named

Sally from the office about five times. Somebody named David. An old friend, he'd said. My friend Bev what's-her-name had seen him at a party in Dallas last night and had told him about Sudy. Everybody in the world knows but you. And who is Ned? Almost filled up the entire machine with his calls. And where had I been?

I didn't try to explain to my aunt. I didn't tell her that my showing up in Rollins was the craziest of coincidences, founded not on intuition but only a foolish quarrel. I just stood there and nodded into the telephone, the reproach in her words deserved.

With great care I replaced the phone and with equal care filled a glass with water as if anything I touched might splinter in my hands. My first instinct was to return David's call—he knew my history with my mother—but I resisted.

Instead, I decided to call Keith, my first husband. Keith would understand. Dependable, supportive Keith. "Don't be a fool!" I could hear my mother scold. "He's a married man with a family." She was right. I would not call. But wasn't that the progression? As before, from Sudy to David. From Sudy to Keith. From Sudy to somebody.

As a little girl, a few months after moving to Texas, I spent the afternoon with a new friend. We sat on her front steps while I tightened my roller skates, and she talked about my half-orphaned plight. How horrible it would be, she said, if something should happen to my mother. "It must be like losing your legs," she went on. "You've already lost one. You lose the other and you can't walk at all."

"That won't happen," I mumbled as I twisted the key one final turn in the skate. "That won't happen," I said into my knees and concentrated so hard on keeping away emotion that I can still remember precisely the location of a scab on my left kneecap. I still remember refusing to look at that friend; remember pushing myself off, my friend's voice telling me to come back with her skate key.

Those next few nights I spent awake, alert, eyes locked on the ceiling as I waited from one second to the next to hear my mother's sleeping breath.

By way of controlling my breathing now, I drank the glass of water in even, slow gulps. The last drops of water I poured into a pot of English ivy cascading down the beige kitchen counter. The ivy was the only color in the small kitchen; everything else was in shades of beige and brown, including a few strips of wallpaper featuring fat teapots. The wallpaper helped differentiate the eating area from the kitchen.

When my mother moved back to Rollins after her retirement, she rented this almost-new house with its tiny rooms, very much resembling the apartments she had lived in after we left this town. Though never interested in gardening, she had been pleased to have a yard again, especially since she wasn't responsible for maintaining it. "The owners have to mow," she'd said as if this made her box a bargain.

As I stared at a tarnished silver water pitcher brought with us from Kentucky, I tried to imagine what awaited me at the hospital and how I would respond. Aunt Stella had warned of what was in store: a temporary loss of speech, already beginning to return; partial paralysis of the left side; possible hearing impairment.

Aunt Ruth and Aunt Stella met me at the hospital, but nothing really prepared me for what I found as I stood by my mother's bedside.

My first reaction had been one of surprise over how sunny the intensive-care room was and how many machines were in it. Creating an atmosphere of hard brightness, the sun glanced off the shiny white walls, the metal frame of the hospital bed, shone on the enameled monitors hooked up to the frail, still figure of my mother. I concentrated on that brightness for as many seconds as I could before accepting her transformation.

She slept, giving me time to compose my face, if not my emotions. My aunts came and went at prescribed times, but so intent was I on willing her back to us, I hardly noticed them. Even the doctors made no real impression on me. What could they tell me that I couldn't already see?

Tubes sprang from her arms, her nose, her urethra. Her hair, unteased and stuck to her head, looked thin, lifeless; her mouth, without her false teeth, shrunken—an old woman's mouth, not my mother's. Nothing could have readied me for this. Terror— a falling, a crumbling—engulfed me. I held her hand and silently promised that I would become the flawless daughter we had both once set our hearts on.

By the time she opened her eyes, I could smile. "Hello, Mama," I whispered. Her eyes filled with tears. She clung to my hand; I clung back.

Since my flight from Texas almost twenty years earlier, our meetings were charged with the sure knowledge of a parting, painful to us both. She never quite forgave my leaving the state or my first marriage or my first career and could not overcome her disappointment. My going served as a reminder of all the old dangers lurking around the corners for the two of us. Without her instruction I could still fall down. I confirmed her fears: I was flighty; I was soft. Disillusionment with a marriage or a career gave me no excuse to flee; I should have stood my ground.

Usually, times we were together, we had about twenty-four hours before she began to find reasons to lash out over a real or imagined slight, or a real or imagined fault.

"You never visit," she accused. "You might as well be a stranger. I don't know why you can't settle down like a normal person. You are so particular God couldn't please you."

Because I refused to reveal anything about myself of true consequence, I botched any chance we might have had at coming to some real understanding. So we met and we quarreled and we made up and planned another meeting. Usually away from Texas; usually with the same result.

＊　＊　＊

That night, after everyone else had gone, a young, blond nurse, large-boned and ample of face, took me into a conference room with a small oak table and four matching chairs. What a dreary way to be given bad news, I thought, imagining a family hunched forward, elbows on the table, hanging on the doctor's every hard-to-follow phrase. Had that been how it was for my mother when my father died? A hard chair, a hard table, and a doctor's hard, clinical words?

Had she received the news all alone, or had she been in the room with him? Comforting him as she later tried to comfort me. I did not know. I had not wanted to know. My own nightmare was enough without sharing hers, too; a reason, perhaps, she never told me.

The nurse pointed to a beige vinyl two-seater couch pushed up against one wall. "You'll have to curl up," she said, "but maybe you can sleep a little." She unfolded a blanket she had been carrying in her arms. "I've warmed it for you."

"Thank you," I said, more grateful to this woman than she could ever know. I lay on the top half of it and allowed her to wrap the other half around me. For all her gentleness, I might well have been her patient.

"Want the light out?" she asked at the door.

Her kindness overwhelmed me. Only then did I realize how much I missed Texas, missed Rollins, missed my family.

Visiting

Hours

On one empty night Beverly Connors Renfro, my old school friend, arrived at the intensive-care waiting room. I didn't recognize her. The few extra pounds in her hips, the strident ash-blond coloring, the makeup too contrived for her delicate features—slight alterations, really—changed her appearance more than the adjustments warranted. The biggest difference had to do with presence: this Bev had lost her poise and confidence. I didn't know how to respond to the person in front of me, but full of longing for the old, I embraced her.

"My mother called," she said. "I'd have come sooner, but school and the kids . . ." Her voice trailed off, unsure of itself. Up close her face looked drawn and more lined than I remembered. This past year she had divorced her husband, and I had made a cursory phone call. I wished I had done more.

"How are things for you?" I asked before she could start in on condolences. I was sick of condolences. "And the girls?" I added.

"Better. Janice is a freshman in college at Tech. Sonya's a junior in high school. At first they hated the move to Dallas, but they've adjusted well. Faster than I have. All these years I wanted to leave that damn ranch. . . ." She paused, then went on, "It's funny what I miss. Not the swimming pool or the tennis courts or the helicopter—you knew about that? The helicopter?" I shook my head, but she had already lost interest in it.

"I don't miss anything," she said as she gazed at her hands, "but the cows. I miss the cows." Now she focused her eyes on me. "I'd turned them into people," she went on. "If you watch them long enough, you find their personalities are every bit as interesting as most of those around you. I was so lonely." She was sitting on the edge of the couch, hands clasped on her knees, as if she might bolt at any minute. "The girls have been a great comfort to me. They keep me busy. I don't know what I'll do when they leave home."

"My mother used those words about me when I was growing up," I said. "But you'll get better, then wonder why you stuck it out so long." I believed that. And what good would it do to speak of the other side? The bouts of loneliness that hit out of nowhere, reinforcing all the self-doubt, the fears. I'd had plenty of all that, in slightly different forms, whether married, involved, in love, or alone.

"I'm talking too much," she said and sat back into the couch. "Here Aunt Sudy is sick and all I can do is rattle on about me. I broke down and cried when I first heard about her. Believe me, I've thought about Aunt Sudy a lot—how strong she was for all of us. All by herself, too, yet she gave so much. She *liked* us." Bev looked down at her hands spread wide on her lap. "Herds have a lead cow, one the others follow. She makes the decisions even for the bulls. I've often thought of Sudy as our lead cow.

"I kept telling myself I was coming up to talk to her, but I think I was a little embarrassed. You know? She wouldn't understand why I couldn't be strong, too."

"You're doing fine. You're making a life for yourself and the girls."

"Am I?"

I quickly changed the subject. "How is your mother?" I asked and realized how little news Sudy had been giving me. Had she been withholding information or was it that she simply sensed disinterest on my part?

"I dreaded telling her I was leaving Jack. She's always said she doesn't believe in divorce. She thinks you just make the best of your situation. But she's been great. She went so far as to say she thought I did well to put up with him as long as I did.

"I think his miserliness bothered her more than the affair he was having," she went on. "It probably did me, too. Oh, he liked to play Mr. Big Shot with his helicopter and things like that, but the rest of the time he quibbled about my accounts—how much I paid for toothpaste and cleansing cream—silly items. I could forgive his stinginess with money but not with life." She put her elbows on her knees and cupped her face in her palms, a girlish and confiding position. Her words spilled out as if she had not talked to anybody in years.

"When our calves were seven or eight months old, we separated them from their mothers and took them to slaughter. For a week afterward, the mothers would go to the place of separation and bellow all night. I mourned with them. After about a week, the cows appeared to recover, but I would grieve for another month. Sometimes my depression got so bad I'd go to the doctor for pills.

"Then two winters ago a calf was stillborn, its body frozen to the ground. For two weeks the mother, trying to revive her baby, licked the corpse. Every time I checked, that cow was out there licking. One day as I watched I began to think, I am that cow and my marriage is that frozen body and there's no way in hell either she or I can save what's already dead. That's when I started making my plans." Her face bore the expression she must have worn when she announced her decision: grim, determined, defiant, the spunk of her forebears prevailing.

As if on cue, she began searching her purse for something. "Before I forget," she said as she looked, "you're to expect a call from an old friend of yours. I wrote his name down. I met him at a party the other night. Started flirting with him—he's married, but what the heck—then he found out I'd grown up in Rollins and one sentence later we were on to you. We figured out we had even met before. I think he's still a little in love with you." She rummaged some more in her purse before closing it. "I can't find his name, but it's David something. You dated him in college. Wasn't he a big romance of yours? I vaguely remember your talking about a David."

"David Wright?" I asked, already knowing the answer.

"That's him. He's worse for the wear but still cute enough to flirt with."

"He happened a long time ago."

"Well, I'm using you as my inspiration. You aren't beauty queen material and you keep finding men." She looked upset. "I didn't mean to insult you. I just meant—"

With a wave of my hand I cut her off. "Bev, stay away from married men. At best, they're stopgaps. And you're too vulnerable. They almost never leave their wives."

"I know! But they seem safer. I'm scared to death of catching something. AIDS is just the worst of the things I worry about." Her eyes widened as if to release the tumult stored in her head. "To tell you the truth, I am seeing somebody, but he drives me crazy talking so much. He's pretty good at sex, but it takes him forever to get around to it."

I laughed. Bev grinned. "Marge Dalton warned me that most men talked either too much or not at all. She also warned me against small towns, including Rollins. Said it was awful for her after her divorce. Married friends drop you. I've thought about your mother and how hard it must have been for her."

I had never thought about it myself, for we'd been surrounded by plenty of family and single women friends, although Bev was right, of course. Seldom did my mother go to the houses of married friends. No wonder she had been so ready to leave Rollins.

"Are you finding this a problem in Dallas?" I asked, wondering what my life would have been like had I chosen to stay there.

"Not really," she answered, but I could tell she had other things on her mind. "You know, we had the most romantic bull. He courted his cows carefully. And when he was in the thralls of one, he'd have no time for any of the others." With the telling, she became more cheerful. "He'd graze with her and lick her ankles, then all over, taking all the time in the world. I keep thinking there has got to be a man out there as good as that bull, but so far I haven't found him."

As she stood up to go, she grabbed my hand. "We don't fit anywhere, you know. We don't have the protective traditions of older generations or the street smarts of the younger. We got caught in between. We were so *stupidly* innocent."

"I know."

"But you think the world can work for us anyway?"

I nodded yes, not sure I meant it.

After Bev left, I switched on the TV but couldn't get the gist of the images. They came out only as shapes with color, a not especially interesting kaleidoscope. Beverly Renfro's visit had unsettled me. If there was one man in this world to avoid, it was David Wright, of the lusty prick and promises of everlasting love—a romantic bull if ever there was one, off and on through more years than I liked to acknowledge.

David

Seduced

On a late June morning of our graduation summer, David and I picked up the clothes we had strewn in three minutes flat from the front door of his apartment in Fort Worth to his couch some eight feet away. We knew it was three minutes because he had checked his watch as he opened the door, then again when we landed on the couch. One of David's more annoying traits was to fancy himself time-efficient. Granted on this sticky, sweltering day, we weren't overly dressed to begin with.

Three weeks after upholding my virginity, David had solemnly declared we should renounce celibacy. Though this did not

make for an auspicious, never mind sexy, beginning, we found
ourselves apt, if earnest, students of copulation. In no time at all—
two to be precise—we had gotten the hang of it. "Insatiable"
described us pretty well. Even so, we managed to find other areas
of disagreement.

"You've got to tell her you're leaving," David said, pulling
on his boxer shorts.

"I'm going to. I just need to think of a reason, other than
the obvious." As soon as the words were out, I knew he would
pounce and he did.

"Tell her you're leaving with me."

"I'm not."

The spring had proven eventful: David got the hang of making love and my mother took a traveling job with Western Auto.
When she told me about the job, she looked more pleased than
I had ever seen her. "This means a transfer to Houston. Time to
get out of this one-horse town. I'm selling the house—I've just
been waiting for you to graduate—and we'll find a nice place
there. An apartment would be fun for a change. With your working, too, we could have a really nice one."

I had made an effort to bring my enthusiasm to proper pitch
and, at the same time, assimilate all the messages delivered. In
one fell swoop, she had determined where I would live and ruled
out graduate school. The apartment was a sop to me, for I had
always been taken with them. Lives appeared self-contained there,
all things manageable, not subject to the sprawled emotions en-
couraged by houses. She shouldn't make me find out differently,
I thought.

"Can you imagine anything better than what we did a minute
ago?" David asked. "Truthfully, now?" I shook my head no.

"So what's the problem? Thousands of great screws and you
can see the world, too."

"Your world. You'd be gone for months. I wouldn't make a
good military wife, you know that. And what would I do?" I
started picking up my clothes.

"You would be my *wife*, damn it!" he shouted. Then, in a

more reasonable voice: "And work math problems. Aren't you giving up philosophy for math?"

"I said I *might*." I wadded my clothes in front of me and leaned against a chair. "At least with math you know where you are. You can recognize patterns." David was staring at me either with incredulity or sympathy, I couldn't tell which.

"You'd better marry me," he said. "Nobody else is going to put up with your . . . your oddities."

I stood up and started toward the bathroom to dress in private, but he blocked the door.

"If you loved me, you'd find some way to accommodate us."

I threw my clothes at him. "If you loved me, you'd find another life."

"Don't just stand there like that," he said.

"Like what?"

"Naked."

"David, we don't have time."

"Turn around."

I started not to but watched his eyes and changed my mind. He came close. "It's your ass that drives me crazy," he said, stroking it.

I put my hands behind my back and pulled down his shorts. "You've never used that word in front of me before," I said.

"What word is that?"

"You know."

"I keep trying to save things for our marriage," he whispered.

The

Waiting

Game

A lifted finger, a recognizable word, an extra spoonful of food—these tokens of progress measured my sense of time. After the immediate crisis passed, I confined my hospital vigil to fourteen-hour watches. Though a steady stream of visitors called, Sudy was not ready to receive friends and only saw her sisters for a few minutes at a time.

Those first days, Aunt Ruth and Aunt Stella had been in constant attendance, and Aunt Clara came from Dallas as often as she could. They would provide the backbone until Sudy was stronger, but now she was doing just fine on her own. The doctors marveled at how rapidly she was rebounding. "Not out of the woods," her internist kept saying, "but on her way." Neither he nor I was ready to address the question of on her way to where.

I tried to imagine the two of us sharing a place in Boston. On my turf, she always grew restless, hated playing second fiddle to me. Hated the New England brusqueness of speech, the efficiency of manner. She mistook reserve for unfriendliness and considered everyone, including clerks, a little snobbish.

But the worst of it, whether in Boston or Dallas or Rollins, was going to be her loss of independence, and I hadn't any idea how either of us would deal with that. Anything less than total autonomy she perceived as defeat. I could not see my mother accepting defeat.

Most nights I stopped by for a warmed-over supper with Aunt Ruth and Uncle Ben, took comfort in the good-natured banter my uncle dutifully produced for me, but sometimes I felt too weighed down—not so much by the day as by all the days to come. On those occasions I resorted to chili from the Taco Bell and settled in alone at my mother's with old scrapbooks.

For hours I sat in her living room filled with furniture from different periods of our lives: from Kentucky the Victorian rocking chair upholstered in burgundy velvet, the oak end table from her parents' home, the gray-and-pink-striped couch purchased after she moved to Dallas, the TV acquired on her return to Rollins—and everywhere pictures, mostly of me when I was young, before my father died and I became entirely her concern. The room was small, but she had managed an uncluttered look despite all her treasures.

Over her couch, the place of honor, she had hung a picture of three horses in a field. The colors were muddy and the composition questionable, but none of that concerned her. This was a real oil painting, she was fond of saying, painted by the credit manager in the Western Auto in Gurneyville. The barren winter field and the undistinguished horses had a familiarity to them hard to escape: the field and the horses could have been my grandfather's. But she was getting better, I would remind myself. She would not die, and together we would set her right again.

On the day she sat up and smiled and made a joke, Ned called. Although I had spoken with him on business matters since my arrival in Rollins, we had not discussed our quarrel, both of us embarrassed by its overtones of a lovers' spat. We had polite interchanges and he never failed to ask about my mother. This time he was more expansive.

Not to worry about anything, he said. The campaign looked good. Mary Cardigan rumors abounding. Press investigating. Lucky us. At the risk of stirring up trouble, I reminded him that Stone could have had a hand in starting those rumors. "He lies so much about small inconsequential matters, he could lie about the big ones, too. Be careful."

"Everybody lies but the two of us," he responded with something close to warmth.

"Be careful," I repeated.

I promised to return as soon as possible. For a day or so. Hard as it was to wrench myself from Rollins—physically and emotionally—I had to check up on Ralph Stone's mischief. That it was his was no longer a question for me. Getting away had served to strengthen my suspicions. But I had time. A few weeks if I was any judge of these matters.

"I miss you," he said before he hung up, and I was pleased he said so.

Naming

Names

We drank iced coffee in Ralph Stone's garden in the middle of snapdragons and baby's breath and dahlias sassing one another. Arborvitae stretched in elegant columns as we talked of smut. There was a rumor about a secretary and Mary Cardigan. Supposedly, the secretary claimed that Mary Cardigan had seduced her and broken up her home. As of now, the media hadn't picked up the story.

"Certainly a new twist on an old tale," I commented after Ralph and Ned sketched in a few of the pertinent details.

"You sound skeptical," Ralph said. He stopped gloating.

"That's putting it nicely."

"I'm only telling you what we've heard. I didn't have anything to do with this and don't want to be accused of negative campaigning." He laid his hand on his knee and leaned toward me. "Frankly, I feel sorry for the woman. We don't want or need this kind of revelation."

Was this the royal "we"? I asked myself, unpersuaded of his innocence, his wide-open hazel eyes notwithstanding.

Rachel, flushed and glistening from a tennis game, strode toward us. She nodded to Ralph and me but kept her eyes on Ned.

"I haven't seen you in an age. Where have you been?" she asked him as she dropped beside where he sprawled on the lawn.

"You'll get grass stains on those white shorts," her husband cautioned.

She reached to pat his hand but kept her attention on Ned: "Answer," she commanded.

Ned's presence swelled to fill the tribute, and I strove to be more amused than jealous. "Your husband is a hard-driving man," he bantered, diplomatically establishing Ralph's proprietorship, but neither of them was paying much attention to the conversation itself.

Suddenly, Rachel jumped up and sat on the arm of my chair. "My God, H.A., forgive me. How is your mother? Ned told me. I'm so sorry." She took my hand in both of hers, then stroked my hair off my forehead. My aunts could not do better. No wonder she enchanted Ned.

"She's not out of the woods, but she's much better, thank you." With an effort, I drew the conversation back to the matter under discussion before she arrived. "We were talking about Mary Cardigan," I said and deliberately did not look at Ralph.

"We'll beat her, won't we?"

"I believe we will. What do you think of the charge against her?"

"What charge? Every day Ralph comes home with a new one." Her eyes remained friendly, but a wariness registered in them.

"I had in mind the lesbian-homebreaker one," I answered, not bothering to keep the sarcasm out of my voice.

She laughed. "Sounds preposterous, doesn't it?"

73

"And untrue, don't you think?"

She looked to Ned instead of Ralph, but her husband answered for her, anyway. "What does it matter what she thinks? I've told you this isn't our doing." He began pacing. "Nor is it our responsibility to stop. Why look a gift horse in the mouth? I'm beginning to wonder whose side you're on, H.A."

"Ralph wouldn't make up a story like that," said Rachel. "Tell her, Ralph."

"I just told her."

"H.A. isn't accusing you," Ned interjected, giving me an exasperated look.

"I'm not accusing. I'm saying I don't want this campaign to be part of a smear, and I think a few phone calls from you would help stop the rumors before they get out of hand."

"If she's right, I think you should do it, Ralph," Rachel said softly without looking up.

For a minute he had the same steeliness, the high-pitched hostility he'd had with Annie the day she disobeyed by playing with his file-cabinet key. Which key were we playing with now? As he had with Annie, he suddenly calmed down.

"Oh, all right, you two. I'll make some calls. Do what I can to clear this up—though it's *not* my doing."

Rachel gave him an effusive hug, and I smiled and thanked him. I could afford to be a gracious winner, although the kernel in my stomach did not diminish one bit as we all sat down to sandwiches and a strategy session, compressing three weeks' worth of meetings into an intense few hours.

Thinking back to that day with Annie chilled me. At the first opportunity, I wanted a look at his contributors' list, the one he kept so confidential I hadn't access to it, couldn't be sure of its location although I felt certain that key Annie was playing with had something to do with it.

Since Ned and I had afternoon appointments set up in Hartford at campaign headquarters, we left after a phone call to check on my mother. As they had earlier, the Stones expressed delight at my mother's recent progress. To their credit, neither appeared to begrudge me more time in Texas.

Ned, once out of the Stones' sight, was all solicitousness. He does care, I thought, and surprised myself with how much I cared about his reaction.

"Everything all right in Rollins?" he asked.

"I don't have to be back until the day after tomorrow. Aunt Stella convinced me I might as well make use of this time while Sudy is still in the hospital."

"Then I'll take you to dinner."

As it turned out, when we began closing down the Hartford office for the night, I remembered an early-evening appointment I'd hastily made when I knew I was coming north.

"Can't you cancel it?" Ned asked, impatient to get back to Boston and on with our plans.

"Not likely. But you fly ahead and take care of the Boston contingent. I'll catch the last plane out, and we'll have a late supper."

"That's not fair to you."

"Just leave me the keys." I held out my hand and he threw them to me.

When I heard the outer office door slam, I went directly to the small key Annie had played with.

The contributors' list was where I had watched Stone put it during our first meeting, and over the next two hours I sat there laboriously copying names, addresses, and pertinent information that could cause him big trouble if leaked, including a letter attached to the file of Jack Stoddard concerning the dismissal of one Gary Boatwright. According to the records, the man had been thoroughly investigated, as had many others whom I came across. Big Brother was, indeed, alive and well, but he was corporate America, not government. A chilling thought. No wonder Ralph was so protective of these files.

My fingers cramped and my head ached, but I was determined to go through everything. In the first place, I hated surprises, and, from the looks of these papers, I could have been in store for many. In the second, I wanted to be ready if Ralph did not make good on his promise to call off the dogs on Mary Cardigan, for as he had the power to ruin her, I had the power to ruin him. Ralph Stone might be ruthless, but I had a vindictive streak. I didn't use it very often, but I knew how to use it well.

Consolations

After my move to Boston I was fine most days except on the mornings when I awoke wondering if my heavy periods meant I was going through menopause. At forty-five? Much too young, I'd assure myself and pour a cup of coffee before settling back in bed with the *Times*, the *Journal*, the *Globe*, the *Post*, and my remote control for the morning shows. Already feeling better, I would anticipate the next hour with the headlines and tell myself age didn't mean anything, not until eighty.

Scanning the papers, I'd opt for hope and curiosity to keep me young. Age is attitude, I'd say as the nice faces and soothing voices spoke to me from my television set. But weren't my fingers slightly stiff? And there was no ignoring the periods. My body definitely had its own agenda and the agenda had to do with age. And what was I doing with my life? Then after a few more sips of coffee and an occasional editorial that I agreed with, the world promised more pleasures.

However, since returning from Rollins, my morning panaceas weren't working. I could not get much interested in the outside world, nor did I look forward to going back to Texas and the decisions regarding my mother. When Ned called to ask if he could take me to the airport for my noon flight, I propelled myself from bed to start packing.

He arrived three hours early. "You sounded . . . down. I thought maybe . . . I'm good at closing suitcases." He followed me into the bedroom and watched me pack a couple of blouses. He thinks I'm old and broken, I thought. He thinks I can't close a suitcase.

"Sit down over there." I pointed to the one chair in the room. "It's not too comfortable, but I only use it to put on my shoes. I usually lounge on the bed. I . . . but I'm jabbering." The voice and the words had nothing to do with me. The room and Ned didn't either. Neither the cheerful quilt nor my beloved books helped orient me.

As if reading my mind, he took a step toward me. I spun around and headed for the bathroom. "Almost forgot my toothbrush." The last thing I needed was pity. I gathered up my creams and blushers and mascara and lipsticks and deliberately did not speak or leave the bathroom until I felt under control again.

When I came out, I found Ned in the kitchen making toast and a fresh pot of coffee for us. He had set the dining-room table and put out four or five jams. "Do you like jellies or what?" he asked, referring to the dozen jars in my refrigerator.

"I can never remember if I have any. I think it's my excuse to justify buying another kind."

"Couldn't you buy them even if you didn't forget?"

"Too extravagant." I took the cup of coffee he handed me. "Now, be sure to call Sally Cummings to get that latest poll. She can call me, or you can. I don't have a fax, remember? And you'd better brief Ralph about tomorrow night's fund-raiser."

He held up a hand to stop me. "You told me all that on the phone. I have a very long list of dos and don'ts. Sit down a minute and eat something. You need to eat."

"Most of that stuff you can give to my assistant when she's over the flu," I said as I sat holding the piece of toast he handed me.

"Don't worry about it. Just eat. You're going to make yourself sick."

The combination of tenderness and scolding in his voice was too much for me. I made a little sound, somewhere between a laugh and a cry, and pushed myself up. "Time to go," I told him, but he put his hands over mine to restrain me.

"H.A., you have hours until your plane. Just sit here and eat your breakfast. We can go over the list again if you'd like. Or you can tell me about your mother." He pulled several sheets of paper from his pocket.

I shook my head. "No on all counts."

He smiled. "I'm going to remind you of that answer the next time you nag me to talk more."

And what if there's not a next time? What if I can never come back? Or I come back irrevocably changed because my mother has died?

I took another sip of coffee and stood up. "Let's close that bag now."

"Sure, but we've got over two hours. If you want me to make some phone calls . . ."

"I don't want you to make phone calls," I snapped.

"Would you like a drink?" he asked as he followed me back into the bedroom.

"At nine-thirty in the morning? I only do that when Ralph force-feeds us champagne."

As he closed the two suitcases, I said, "I don't want you to feel sorry for me."

"How can I feel sorry for you? You're the most together person I know. Half the time you still intimidate me, you're so . . . so . . . in control." He paused. "And sweet, too."

I walked to the window. "No sun here today," I said. "In Texas I'll find sun and good dry heat. I love that heat, the intense absoluteness of it, dry and strong enough to warm you through, to make you feel inseparable from the land and surroundings, even when the demons attack."

Ned had come up behind me, and I turned to him. I don't know which of us reached out first, and I don't know who held on to whom, but we stayed that way for a long time, our bodies swaying gently. I also don't know when the friends' embrace turned into something else or who turned it first.

I became aware of Ned kissing my temple and of my body responding, and I made a conscious decision to turn my face enough to find his lips. He brushed mine, almost casually, as if we kissed all the time. And why not kiss? Why not be greedy just this once? For a while we stood and touched like that, exploring each other's mouths, bodies. Then he led me to the bed and was no longer younger or intimidated or deferential.

On the ride to the airport Ned made plans for when I got back and I tried to forget that my life might be changing forever. He went over my lists, and I tried to pay attention. He told me I was wonderful, and I tried to be responsive. For once Ned felt like talking. An easiness settled on him, and I realized how much I had missed his company.

He spoke of the rumors circulating about Mary Cardigan. Ralph had assured him that he had made those phone calls I'd asked him to make, reiterating that he was in no way involved. Still, our candidate felt the stories were true and hoped that "the truth would be triumphant."

"What an ass. My instinct tells me she's innocent. Just please be careful," I told him and made a note to call Ralph with another warning to cool it on her as soon as possible.

Ned swung my suitcases from his trunk and lined them up on the sidewalk. Next to them he deposited a brand-new fax machine, the box carefully tied in butcher's twine with a small carrying handle at the top.

"Now there's no limit to our contact," he teased, pulling me against the rough tweed overcoat that smelled like him and a little bit like the sea.

"You're a good friend," I said, biting my lower lip and feeling suddenly teary. I pulled away and motioned for a porter.

During the flight to Texas, I vowed again to do whatever I could to stop a rumble on Congresswoman Mary Cardigan. The viciousness of the rumors would destroy almost anyone. Granted she had a lackluster legislative record and an abrasive manner. In fact, as far as I was concerned, she had little appeal as a candidate or a person, but she didn't deserve this—our country's political bile.

The process begins with the innuendos—slime spread on half-truths. Opportunity is all in these matters. That and our ability to be shocked, or pretend to ourselves that we're shocked, or to tell ourselves (those of us assuming some sophistication) that it's not the deed so much as the lying about it. With the ease of ill-tempered children given a box of Crayolas, we break reputations and ruin lives. We are repulsed and drawn at the same time, and none escape.

In

Their

Footsteps

Buffaloes and bears trampled the first path through Rollins, a prairie covered with dancing grasses in uneven shades of green, mingled every now and again with trees of inconsiderable height. Not far from the path, a man excavating for water discovered the skeleton of an Indian. The wolves and my grandmother did not take over the road until five centuries later.

In a tough fight, my grandmother finally beat out the wolves. Hardy stock, these women, migrating to Texas from the Carolinas and Virginias, sometimes stopping off for a generation in Tennessee. A majority of their mothers or their mothers' mothers had landed on Southern shores as indentured servants from Ireland and Scotland without benefit of protectors. They had learned to fend for themselves early on.

To their granddaughters they imparted a certain cunning, a resourcefulness hidden under the veneer of sweet Southern womanhood, although the ones who ventured on to Texas seldom bothered with the veneer. Style, what there was of it, took more time and energy than these frontier women had. Only *their* granddaughters gained the luxury of learning sweet manners. Still, such amenities never held the same premium with Texas women as it did their Deep South counterparts. Over the generations a secret sense of freedom had crept into the canon and flourished—for a time and up to a point.

✳

"She's going to be all right, H.A. I know she will." My cousin Will, whom I could no longer wrestle to the ground, was driving me to the doctor's office in his racing-green Porsche. Growing up he had made my life miserable and wonderful with excitement. Only after my father's death did I begin to fight back—making him pay for feeling sorry for me. Years passed before I noticed he'd outgrown me by two heads and hadn't been a brat for a long while. From time to time he came calling on me in the various cities where I lived, usually when we were both between lovers of consequence.

We had come to have a conference with Mama's doctor, rather than just another hurried exchange in the hospital corridor. The doctor was planning to dismiss Sudy by the end of the week, but none of us knew quite what that meant in terms of follow-up care.

"She'll hate it when she finds out I've gone round her and talked to the doctor," I said.

"We can't assume, Ms. Reese, that she'll ever be better." The doctor's large Adam's apple kept moving hypnotically up and down as he talked. When I first met him, he looked younger than Ned—not a reassuring sign—but now I'd come to admire his care and compassion. Sudy could have been a young girl beginning life for all the effort and attention he gave her. I was not prepared for his suggestion that she go into a convalescent home for stroke patients.

"She'll get supervised care there." He was talking about a place in Dallas.

"Do you mean a temporary arrangement?" I asked. "Until she's well?"

He and Will were looking at me with pity, and I realized he had already said she could never again take care of herself. He had been saying it every day in so many words, and I had chosen not to hear them.

"She has always said she wouldn't go to a home," I explained.

"But she requires around-the-clock care. She needs therapy—a lot of it. Unless you put her in a home, the cost is prohibitive."

"More expensive than the place you recommend?"

"Yes. Plus you have the added problem of finding qualified help."

I shook my head. "I can't do this."

"After we explain, your mother will probably insist on it herself."

"I'm not about to tell her she'll never get better, and no one else is either."

The doctor pulled himself up. "Look, she dealt with her oncoming blindness with as much grace and spunk as I've ever seen. She'll do the same with this."

Will and I looked at each other. "What do you mean her oncoming blindness?" I asked.

The doctor flushed red. "I thought she had told you by now. Three years ago she started to go blind. Her ophthalmologist in Dallas gave her five years before she'd be incapacitated by it. That's why she decided to move back to Rollins." He paused. "You never noticed her poor eyesight?"

I had noticed she didn't read anymore and missed incidents in television stories. I hadn't thought much of it since she still criticized the split ends of my hair. "But she drives," I answered defensively.

"I know. I told her to stop over a year ago." He looked a little defensive himself. "She didn't want to be a burden to you. She was afraid you'd insist she move to Boston and she wasn't about to do that. She wasn't moving in with any of her sisters either. Said they would try to boss her around." The doctor coughed, swallowed. "She made me promise not to tell. Your mother is very independent, but I don't have to tell you that."

We all agreed not to mention the nursing home as anything but a temporary answer, nor would we discuss her slim chances of any but a slight recovery. And Sudy was Sudy. Who knew what she might be able to do when she set her mind to it?

This last was my observation, not the doctor's, but it cheered me a little as I got back in the car, suffocatingly hot from sitting in the sun.

Will and I headed toward the Holiday Inn, one of the only two bars in town—and those no more than five years old. Rollins voted "dry" for a long time.

After buying a lifetime membership in their club for five dollars, Will ordered a beer and I asked for a dry martini, a drink I had not had in fifteen years. The room smelled of stale smoke and beer and was every bit as cold as the car had been hot. The darkness inside seemed intent upon erasing any reminders of the harsh brightness outside.

"Think of it, Will," I said, no longer able to keep back the tears or hurt feelings, "she is going blind and won't even tell her own daughter."

"All she told me was she wanted to move back to Rollins," he said, shaking his head. "She'd gotten pretty forgetful and had messed up on the books a couple of times. I didn't say anything to her about it—hell, she could have stayed there forever as far as I was concerned—but she knew and she was embarrassed. Or I think she knew. She didn't mention that to me either."

"Well, you can be sure I didn't know."

"She made the decision alone. She doesn't think any of us have sense enough to get in out of the rain," he said, quoting one of her favorite put-downs.

The waitress appeared with our drinks, and after a few pulls on his beer, Will spoke again. "I think losing her car may be harder on her than any of the rest. She's always been such a go-er. She once told me she could hardly wait to get back to work after you were born. The only reason she quit at all was to please your father. Did you know this?" I shook my head no.

"He thought she should stay home with you, so she did as long as she could stand it. 'How long was that?' I asked her. 'Three months,' she answered."

I smiled. "Work has always been so important to her. You

gave her a new life, you know, something I was never able to do."

Twelve years ago Will made a great deal of money building luxury apartments for the wealthy young professionals who were spilling into Dallas. He quickly gained a reputation for quality, building solid walls and installing plumbing that lasted and fireplaces that burned real wood.

To his aunt Sudy he attributed much of his success. Upon her retirement from Western Auto, he hired her as his bookkeeper. But she didn't confine herself to his books, of course. After all, he was her nephew, starting up a new business, and he needed her guidance.

As it turned out, he did. She inspected the building materials. Badgered the contractors. Supervised actual installation. Chatted up foremen and workers. No one knew where she might turn up. "Keep them on their toes," she said, determined that Will would get a day and a half's work for a day's pay. She continued her vigilance after a building went up, harassing management to provide superior service, checking with tenants on their complaints. Her curly black head (helped along by a rinse) could be found looking up chimneys, poking under sinks, bent over carpet stains. In between she kept her eyes on the books—and on Will.

"The workmen always ask about her. The more trouble she gave them, the more they took to her. She could make them madder than hell, but it never lasted long. Probably because she never stayed mad. Lost her temper, but then"—Will snapped his fingers—"it was over." Tears came to his eyes. "H.A.," he began but couldn't go on.

I took his hand. "Let's talk about something less depressing. Are you bankrupt yet?" We both laughed, but for the next hour I sat listening to his litany of woe, as he dropped all pretense of trying to maintain a sense of humor about his problems. He was struggling to keep going because his business had been hit hard by the recession. He hoped to sit tight until the economy picked up, for, more than anything, he wanted to stay in Texas.

"I guess you don't understand that need, huh?" he asked.

leave, visiting his wife's parents, and we ran into each other at a party. He looked exactly the same as when I last saw him except his crew cut was longer. My appearance had altered considerably, what with my no-nonsense suits and chopped-off hair.

Nevertheless, he proclaimed me his same true love and spent the next three weeks proving it in the back of cars and in cheap motel rooms and twice against a tree in a suburban park. All through the late winter, we had a high old time, playing lusty teenagers. He insisted I not wear jeans or stockings, the better to feel my legs.

Yet neither of us seriously considered leaving our spouses. After all, he had young children, and I had no desire to break up my marriage, as difficult as it already was. When David's stay was over, our leave-taking was filled with tears and vows not to put ourselves through anything like this again. Neither of us believed it for a minute.

David found me next through an alumni publication after my divorce from Bill. This time I had given up stockings and panties and bras altogether to become a late-blooming flower child. This time we both lived in Washington, and more than once it occurred to us that I must have known he would eventually do a stint there. This time we broadened our repertoire of places to meet, including movie houses in the afternoon, trains, planes, an alcove of the National Gallery of Art, a taxi, a rowboat, and the Thomas Jefferson Memorial. We gave spontaneity a new luster. Though these bold couplings were done for the thrill, we also enjoyed our old game of keeping score. We liked statistics.

Trying to prove my love, I gave up the man I had been seeing, although a future with David was by no means certain. We discussed endlessly when and how he would tell his wife and children, but, more often than not, guilt overwhelmed us. Futilely, I tried to assuage both his guilt and his jealousy over former husbands and unimportant lovers—a jealousy that filled him with a rage I couldn't calm.

I pleaded with him to believe we could last and promised to marry him if only he would trust us. But his obsession with my sexual history proved too strong for our love. He wanted details and, fool that I was, I gave them to him in all their shameful splendor.

That we were demented crossed my mind more than once, and we became particularly fond of calling each other crazy. Anyone overhearing us would have agreed. Still, no matter what terrible things we said, we would call a truce to make love again. Had we ever finished an argument, maybe we wouldn't have had so many. As it was, we were too far gone to be rational.

When we weren't together, he wanted to know what I was wearing and what I had for lunch and what my thoughts were. He remembered the clothes I wore on which dates all the way back to college. He knew the location of every mole and every freckle and the unexpected places that excited me. He memorized me. I had no protection against such fierceness.

The third time is the charm, we would say. But it wasn't. He came to feel he couldn't trust me. He had put all his faith in me once, he said, and he had paid a terrible price. Now all I could offer was my own raw need of him, and obsession does not purchase stability. So once more he left, and this time I determined never again to open myself to him, emotionally or otherwise.

Tonight I had come as a favor—"the last thing I'll ask of you," he pleaded. "No games and no rehashing. I just need to see you." His voice had lost its resonance, making him less of a threat.

The man framed in the entranceway was not who I expected. He looked more like David's father than David. Before he closed the door to the brightness of the outside lights, I saw that the body was thinner, the hair grayer, the eyes sadder, but the face—heavily lined with flesh loosely and carelessly slapped on the bones—alarmed me most. Had his cock suffered the same fate? I wondered.

Afraid he might read my thoughts, I leapt up from the booth, shook his hand, and started talking about the darkness of the room, the stickiness of the weather, and the excellence of the margarita. He took in my words with his eyes, waiting me out until my voice slowed and got thick with the seduction I was fighting against.

"Do people think you're pretty?" he asked.

"Even for you that's a strange opener."

"But do they? I've never known. To the best of my knowledge, I've only had one objective look at you, and that day you were a mess."

"Cut it out, David. This is not about old times." He had already provoked me with his stare.

"What is it about?"

"You're the one who asked me. You said you needed to see me about something crucial. Remember?"

"I wish this were a nicer place, something gayer, more attractive."

"We've never eaten in a nice place. You were always either broke or hiding from your wife."

"Don't let's start," he said and put his hand on top of mine.

"Let's don't," I agreed and moved my hand away.

"Is this going to be the first meal we've ever sat through where I haven't felt you up?" He smiled.

"Yes," I answered through clenched jaws, refusing the joke.

He continued to look at me, then shook his head as if trying to come out of a trance.

"H.A., if only you could have let us just be in love."

"I hate it when you start that melodramatic stuff. It was bad enough when I was in love with you. I did not come here to rehash old times. You promised." I took a sip of my drink. "I would remind you, however, that you are the one who left *me*."

"We didn't have a snowball's chance in hell."

"I remember that line. I have, fortunately, forgotten my reply."

"Don't be bitter. Surely you know enough about yourself by now to know you only made that commitment when you knew I couldn't. We keep each other in a fantasy world to avoid real loss, whether it's our romance ending or natural catastrophe striking one of us."

"Is this why you brought me here? To justify?" He shook his head no and looked ready to cry. I hushed.

Already drinking too fast, I switched to a Carta Blanca when the waiter came; David ordered a Coke. We ordered a few things from the menu, then began playing catch-up—my mother, his family, my work, carefully avoiding my marital status or involvements. I didn't notice I was swinging my foot under the table until he winced. Then my fingers tapped the table until he clasped his hands over mine.

"Slow down," he said and, after a pause, added: "We can go to bed whenever you want." Too angry to speak, I jerked back my hand.

"Your fidgeting is always about sex. Don't act as if I've insulted you."

"Just maybe you don't know everything about me anymore." I made up my mind that if he kept to this line of conversation, I'd leave.

Without urgency, he leaned forward. "You change not at all. Your need for control is too great."

"Any resemblance between me and that twenty-year-old girl you knew is gone. The way I live my life is proof of that."

"The way you live your life tells me you are as elusive as you ever were."

"I'm not listening to this . . ." I began. He interrupted me:

"Then why always two men around?"

"David, for God's sake, don't start this. You know better. The exception has been you."

"The point is you keep somebody else waiting for you. Including me, even these last few years. You always know I'll be here for you."

"In every way but the way I wanted."

"Exactly as you wanted."

The waitress served plates of enchiladas, tamales, rice, and beans. We used the food as a distraction, tried to ignore the silence flopping all around us. Safe topics were hard to come by, and we wanted to be careful with each other, not an easy or familiar task. As a result, I pushed the food around with my fork a while longer before broaching the question again: "Why are we here?"

"I understand you are involved with a young buck."

I picked up my purse and started to slide out of the seat. "You are not doing that to me ever again."

He grabbed my arm. "My question is 'Why?' "

"Maybe because I love him," I said, wanting at that moment to hurt David Wright more than anything in the world.

"You loved them all. Or some of them. For a while. Now you've chosen someone young to ensure you won't be left alone. With any luck *he'll* outlive you."

I didn't answer, but something in his earnestness alarmed me. I could not get at the unfamiliar feeling surrounding us. These were not precisely the old words after all. Something was wrong and I decided to stay and find out what. For a few minutes we went back to playing with our food. Then he put his fork down and began again.

"Mutual friends tell me you're settling easily back into Rollins."

"I have to be here right now. Besides, Rollins comforts me. I know what I'm doing."

"Baby, you always think you know what you're doing. I'm telling you, you don't." He gave me one of his charged I-see-your-soul looks, and I dropped my eyes. For a long time now I had been questioning my change-partners-and-dance habit and also my dependency on those partners. I indulged my irresponsibility in this area because the alternatives felt worse.

"I always hoped I could give you whatever it is you are missing. If I had thought it possible, I would have hung around."

I shook my head. "I'm not looking to *complete* myself, if I ever was. I would like to know what I could have been like if my life had gone differently—with a . . . father, even a grandfather."

"You've hardly spoken of your father before."

"Until recently, I've never thought about him much. Or my

grandfather. Too angry, I guess. Anyway, I'm just beginning to understand how . . . lopsided? . . . I am."

We sat through another long pause, then abruptly he said, "You think I look old. You aren't attracted to me anymore." He said it so bluntly, without defenses, I knew he wasn't seeking assurance. I gave it anyway.

"When we're a hundred and two, I'll still find you attractive, but I'm not going to bed with you again." The first part of the statement was true enough, although he did look old.

He once more took my hand. He turned my palm up and traced my lifeline with his finger. Years ago he'd learned to read palms, a claim which always made me nervous.

"And if I don't make it to a hundred and two?"

"David, why are we here?"

"I needed to see you. Maybe to tell you I'm sorry for all the pain I've caused you." He looked at me. "To tell you I love you."

I laughed and took my hand away, gently this time. "I like it better when we're tossing blame."

"Will I see you again?" he asked.

Something in his forlorn manner stopped me from giving a definite no.

"We'll see," I answered.

He smiled. "That's what I tell my children when I mean 'no.'"

"We'll see," I said again.

On the way out, he whispered sadly, "Let the record note I didn't feel you up."

I reached up to kiss his cheek. "Take care," I said, surprised that I had had no desire to make love.

"I love you," he repeated and turned abruptly away.

Driving home, I played the evening's tape over and over in my head, but I couldn't digest his unsettling statements. Nor could I find the clue to explain his new secrets. All evening I felt we were reading lines for the wrong story. Something terrible must have happened to him.

Women

Alone

Will and the doctor and I stood around my mother's bed. We let the doctor do the explaining. By now he appeared as nervous as we were.

"I'll see you in hell first," she said almost before he got all the words out of his mouth. She glared at me. "H.A., this is the worst damn fool idea you've ever had. I'm not going."

"Only until you're better," I pleaded.

"I'm already better. And if you try it, I'll check myself out."

"Mother, please."

The night before, I had churned and worried about Sudy's indomitable will. All her life she used it to fight her battles, but under these circumstances I wasn't sure it would serve her well. In most cases, she carefully examined all her alternatives before coming to a decision. Once made, she put formidable energy behind it. She relied heavily on her instincts to guide her, but boundaries between instincts and emotions can blur, and never more so than with Sudy.

The doctor started again: "Maybe if you think about it, give yourself a little time, you'll—"

"You might as well leave now. All of you."

I saw a tear in her eye just as I hardened myself to bring up the financial side of it: Medicare won't help us at home; we can't afford this for long—money concerns disturbed her.

"At home we'll have to have round-the-clock nurses," was the best I could do.

"I don't need anybody! Including you."

Will had walked to the window, his back to us. Understandably. The sight of all that anger and spunk flying from that impotent body was almost unbearable.

"I know all of you think I'm just an old woman, but I'm not." She began to cry.

I put my arms around her and kissed her forehead and agreed she could come home. Will and the doctor stared at me.

"But we have to have help," I said.

She looked at me like a little girl unfairly treated. "H.A., you know I can't stand to have anybody but you there all the time. It'll drive me crazy."

I ended up agreeing, at least in part. If I took a nursing shift, we could stretch the money out. I would have to stay here for a while longer.

After leaving the hospital, Will and I did not discuss what had happened. Instead, we stayed out late and drank too much, but my anxiety remained unquenched. The bars themselves tapped an uneasiness in me. Reaching over the blaring music the too-eager voices left me feeling ancient and sad as they shopped for a fix to their loneliness. The most uncomfortable part was knowing that their shrillness mirrored an emptiness in me.

On the way to my door, Will and I held hands.

"I guess I've signed on to hang around for the duration," I said, breaking our silence of the evening.

"So it seems. Can you afford to do that?"

"No," I answered with more emotion than I intended. "Actually, I could be in so much trouble, it's probably just as well I'm here."

"Want to talk about it?"

I shook my head. I couldn't tell straight-arrow Will how I was trashing my own candidate because he hadn't kept his word; because he was trashing someone else; because I was sick of sleaze. Instead I laughed and said, "The last time I confessed, you promised to haunt me if God got hold of you by mistake."

"You told awful whoppers."

"The trouble is I still do."

"But you get paid for it."

"Will," I said, opening the door. "I know she's going to get better. I just know it." Because, I thought, sick with my own selfishness, I don't want to decide how she ends her days.

My cousin waited only seconds before answering. "It looks like she has to."

After Will left, I considered looking through my mother's papers for clues to insurance and her financial state but knew she would hate that, having never confided her business arrangements. Now I couldn't bring myself to ask her or find out on my own. In a family of two, an intensely private two, the codes are necessarily strict.

Instead, I pulled out the scrapbooks again and studied the pictures of my mother and me with her friends at a fishing camp in Louisiana. In most of the pictures, they wore pedalpushers and clowned for the camera or one another, a small fish appearing to be their favorite prop. In most I am watching from a short distance.

One of the women had a son along; all of them were single. They always told one another they were a lot more fun to be around than men, but I had never been sure they meant it. I *was* sure none of them would have stepped into anything resembling tonight's bar scene, and not because they didn't enjoy a good time.

Smart, funny women with an irreverence for much of what passed before them, they were like my aunts except more career-oriented. They spoiled me forever for a certain feisty way of looking at the world.

They used their wicked tongues to laugh at the bastards and with one another. They fought all manner of heartaches and disappointments with their humor, and I imbued myself with their spirits to fight my own.

✳

On my bedside table, Aunt Stella had left messages that a Ned and a David had called. She started to ask them, she wrote, why they thought I would know which David and which Ned. Serve them right, she felt, if I didn't call either back. What we needed, I concluded as I smiled at my aunt's sauciness, was to make Sudy laugh again.

When

Their Hearts

Were

Young

The Justin sisters loved picnics, had many, and this was to be one long, lovely picnic after which my mother and I were to live happily ever after with her father, whom we all called Papa Bear. The sisters had grown up in a big old house where Papa Bear now lived all alone. The sisters had decided that my mother and I could solve several problems at once if we went to live there. All that was left to do was to convince Papa Bear.

Aunt Ruth, Aunt Clara, and I arrived at Lake Texoma before the others, who had stayed to watch Uncle Ben play softball. Aunt Clara hadn't wanted to wait. "If we're paying for cabins, we might as well use them," she'd said. Aunt Ruth agreed; she had seen enough softball games for one summer. Since my mother didn't want me riding with Papa Bear, I got invited to join my aunts.

"H.A., cover your face," Aunt Clara said as she picked up the spray gun to get rid of the mosquitoes. I obliged by rolling onto my stomach and burying my face in our pallet. Aunt Clara always acted like those blondes in the movies who live in big white houses and have horses and dogs and butlers to answer the door.

"If it gets any hotter, we might just as well get on with hell," Aunt Ruth said. "Ben is going to have a stroke playing in this heat. Damn fool men!"

She fanned herself with the afternoon paper and looked down at her slender, tanned legs sticking out from her white shorts. Her starched white halter showed her August tan to good effect. She was the smallest of the sisters and darker than my mother. She also didn't argue as much. Maybe because she was a little quiet, or because she didn't push herself on me or ask dumb, grown-up questions, I especially liked her. I would talk on and on to her every time I had a chance. She had sleepy eyelashes and almost brown eyes that looked right into you without disturbing whatever was trying to settle there.

The slow rhythms and soft sounds were usually pleasant enough to while away a sultry summer evening, but not tonight. The day had been a scorcher; by noon the temperature topped one hundred.

I turned back over and jabbed at the sky with my index finger.

"How many stars so far?" Aunt Ruth asked.

"Three hundred and forty-six."

Earlier they had been giggling like schoolgirls. After we had unloaded the food, beer, and bedding, we took a walk along the lake and sang all our favorite songs: "Paper Doll," "Don't Sit Under the Apple Tree," "In My Adobe Hacienda," and "Chatanooga Choo Choo." When we got back, they had served me milk and Aunt Stella's chocolate cake. We had planned to stop for a picnic along the way, but hungry and excited about our trip, we had eaten our tuna sandwiches and potato chips in the car.

Now they were drinking beer and talking about my mother in code while I pretended to sleep. The subject was her temper and her need for a job.

"Needs something to keep busy with—always has—before everybody goes c-r-a-z-y."

Aunt Ruth agreed: "She's too smart and too . . ." She hesitated. "*Good*—the most unselfish person I know. Anyway, she gets things out and gets them over with. Everyone loves her."

"Except the ones she attacks," Aunt Clara said.

"Sometimes even those."

"I just think somebody should suggest a job."

"Then, sister Clare, you do it."

"You're the one that gets to put up with her stomachaches and headaches and sinus problems when she's not working. It's in your interest to tell her."

"She's fine," Aunt Ruth said firmly and stubbed a cigarette into the ground. "As soon as she gets settled you-know-where, she'll be able to get on with her life."

"Do you really think this plan will work?"

"Why else are we here? Of course it will work."

These last words relieved me, though I had no doubt that we'd have our lives resolved by the end of this camping trip. Since our move back to Texas, we had been living with Aunt Ruth, Uncle Ben, and my cousin Joey. At first the easy access to one another's lives and houses had delighted me. I filled my life with the bustle of gossip and games and the attention of my aunts. I soaked up the confusion and companionship with an uncritical eagerness. But permanent arrangements of an unnatural order wear, and came too late in my life to sit easily, even at my young age. Nothing felt like our own anymore, not even us as the Reese family.

My grandfather's house offered release. I had begun to plan my own bedroom, the corner one over the kitchen in Papa Bear's house. In my dream, I filled it with sunlight and peach flowers running up the walls and splashing the skirts of my dressing table and the bed we'd finally take out of storage. The white organdy curtains would be the same ones I'd had in Kentucky. What I did not want to hear was any question that this wasn't to be.

For a few minutes, my aunts fanned themselves and me and were quiet. Then Aunt Ruth asked, "Do you want another beer?"

Aunt Clara giggled. "I have a better idea." I heard her go into the cabin.

"Bring milk, too," Aunt Ruth said.

"And ruin good whiskey?"

"The milk will coat our stomachs."

After settling with their drinks, they began talking in stage whispers that only a deaf person couldn't have heard.

They weren't telling secrets, just talking about how they used to slip around to smoke. I knew all about that and about my mother herself slipping around, so I did doze off for a while but woke to hear Aunt Ruth ask in a low voice: "Do you think we're drunk?"

"On one drink?"

"Clara, I think we are. My head already feels like a cloud floating by."

"You watched too many birds fly away this evening." This last remark struck them both as hilarious, but Aunt Ruth began to sound like she was crying, too. She blew her nose.

"Come on, Ruthie," Aunt Clara said. "You need to have a good time."

Aunt Ruth started to object, but took a sip of her drink instead. "Okay," she said, "but I'm worried we'll get drunk and go off and do something awful."

And leave H.A., I thought. Don't forget about H.A.

They sat together in silence for a few minutes until Aunt Clara got an idea: "We'll drink only until we can't walk a straight line anymore. Every thirty minutes we'll test ourselves. Then we'll know when we've had too much to drink."

Their back ends in the air, they worked hard to lay sticks end to end to make a straight line. They looked so funny that I forgot to close my eyes when Aunt Ruth looked over at me. With that discovery, we all went inside and I was put to bed, though I insisted on their leaving a crack in the door.

Soon they forgot about me and began using the red and yellow squares covering the floor to walk their line. I was relieved to see that neither of them had any trouble doing it. They didn't look or act like aunts, though. Even barefoot, Aunt Clara, wearing a black cotton sundress, looked more like a movie star, and for the first time, I realized Aunt Ruth could be one herself, she was so beautiful.

After the next line test, Aunt Ruth turned to Aunt Clara. "We have to look after H.A.," she said. I wanted to tell them it made more sense for me to look after them, but she kept talking. "We'll lock ourselves in, that's what. That way we can't leave H.A. or do anything else wrong." This time she reached for the bottle.

"Ruthie, I've always wanted to get drunk with you," Aunt Clara confided. Again they both giggled.

Until then a part of me believed my aunts were not really drunk. But once they admitted it, I began worrying about how Aunt Stella and Uncle Curtis and Uncle Ben and my mother would take to this new sister act and wished they would go to bed.

Uncle Curtis and Will showed up first, having driven straight from Dallas after attending a father-son Boy Scout cookout. The troop had run out of food, and they were hungry.

Aunt Ruth and Aunt Clara decided to fix them breakfast. For the first few minutes my aunts behaved themselves. Both were extra quiet, but their breath was the first giveaway.

"Have you ladies been tippling?" Uncle Curtis asked, smiling and putting his arms around them both. He liked to say that if he'd met Aunt Ruth first, he would have married her and had an easier life. He was tall and the family accused Aunt Clara of not feeding him enough because he never gained a pound. He had started an electronics company, which made him and Aunt Clara a lot of money.

Now Aunt Ruth, in her wide-eyed way, confessed to putting
a splash of whiskey in their milk to help them sleep in a strange
place.

Uncle Curtis spotted me staring through the crack in the
door. "And you, H.A., have you been tippling with your aunts?"

Will, seeing me, spoke up for the first time: "Did you bring
any funny-books?"

I had to shake my head no and suffer his scorn. He had a
large cardboard box filled with every imaginable war comic
book—none of which were funny. My mother thought they were
a waste of money and time. At least *my* mother wasn't drunk, I
thought to myself.

Aunt Ruth fried sausage while Aunt Clara beat the eggs. The
two began humming "The Charleston," Aunt Clara moving her
feet to the tune.

"You're not as good as I am," Aunt Ruth told her, swinging
her feet, too. Instead of using a fork or spatula, she daintily turned
the sausage with her fingers. When they began to sizzle, Uncle
Curtis looked at her with some concern.

"Careful, Ruthie!"

Aunt Ruth acted as if she had just discovered what she was
doing and quickly covered up. "Oh," she said, holding out her
smooth, delicate hands, "these are very tough."

"Why don't I just finish this while you show H.A. and Will
your Charleston?" Uncle Curtis said.

Aunt Clara turned to him. "I thought you liked *my*
Charleston."

"All right, Clare, why don't you show us yours, too."

"No," she answered. "I'm fixing the eggs."

"You aren't as good, anyway," Aunt Ruth said, moving her
legs and arms in time to the music in her head. "Why doesn't
Sudy get here? She's good."

"I hate it when you and Sudy show off," Aunt Clara told
her.

Will had not smiled once at any of this. I felt sorry for him.
"Did you bring funny-books?" I asked.

He jerked his head toward the door. "They're out there."
We got up to get them.

"Don't start that now!" Aunt Clara called after us. "Your
supper is ready."

"Breakfast, Clara. We've fixed breakfast." More giggles, and
Will said, "I'm not hungry."

Before a fight could start between them, two cars drove up
and a horn honked.

"Good!" Aunt Ruth said. "Everybody can have breakfast and
we won't have to worry about it in the morning." This logic
made even Aunt Clara look puzzled.

It turned out that Papa Bear wasn't coming up until Sunday—
business, he'd said, but the sisters doubted it—and Uncle
Ben's team had lost. But once the bad news was out of the
way, the picnic spirit filled the cabin. Uncle Curtis got a big
kick warning everyone about my aunts. "Clara and Ruth are
higher than kites. Don't give them a drink and don't let them
cook."

My mother was the only one not amused. "I trusted you to
take care of my baby," she told them.

But anger was hard to hold on to. When Uncle Ben dozed
off sitting in his chair, Uncle Curtis stuck a match in his shoe
and lit it. I told Joey and Will I had caught a fish two feet long
and eaten it for supper. Challenged, Aunt Ruth and Aunt Clara
backed me up. Uncle Ben said the lake was full of fish like that
and tomorrow the boys, if they were any good, could catch some,
too.

We all sat around, the uncles telling stories on their wives
and one another, the sisters remembering earlier times. "Remember, Stella, when you were twelve and took us for a ride?" Aunt
Ruth asked.

"It was Dad's car and she took us all over the countryside,
not bothering with roads or bridges at all, up and down creek
beds," my mother added.

"Yeah, and plowed fields, too, and through high grass and

past scared cows," Aunt Stella said. "I was afraid Dad would string me up for what I'd done to the car—"

I thought Aunt Stella as glamorous and worldly as anyone could be. She had auburn hair, blue eyes, and mink tails she threw around her neck on any day the temperature fell under seventy-two degrees. My mother said when the two of us got together, she couldn't tell which one was the child.

"Except he never noticed, he mistreated the car so much himself," Aunt Clara ended. Everyone laughed.

And then there was the one about my father getting happier and happier on a Christmas Eve as my mother got angrier and angrier. When my mother finally got my father to go to bed, he sat down to take off his shoes and the bed fell in. "Sudy," he said in all seriousness, "I knew you were omniscient; I didn't know you were omnipotent, too." I was pleased to see my mother could laugh about him without having to leave the room to blow her nose.

Aunt Clara's and Aunt Ruth's opening performance set the weekend's tone: the difference between parents and children grew less and less. After one perfunctory warning not to drown in the lake, my mother pretty much ignored me, and the weekend became an unending dream of uncles teasing and sisters dancing. My cousins and I disappeared for hours without anyone caring.

I made it all the way to Sunday morning without worrying about anyone, and that day started as another party. Everyone had moved out under the trees for coffee or milk. Uncle Curtis offered to pay my mother five dollars if she would fix him her special pancakes.

"I want some, too," Aunt Stella said.

"For an extra dollar."

"Damn it, Sudy," Uncle Curtis said with admiration, "I always say you're the best businessman in the family."

"I am a charter member of the Rollins Business and Professional *Women's* Club."

"Suit yourself, Miz Sude, just get my pancakes going."

While Uncle Ben and Aunt Stella got a fire going outside for their scrambled eggs, my mother went inside to make up her batter. I trailed after her.

"Come on, H.A., we're going to play a joke on your uncle. See that box of salt? See that flour? Well . . ." We were in the process of putting in a whole lot more salt than flour when we heard Papa Bear's car drive up and I ran outside.

To begin with: the Old Bad Woman, Papa Bear's sweetheart, had come with him. Because of the expressions on my aunts' faces, I knew who she was, even though she didn't look so old or so bad. At least not to me. I couldn't see what the fuss was about.

She had big bosoms that made her look fat and skimpy pants that also made her look fat. She had what my aunts called "country-permed" hair—frizzed with too many waves too close to the head. She had bright red lipstick and two bright red splotches on her cheeks, but they didn't hide the lines, the kind Aunt Stella warned could happen to me if I stayed out in the sun too much. Still, she looked a lot younger than my grandfather, whose jaw muscle kept twitching.

Since his grandchildren were the only ones who had come up to him, he began by introducing us to Violet Durham. Until then, I'm not sure I knew she had any name other than "the Old Bad Woman."

"Call her Aunt Vi," he said to Joey, Will, and me. "The rest of you know each other." He looked hard at his daughters. They looked hard back.

My grandfather had a full head of uncombed sandy hair with very little gray, which my aunts were always remarking upon. He said what did they expect? At sixty-four he wasn't ready for the grave, even if that's where they kept trying to put him. Sometimes he'd say this in good humor and appear to be flattered; sometimes he was accusatory and one of my aunts would cry. My mother said this was a way of talking about other things without really talking about them.

He had young blue eyes, too—filled with mischief and curiosity but not a bit of warmth. When he was angry, his eyes sliced right through their target. Everybody said he and my mother shared an Irish temper, but that was about all they shared unless stubbornness came under a separate category.

Uncle Curtis stepped forward and put out his hand. "Curtis Little. I don't believe we've met."

Vi held out her hand but seemed as incapable of speech as my aunts. Without a word the three of them walked into the cabin where my mother stood by the window.

Aunt Clara burst into tears.

"Why did he bring her?" Aunt Stella asked.

"I'm not going out there with that b-i-t-c-h," Aunt Clara said.

"She can spell," my mother said, indicating that I wasn't as invisible as I'd hoped.

Uncle Curtis poked his head inside the screen door. "Where's my breakfast, Sudy? I'm a hungry man."

"Go to hell," my mother replied.

Uncle Curtis came in. "You all don't act this way. Don't spoil the weekend."

"*We* haven't spoiled it."

"How could he?" Aunt Stella said again.

"We're not going out there, Curtis. Not while she's here," Aunt Clara said. "You can go tell him that."

Uncle Curtis drew himself to his full height. "No, I won't. You'll just be driving him away. Now, Sudy, fix my goddamn breakfast." At the door, he added, "And grow up! All of you."

For an instant, I thought they might attack him, but suddenly my mother went back to her batter and my aunts, taking their cue from her, began taking out the paper plates and picnic blanket.

My mother served Uncle Curtis, Aunt Stella, Papa Bear, and the Old Bad Woman the five-dollar pancakes without speaking to any of them. Each one thanked and praised her before putting the food in their mouths. As they began to chew, their expressions of anticipation changed to glumness. My grandfather was the first to say anything: "Sudy, have you poisoned us?"

"My God, Sudy, you should pay me for eating these things," Uncle Curtis chimed in. My mother winked at me.

"Maybe we just need water," Aunt Stella said, picking up a bucket of water that had been drawn to boil for tea. She splashed some on my mother's head, then, lightning-fast, she doused the pancake eaters, including, of course, the Old Bad Woman. She looked a lot worse wet than dry.

"What the hell, Stella!" Papa Bear said, jumping to his feet. "You and Sudy both gone crazy?"

In a second, everyone was laughing, except for the Old Bad Woman. That may have been because no one had spoken to her since Uncle Curtis's handshake.

Will and Joey stayed right by me, and I felt we were a lot older than anyone else around. When everyone stopped laughing, Papa Bear turned to Aunt Ruth. "What say, Ruthie, how about some real breakfast?"

"Oh, we're all breakfasted out."

"Well, my grandchildren have to eat, if I have to fix it myself. Come on, Vi, we'll show 'em how."

Vi seemed to understand that this was not a good idea, but she smiled lamely and went over to help.

"No one is hungry," my mother said.

"How 'bout you, H.A.?" Ignoring my stomach, I shook my head no. "Will? Joey?" They were no fools. They shook their heads no, too.

"I think," Aunt Clara said, looking at the cloudless sky, "that it might rain. Time to pack up and start back."

"Suit yourselves," Papa Bear said as the rest of us started packing up. The Old Bad Woman told Papa Bear she thought she'd take a walk. Her voice, I realized, sounded just like anybody's.

Aunt Stella reappeared before Uncle Curtis, who was swimming somewhere in the lake. Aunt Clara honked the car horn to call him.

"Go on. All of you go on," Papa Bear said as we climbed into the cars. "I'm going to stay and have myself a goddamn picnic. I don't care about the rest of you."

"We've noticed that," my mother shot back.

Next week, I thought, I'll talk to him and arrange the move by myself. He and I can surprise Mama. As we pulled away, Papa Bear, hands in his pockets, stood looking out toward the lake.

On the ride home, the wind stung my sunburn and Will couldn't resist "frogging" my arm a couple of times. But I didn't care. He still believed I had caught a two-foot-long fish.

The

Women

Warriors

Summer stayed late into the fall. Azalea buds appeared, and my aunts worried that a cold snap would kill them. Will and I continued to go barefoot. My mother washed and ironed my shorts and decided to go back to work. I began to plan a Christmas in Papa Bear's house. And Papa Bear decided to redecorate without mentioning it to any of us.

Miss Lena was the one who told us. She was a friend of the salesman in Klemm's Furniture. While Papa Bear visited cousins in California, the Old Bad Woman had gone in and ordered new furniture for him. The old stuff would get stored in the barn, she told the salesman. Papa Bear had signed a note saying she could charge to his account. This Saturday was delivery day.

My mother, Aunt Stella, Aunt Ruth, Will and Joey, and I opened Papa Bear's front door without knocking. They didn't believe in knocking, but in this case nobody cared. Papa Bear was still out of town. We had come to take my grandmother's furniture ourselves before it got stored in any barn. Aunt Clara, who had the flu, had given her sisters permission to make decisions about which pieces to take. They would sort it all out later.

"I would love this desk," Aunt Ruth said, running her fingers around the corner of the big rolltop standing in the hallway, "except I don't know where I'd put it."

"The desk stays," Aunt Stella said. "Dad couldn't function without that desk."

"Look, she hasn't dusted in a month, I'll bet." Aunt Ruth held up her fingertips to show us. We had heard the Old Bad Woman was "keeping house" for Papa Bear these days. Since we heard that, none of us had been to see him for fear of running into her.

"What do you expect from a slut?" my mother asked.

"What's a slut, Mama?"

"Nothing you need to know about," she snapped.

"What will it be like coming here and not sitting at that dining-room table? Do you remember the time Mama climbed on top to show us how to dance a jig?" Aunt Stella had tears in her eyes.

"That's why she left the Methodist Church," Aunt Ruth said.

"Why?"

"Because she liked to dance, and in those days Methodists didn't believe in it."

"Everybody knows that story. I thought you were telling us something new," my mother said. "We can't stand around here all day. Let's get on with this. Besides, we're not going to eat here anymore."

"Don't say that, Sudy," Aunt Ruth responded. "We're going to have you in here by the holidays."

"Not if he is still seeing her."

"He won't once you get in."

"I should have married Bob Watson," Aunt Stella said to no one in particular. "He was going to be a Methodist minister. I would have made a good minister's wife."

"Ha!" my mother said.

"If Dad and Mama hadn't been so dead-set against Methodists! Nowadays you can hardly tell the difference between them and us, but back then you would have thought I was marrying a Catholic."

"You wouldn't have gotten along with him any better than you have with the two husbands you've lived with."

"Dick was a fine man. I will remind you I am a widow just like you, Sudy."

"Then who is Jeff Carter?" Uncle Jeff was Aunt Stella's second husband.

"Both of you hush," Aunt Ruth said. "Sudy's right: let's get on with this."

My mother surveyed the furniture. "The dining room stays as it is. Nobody has a house big enough to hold the table or the hutch. It's been good enough for him this long; it's good enough for him now."

"I can understand why he wants a little change. Seeing Mama around here all the time . . . We ought to take some of this. Don't forget, when you move in, you may want to bring some of your own furniture out of storage."

"I'll take the breakfast table if nobody wants it," Aunt Stella said after walking into the kitchen.

"If I could move the window seat, I would take it. I've spent enough hours dreaming on it." Aunt Ruth picked up the pillow cushion from the seat. "Look, she's re-covered it in this tacky brown."

"*I* re-covered it," Aunt Stella said.

"The couch has to stay, too," my mother announced.

"All the living-room furniture stays," Aunt Stella added. "Mama decorated this room when we were little girls."

Aunt Ruth called from upstairs, "Dad is staying in Clara's and my old room."

"We're not taking one stick of furniture from Mama's bedroom," my mother said, then asked: "Why are we doing this? Do we want her to fill this place with junk?"

Joey, who had been playing in the yard, ran back inside yelling, "The Old Bad Woman's coming! The Old Bad Woman's coming! And she's brought a truck with her."

Without another word, without so much as a look, the three of them turned back downstairs.

The Old Bad Woman looked at our car, then looked at the house. She hesitated before motioning her son and the driver of the truck to follow her. As she started toward the house, the two boys opened the back of the truck. My aunts and mother stepped onto the porch. Joey and I stayed just inside the door.

"Sam back yet?" the Old Bad Woman asked. She kept twisting her purse, but her voice was friendly; firm, too.

"What's going on?" my mother countered, nodding her head in the direction of the truck, where the boys were unloading a coffee table.

"I asked if Sam was back." She wore a bright pink suit and the highest heels I had ever seen. The suit looked cattywampus on her, and she moved in the shoes as if she were playing dress-up.

"And I asked what you think you're doing with that furniture." By now a couch and an easy chair had come off the truck.

The Old Bad Woman turned to the boys. "Come on with that stuff," she told them.

"There's no room for it. We didn't take anything." By now the boys were on the porch. Aunt Stella blocked the door. She was wearing an old brown shirt and a blue sweater she'd bought back in high school; the sweater brought out her blue eyes and fit her well. Standing there with her red hair and fair skin, she could have been a heroine in one of my books. She also looked ready to take on the world. The boys must have thought so, too, for they put the chair and table down on the porch. When they turned toward the truck, Aunt Stella pushed the chair onto the ground. She had picked up the table to throw after the chair, but the Old Bad Woman leaped up and took hold of Aunt Stella's shoulders.

"You filthy bitch!" the Old Bad Woman screamed.

My mother stepped closer to them. "Don't you touch my sister!"

With Aunt Ruth now blocking the front door, the boys set the sofa on the porch. Like his mother, Junior had a stout blunt-featured look and small eyes that didn't want messing with. From the swagger, it was clear that he and the driver had seen a fight or two. Including Will, Joey, and me, our side still didn't add up to much compared to theirs. Junior moved to his mother's side. "Leave her alone, lady," he said to my mother.

"You go to hell!" my mother answered.

"Junior, put that couch inside."

Just as Junior started to do as he was told, my mother pushed him backward over the sofa. Maybe he was already a little off balance. Anyway, he fell. His mother screamed. The driver clenched his fists. But who could he hit? Even angry, the three sisters looked more suited for a tea party than a brawl. Besides, I had picked up Papa Bear's walking stick to clobber somebody if I had to. Junior stood up dazed.

"Get that trash out of here!" Aunt Stella shouted at him.

"It's not his fault, Stella. Don't be too hard on him," my mother said in a quiet, reasonable voice.

Whether it was the fall or my mother's unexpected defense, Junior stalked off the porch and climbed into the truck. The driver followed. The Old Bad Woman looked around dazed.

"Don't think I won't tell! Sam will disown every damn one of you."

"Gold digger!" Aunt Stella hissed.

"Home-breaker!" Aunt Ruth added.

"He came sniffing after me. I was a married woman minding my own business when he showed up. *He* corrupted *me*. Not the other way around. If there's a home-breaker here, it's your very own daddy. And don't all you Miss high-and-mighties forget it."

Left alone, the sisters pushed the couch off the porch to join the chair and table. Afterward, the three of them sat on the top step.

"How could he have done it?" my mother asked.

"That's just men for you," Aunt Stella replied. "Mama—"

"Mama wouldn't have been so pleased with us today either," Aunt Ruth interrupted.

"John would hate it that I exposed H.A. . . . ."

Aunt Stella put her arm around my mother. "John was the finest gentleman I've ever known, but he'd be proud of you today. He would want his daughter to see how to take up for herself."

My mother started to cry. "Daddy is never going to be there for us; he's dead to me and H.A."

Now Aunt Ruth put her arm around my mother's waist. "Don't be so hard on him. If you can forgive him, you'll see he wants to make up. He's miserable, too; you'll see."

"Ruth is right," Aunt Stella agreed.

"Listen, Sudy, Thanksgiving is only a few weeks away and he's coming to dinner alone. This time we'll talk to him, explain how we feel and how H.A. needs him. He knows he needs you; he's just being as stubborn as you. We haven't made much of an effort ourselves. You know that. Sudy?" My mother shook her head in confirmation.

As if everything was now settled, Aunt Stella pulled a pack of cigarettes from her pocket, and the three huddled together on the porch, smoking. "Did you see her face when her son went flying?" one of them said. "Did you see Sudy's?" They laughed.

"I'd better see about H.A.," my mother said.

"She's fine. I'll bet she and Will and Joey are playing out

back." I took Joey's hand and led him to where we were supposed to be. Will had been sitting on top of the barn roof since right after the truck left.

"Papa Bear is a mean son of a bitch and a home-breaker," I said and picked up a rock to throw at the house.

"I'm going to tell," Joey said.

"I don't care." I threw another rock. "Papa Bear's a home-breaker." Another rock. "Papa Bear's a home-breaker." And another rock.

"Mama!" Joey shouted, running away. But I didn't care. I kept throwing rocks.

I was crying now and my mother was shaking me. A rock remained clenched in my fist.

Family

Lessons

I sat down to a table of possibilities. For this Thanksgiving gathering my mother and I would be at our sparkling, holiday best. After all, I reasoned, Papa Bear had gotten so used to us in our everyday life that he needed to be reminded how wonderful we could be. Under no illusion that my mother would change herself one bit, I needed everyone's help, and from all the week's scheming, I felt I would get it.

As soon as Papa Bear said grace, I would take matters into my own hands. If I could get us through the meal on some happy subject, I knew everything would be all right when the serious talk came up later in the afternoon.

"Did you know the dime store serves duck and oysters now?" I asked him in my best conversational tone as I passed Aunt Stella's hot rolls. "We should go sometime."

"Duck and oysters, honey? I'm not sure you can even get those in Dallas," he answered.

"H.A., what are you talking about? There's no such thing here," my mother put in.

"At Woolworth's?" Aunt Ruth asked.

"They can't even serve a decent grilled cheese there," Aunt Stella said.

"Duke and Ayres, the dime store?" Uncle Ben asked. "You mean Duke and Ayres serves duck and oysters?"

The entire table started laughing. Will snickered openly, and Joey was rolling on the floor. In my holiday-best role, fighting with my cousins was beneath me, but I wanted to throttle Will and Joey.

"I don't know about duck and oysters, but I could sure use more turkey and dressing, Ruth," Uncle Ben said.

"Get it yourself," my mother answered. She turned to Aunt Ruth. "You wait on him hand and foot. I wouldn't do that for any man."

"I'll get it," I said, jumping up. "Any for you, Papa Bear?" My mother frowned at me, but Papa Bear shook his head no.

"Sudy, you still determined to vote Democrat in this election?" Uncle Curtis asked my mother.

"Unless I lose my senses in the meantime, I do."

"I'd think you'd want to vote for somebody to keep us out of war," Uncle Curtis went on.

"Oh, Curtis, hush," Aunt Stella said.

"Roosevelt had to fight. He had to get us out of a depression, too. You think you'd be driving that fancy car if the Republicans were in? You'd still be out walking the streets, selling month-old magazines."

"A lot of Democrats are voting for Eisenhower," Aunt Clara put in.

"Those aren't Democrats. They're idiots," my mother replied.

"Atta girl, Sudy," Uncle Ben said, laughing. I laughed, too.

"Roosevelt and all that bunch were Communists," Aunt Clara said.

"You're a goddamn fool!" my mother hissed.

"I think it's something they ate for breakfast," I whispered to my grandfather.

"Honey, it's mother's milk to them." I had no idea what he meant, but I thought it just as well nobody else heard him.

My mother kept right on talking. "Have you forgotten how they killed cattle and plowed under crops while people in the country starved?" She stood up. "You've turned into greedy, worthless jackasses now that you've gotten sophisticated living in Dallas."

Aunt Clara stood up, too. "I'm not going to take this."

"Is it time for the football game?" I asked Papa Bear.

"It's time," he said to the family. My uncles rose and stretched and drifted into the sitting room to listen to the Humble Southwest Conference broadcast on the radio.

This was an especially critical game because Texas A&M, Uncle Curtis's school, was playing their annual Thanksgiving contest against the University of Texas, the favorite of everyone else, though not one member of the family had gone there. The postures in the room—easy-chair slump, head-nodding, half-closed eyes—belied the underlying charge that any game gave them. No one missed a play.

My mother did not join us until after Texas kicked a field goal and minutes later scored a touchdown. "Who's ahead?" she asked when she walked in.

"You know perfectly well," Aunt Clara replied.

"It's not the Aggies," Uncle Ben said, keeping his eyes on the radio.

Uncle Curtis refused to say anything at all. When Texas made another touchdown, he got up and left the room.

"There's no need to be such a poor sport," my mother said.

"Sudy, you didn't show your face in here until Texas got ahead. Don't talk to me about poor sports!"

Unfortunately, Texas scored three touchdowns right in a row as soon as the second half started. Nobody said a word. After the third one Uncle Curtis appeared in the doorway with his hat on. "Come on, Clare. No sense hanging around here while your whole damn family gloats."

The family sat there with the angelic expression Joey sometimes got when he'd just thrown a rock at a passing car.

"Don't talk about my family that way," Aunt Clara said to Uncle Curtis.

He glared at her and turned to leave. My aunt started to follow.

"I wouldn't let any damn man tell me what to do," my mother said loudly.

Aunt Ruth made everyone hush and sit back down. "We have important matters to discuss," she said, looking at her sisters, but I had no confidence in the outcome considering how quiet Papa Bear had been all afternoon while his daughters fussed. I let myself out the back door and into the yard, where Joey and Will and some boys from the neighborhood were playing their own game of football.

"Shazam!" I shouted and turned into Mary Marvel. "I challenge every chicken-boy here to a knock-down-drag-out!" Then I thought better of it and a few minutes later decided to go back inside just in case I was needed. Joey came with me.

The game over, my uncles had disappeared as planned. My cousins and I quietly headed for the kitchen. If we kept ourselves scarce, we would be easily forgotten and we could listen.

From my place at the kitchen table I could see Papa Bear and Aunt Ruth. This meant my mother, Aunt Clara, and Aunt Stella were sitting on the sofa. My grandfather, sitting in the room's only easy chair, stirred his coffee with his finger.

I looked at Joey, who was punching me and pointing to the cake. He knew he had me, for if he had to ask out loud the show would be over, as Will was fond of saying. If I gave him another piece and Aunt Ruth found out, the show would be over anyway.

"What are you doing?" Will asked as I got down on my knees in front of the window.

"You go on outside."

For once he did as I asked and didn't tease me. Joey had fallen asleep over his third piece of cake. I clasped my hands, crossed myself for good luck, and closed my eyes as tight as I could. "Please, Lord, let that screen be fixed when I open my eyes," I begged. "Please, Lord, and I will always mind Mama and all my aunts and never fight again with anybody and never have any bad thoughts ever again in my life."

I kept my eyes closed. The grandfather clock in the front hall chimed. Papa Bear mumbled a good-bye. The front door slammed. My aunts sobbed. "Hush, hush," my mother crooned to them. I felt my breath go in and out until I was sure God had time to do the work.

The hole was still there. The ragged, ugly hole that lets in flies that give us polio that kills us. God wouldn't even fix the hole, I thought. I now knew with great certainty what I had been trying to avoid: I could not order the universe. My will alone was not enough to make Papa Bear live with me. Or keep my daddy alive.

Well, damn God. And damn Papa Bear and damn my daddy. As far as I was concerned, they could all go to hell. *I* would find somebody for my mama and me. I wouldn't let us be all alone.

Sad tears—the kind I never let come, the kind that had nothing to do with fights and skinned knees—rolled down my cheeks and wouldn't stop. Back then, I had no name for my terror and could not have explained it. I knew where my determination came from, though; as Papa Bear would say, it was mother's milk to me.

Losing

Altitude

David handed me a piece of bread to feed the ducks. "Hurry," he said, "or they'll take it out of your hands." We strolled along Turtle Creek, hoping to have the expanse of green to ourselves. The weather had turned brisk and cloudy, but a young couple with two toddlers were also feeding the ducks.

"I'm in trouble," he had said when he phoned. He needed to see me again. He apologized for bothering me. He had never apologized for bothering me in his life. He looked worse than he had before, I thought, as he gave the rest of our bread to the little girls, bundled in their modern-day, Red Riding Hood coats.

During the period of my miscarriages when I was married to my first husband, Keith, I had been especially drawn to little girls. Was this what my baby would have looked like? Almost any little girl would have been welcome. "Would you be my child?" I wanted to ask all of them.

David looked at his watch and apologized. "When I set this up, I didn't know I had another appointment."

"No problem," I answered, but I was annoyed. I'd gone to some trouble to make arrangements to get away.

"I can't afford to miss the oppor—"

"I said don't worry about it." That came out more harshly than I meant. "I understand," I amended.

"No you don't." He put his hands in his pockets, and we continued walking, stopping every now and again to watch the ducks. Clearly, he had something on his mind, but he was taking his own good time in getting it out. I was in no hurry to hear. I felt comfortable in the familiarity of his presence and realized how much I missed the seasoning of a man my age.

"I wish with all my heart," he finally began, "that we had played our lives differently."

"We've been over all this."

"You should have married me the first time around. How could you have married Keith? How could you have done that to us!"

"Haven't we argued enough about Keith and marriage and leave-takings?" I pleaded, putting my hand on his arm. He calmed down.

"Do you remember the day I left for the service?" he asked and put his arm around me. "I came nine times."

"I remember," I replied and smiled. "I sometimes think that's what bound us together for so long—the prospect of another nine."

"Nine times and nine lives. I always believed we'd have the nine lives. That's what made parting bearable." A sorrow bled through his every word and suddenly I understood: our games were over. I wouldn't fight him ever again.

"I've loved you most," I said in an effort to declare myself in some way.

"I know, but I didn't cost you anything."

"Oh, David, how can you say that?" I pulled back, not anticipating the bitterness.

We stopped and he turned to face me. "We don't get nine lives. This is all we're going to get," he said, taking my hands.

A terrible coldness settled in my stomach. "What are you talking about?"

"Lymph cancer. The doctors say I'll be doing well to make it another six months."

"Liar!" I shouted loudly enough to cause the young family to look in our direction. Some great rumble began in my body that wouldn't be stilled. He pulled me close until I stopped shaking.

"You need to go to Boston," I said into his neck. "I'll make some phone calls. We'll get you in—" With absolute clarity I understood he would be part of my own death.

He put his hand over my mouth to quiet me. "I've been to the specialists. They all say the same thing: with an experimental operation, I have an outside chance. My own doctor doesn't hold out much hope. He's not even sure it's worth it."

"Of course it's worth it. You'll go anywhere. Do anything." I regretted not having ChapStick for his parched lips. A little ChapStick to cure what ails him, I thought as he held me close.

"That's what I need. Your stubbornness and your spirit. Your fight." He pulled my head away from his face to look at me. "I have an unreasonable faith that you'll get me through."

"You bet I will," I said, but I had no such faith in myself or anybody else.

He ventured a smile. "What I've been trying to say these last two meetings is that I'm dying and I regret my mistakes. Now we can only save you, and that's important to me."

We sat in his car and discussed his situation awhile longer. His wife had not really accepted the diagnosis. His children hadn't been told directly, though they knew he had cancer. He wished he were in better shape financially for his family, but they would be pretty well taken care of. We talked at length about the operation, and the more we talked, the more convinced we became of its efficacy.

And to think we once soared, I thought as I watched him move his lips, withered already. Literally soared. The plane's wings quivered as we dove through large scoops of air.

"You understand now?" he had asked. "I love this and I want it for both of us. We'll go anywhere, everywhere—all our lives." His face was deep brown from the summer sun and belonged that long-ago day to some ancient warrior tribe, ready to challenge, to invent, to promise all. Nothing was impossible. Too impatient to wait for military flight school, he had scrimped and saved and learned to fly on his own. To show me, he said, what life could be like for us. "Do you like your surprise?" he asked, meaning his secret flying lessons, meaning our weekend trip to New Orleans.

As giddy as he, I laughed, grabbed his hand, wanted to make

love in the air. But he took his plane seriously, and I knew he had done this for himself as well as for me. He burst to get on with his life, so sure was he of its bountifulness. I could never be so foolish, but the extravagance of his promise that fine morning took my breath away.

The End

of the First

# of Nine

Lives

David and I lay on the bed in his apartment that long-ago summer hardly speaking for fear we'd quarrel again. Our time together was now taken up with "If you loved me's" and "How could you's." I decided I didn't love him, or love him enough. Visions of him laughing as he parachuted out of a plane enraged me.

Though sex was no longer the same, my ardor returned, as did his, probably because we knew this was our last time together. All afternoon we made love, though, true to form, we also counted. And, once more, we couldn't resist turning our lust and stamina into a game. After the ninth come, we lay staring at the ceiling and giggling.

"You're willing to give this up?" he asked. "Confess. You love *it* and *me* too much." He rolled over to kiss, his lips as bruised as mine. "I'm not going to the moon. I'll be here for you. Promise, baby."

My silence infuriated him. "Then you'll never marry me," he said and got out of bed to dress. "If you don't love me enough to marry me now, you never will because it's impossible to love more than we do now."

I tried to put my arms around him, but he walked into the bathroom and shut the door. I put on his favorite sundress, a light pink polished cotton. He liked me in soft colors; his rainbow, he said. I began to cry.

When he came out of the bathroom, his eyes were red, too. "Write me every day," he said.

"As often as I can."

"Every day, damn it."

"You don't have to go. You haven't been drafted." An old argument, but I wanted the blame back on him. By now we were standing at the front door.

"You can't ask me to give up my dream. Not even you can do that. If you can't understand, we have nothing more to say to each other." He turned his back on me as I opened the door.

"Good luck," I said, quickly drying my face.

"Who will take care of you?" he asked, his thin face contorted, his body shaking.

"Nobody." Nobody now and nobody ever.

I watched him walk away with the hope that I would relent and follow in a few weeks. By the time he realized I wasn't coming, he would be busy and half over me. His pride would take care of the rest. Keith, my old reliable high-school boyfriend, would be here for me. And nobody really strangled to death on grief, I reassured myself. At that moment, though, I found myself gasping for air.

In

the

Air

Two days after Ned's last frantic phone call, Ralph and I were on our way to Mexico, or rather, he was going to Mexico and I was going for the ride. He would stay and I would fly back to Dallas. A meeting in the sky suited both our plans.

As soon as the plane's wheels left the ground at the Dallas/Fort Worth airport, Ralph unhooked his seat belt and stepped into the aisle. "It's my own damn plane, I can do what I want," he said.

Learjets being smaller than my transportation of choice, I chose to stay strapped to the overstuffed couch as I gazed around the cabin with its swivel seats facing me and wooden trays and table beckoning.

"You've appointed it well." I paid him the compliment he expected but also deserved.

"I got it for a song when all those asshole Texans lost their oil money." Feeling like a Texas chauvinist for the first time in my life, I didn't return his smile.

"Excuse my French," he said.

"Your French isn't what bothers me," I answered as I accepted a Diet Coke from the cabin steward.

After placing a phone call for Ralph, the steward disappeared into the cockpit and closed the door behind him, leaving Ralph Stone and me alone. I picked up a *Newsweek* rather than watch my host pace, telephone cradled on his shoulder, arms gesturing wildly. More hyper than usual, he had the appearance of a man utterly distraught or utterly performing. In case of the latter, I didn't want to give him the satisfaction of an audience.

"No one needs to know about this," he had said after asking me to join him on the flight, and I agreed to both requests, my antennae alert. If no one needed to know, he might suspect Ned of leaking rumors.

But now his suspicions were taking a while to come out. After hanging up the phone, he began giving me his version of what was happening to him. He knew of three newspapers in the state working on the Stoddard story; others would be. He was making it clear to the world that he had no idea that Stoddard was guilty of ruining wetlands.

"What about the news stories?" I asked. "Wouldn't you have seen those?"

He stopped pacing and sat down, his head in his hands. "Oh, God," he said, "I'd forgotten about those." The man really was an idiot. Thousand-dollar suits and a million employees couldn't fix that. He looked up. "I'll tell them I had already invested and couldn't back out." Crisis solved, he stood up again.

"Anyway, do all that many people really give a shit about these things?" he asked.

"The polls show they do at this moment. Issues come and go, Ralph, but don't underestimate your good voters' ability to get plenty pissed when somebody gets caught out trying to put something over them."

"That happens all the time, too."

"So we're fickle animals. And unreliable in the extreme."

"Meaning?"

"You can't count on people putting up with shit forever."

We moved into clouds and the plane bumped accordingly. Ralph kept up his pacing with no notice of the turbulence, which formed a backdrop to his ranting about the press, the opposition, disloyal employees, disloyal friends, disloyal professional acquaintances, disloyal political acquaintances. Even his wife and young children weren't quite as dutiful as they should be.

This tirade finally exhausted him, and he sat down on the upholstered swivel chair opposite me and pressed a buzzer. The cabin steward reappeared to refresh my Diet Coke and Stone's grapefruit juice.

I had to calculate my questions and answers carefully, for I didn't want any confidences that might come out later in the press. Once he asked what to do, he would not stop with this one admission of weakness. A man like Stone either saw himself as omnipotent or helpless, a baby boy again looking for a savior.

"What do I do?" he asked. I girded myself against the expression that would come over his face—vulnerable, beseeching. In this I got no satisfaction.

"So let's see what they actually know," I said. "One, you invested in a company ruining the wetlands."

He groaned. "Don't put it that way."

"Two . . ." The cabin steward appeared.

"I didn't call you," Stone bellowed.

"Mike asks that you fasten up, sir. The weather is getting a little tricky."

"In which case I'll have a vodka straight up," I said. As we had gotten on the plane, Mike had been charming but did not look experienced enough to pilot in bad weather.

"Later," Ralph snapped, but quickly realized his own boorishness. "I'm sorry. Would you like some lunch also?" I shook my head no. By now we lurched without letup.

"Why don't you mind Mike?" I asked after the steward left. I had an image of Stone catapulting out a window, thus spelling disaster for us all. In typical Stone fashion, he took my request as a show of concern and immediately complied.

"You're not a bad-looking woman," he said.

I deliberately did not make eye contact. The combination mother-and-savior role did not appeal to me even with someone of interest, much less him.

"Two," I began again, ticking off the number on my fingers, "you have admitted nothing to anyone. Three, several anonymous building suppliers have complained they were strong-armed by Stoddard Development into donating to your campaign."

He slammed down his hand on the walnut table between us. "That's not true. Those bastards gave of their own free will and they know it. They know damn well who's going to be their friend."

"That's the point, isn't it?"

He slumped forward. "I guess so."

"Four . . ."

"Do we have to go on?"

"Four, you've got exactly five weeks to convince the world you are innocent."

"I am."

"Will Stoddard go along with us?"

"He's willing to do, to say, anything. I have him by the balls."

"He's saying the same about you," I shot back. "It's important you don't forget that. We need him to tell the world he assured you the problem was taken care of. You trusted him. He let you down."

"He'll own my ass."

"Will he do it?"

"Yeah." He pushed on the buzzer. "Mike, when the hell do we get out of this damn stuff? This is ridiculous."

"Maybe another ten minutes, sir."

"Well, send Sam back. We've got to have our lunch."

"In another ten minutes, sir."

"Sorry 'bout all this," Ralph said with something resembling humility.

"I know Ned is playing up your environmental good deeds."

"Nobody much cares."

"Maybe you should do something dramatic to show your concern."

"How much will it cost?"

"Depends on how dramatic."

The plane smoothed out for a minute or so and Stone was back on the buzzer to the pilot.

"You should also squelch the stuff on Mary Cardigan. How many times do I have to tell you that?"

"And I've told you, I'm not behind any of that."

"Just a thought."

"How would it help?"

"You let up on her, she lets up on you."

He gave me a hard look and a shrug. The lack of turbulence continued, so the cabin steward began composing lunch: white asparagus wrapped in Dover sole, a few baby carrots and green beans in a *beurre blanc* sauce with a ribbon of spinach puree running through it.

"So when are you coming back?" Ralph asked, the question as inevitable as "What do I do?"

"As you know, I can't leave my mother just yet." I hoped Ned had stuck to the story of her being close to death. Nothing less than death would faze this man. "I keep in close touch with Ned by phone. I can keep in close touch with you, too, if you'd like."

"Ned, shmed." He gave a dismissive wave of his hand. "I want you. Besides"—he leaned toward me—"I don't trust him completely. He knows who my contributors are."

"I'm sure there are others."

"My secretary, and she's been with me fifteen years."

I laid down my fork. I had not realized Ned was one of only two people with access to the files I had reviewed. Whatever fun I'd derived from the game was gone.

"I imagine the leak—if that's what it was—came from someone within Stoddard Development," I said.

"Who?"

"A disgruntled employee maybe." I hoped Gary Boatwright, wherever he was, would forgive the innuendo. At any rate, he couldn't be hurt and Ned could. "It's possible a contributor could have an innocent conversation with someone and the rumors started spreading. The opposition was bound to pick it up; they investigated and found your connection to Stoddard."

He jabbed his fork at me: "I want you. And I want you back in Boston."

I knew if the stories started breaking, he'd fire Ned in a second. Ready or not, I was going to have to go back to take some of the heat off Ned. This man needed reassurance every ten minutes.

"Give me a couple of days," I said. "My mother . . ." I smiled, little-girl helpless—whatever it takes, I reminded myself.

"Sure."

The cabin steward reappeared to take away our plates.

"Why don't you stay here tonight? I admire a girl like you."

"I admire you, too, Ralph." I leaned across the aisle and patted his hand. "I don't know many men who are as faithful a husband as you. You're one for the history books." I believe the cabin steward winked at me.

Gloating, he said, "Yeah, I guess I am."

After we landed, I waved him away with a smile and stayed on the plane while we refueled. When the turbulence began on the way back, the steward offered me the vodka bottle, but now weather seemed the least of my worries.

Kind

Men and

Pecan

Pies

At Bob's Café Uncle Ben and Uncle Curtis sat across from me in the booth closest to the door, so we could visit with anyone passing through for an afternoon cup of coffee. Uncle Ben might have the same conversation ten times, on occasion with the same person, but he enjoyed it anew each time. Memory loss wasn't all bad.

He had the beginnings of Alzheimer's, Will confided in me, but Aunt Ruth wouldn't discuss the problem. What could doctors tell her? Certainly no one knew better than she did what to do with her own husband, but she got furious with him whenever he wandered away or became too forgetful. I blamed my own self-absorption as much as my mother's illness for not having noticed sooner how his condition was deteriorating.

Uncle Ben had taught me how to ride a bike and skate. He had listened to my endless stories with more patience than any of my aunts. If he did get tired of my hanging around, he never showed it. When I left Texas, I knew he missed me. I called him once from Washington, D.C., on his birthday. He never got over talking to someone that far away. Calling from the moon would not have pleased him more.

Since my uncles' retirement, meeting at Bob's Café had become the highlight of their week, with Uncle Curtis driving in from Dallas for the purpose of taking Uncle Ben on this outing.

They were pleased with themselves for thinking to invite me along this time, if not quite sure what to do with me next. Being as shy as they were, I realized how seldom these past few years I had visited with them without my aunts.

"Now, H.A., go all out," Uncle Curtis urged. "It's my treat."

"No, it's *my* treat. You can have duck and oysters if you want to." Uncle Ben laughed. Though he had put on extra pounds and his face had a permanent flush from high blood pressure, he was handsome still, with his waves of frosty hair. Alzheimer's had not taken its toll on his looks. He turned to Uncle Curtis. "Do you know H.A. thought Duke and Ayres was—"

"You were a mess when you were little," Uncle Curtis said to me.

"They were all messes. We had all those messes and all those mamas hovering round them. The messes were easier to take than the mamas."

"They were something, weren't they?" I could tell by the way Uncle Curtis's face lit up that he meant the mamas. "You couldn't do anything with them."

"Didn't want to," Uncle Ben said.

Uncle Curtis, who had collected an abundance of wrinkles but few gray hairs, leaned over and removed the hat from his brother-in-law's head.

"This girl thought Duke and Ayres was 'duck and oysters,'" Uncle Ben repeated to the slender waitress of indeterminate age and hair color, who laughed as if she might have heard the story before.

"Have the coconut pie, H.A. That was your favorite when you were a little girl." Uncle Ben may have lost his short-term memory, but nothing had yet touched his long-term one.

"Pecan is the best here. You know that, Ben." Uncle Curtis turned to me. "They make the best pecan pie in Texas."

"She likes coconut."

"I'll have both," I told the waitress, "and vanilla ice cream on the side of the pecan."

My uncles, pleased once again, began to discuss football. I nodded and smiled at what I hoped were appropriate times but let my mind wander.

Most of my life I'd underestimated these men with their genuine relish for Justin women. On the whole, they were not ambitious, but they arranged lives of dignity and gained satisfaction from their families and friends and small pleasures. Because they appeared more pliant than my aunts, I mistook their softness for weakness, failing to understand their sense of security.

None of them tried to dictate terms, nor were they dictated to. They did as they pleased while acknowledging, and often accepting, their wives' advice. They appreciated the drive in women of strong temperament. They were not threatened. They were grown-up men.

Jack Templeton was the first to come by with the topic of the day: the death of a telephone lineman.

"Hear about that guy?" Templeton asked, stopping at our table. There was no question about what guy he meant. "Wonder how something like that can happen, don't you?" He plopped himself on a counter stool directly across the narrow aisle from our booth.

Uncle Ben spoke up: "Man must have thought he was fishing. If you're up in a crane, you ought to have more sense than to forget what you're doing."

"He made a wrong move, Ben," Uncle Curtis corrected him. "Lost his balance. That's what happened."

Uncle Ben looked at me. "If I was up in one of those things, you bet I'd pay attention to what I was doing."

The waitress handed Templeton a cup of coffee and poured us fresh ones. "His kin are from Prosper. My cousins know lots of them."

Uncle Curtis shook his head sadly. Templeton spoke to me: "You know the Allens—lived down by the cotton gin."

"Maybe my mother does," I answered.

"Course she does. How is your mama?"

"She's coming along. Not as fast as we'd like, but she's making progress." In fact, she had been home almost a month and was not much better than when she left the hospital in spite of her efforts, mine, her sisters', and the physical therapist's. Now I worried as much about her sudden temper fits, her crying bouts, her inconsolable humors as I did her physical health. These would pass, we kept telling one another, but so far they hadn't.

"Well, Sudy's one of the all-time greats," Templeton said. Then he got up with his coffee to wander on and find himself a new table for another rehash of the lineman's death.

No wonder I stayed so aware of my own mortality growing up. No death goes unobserved here. People die and everyone is affected. In Rollins the closeness of death is a reality to be lived with daily. Reports of who died and how were related in great detail, whether or not the person was a friend. No one was allowed the luxury of indifference that comes with large cities, those urban repositories of names and faces without histories.

On the whole, I derived comfort from my stay—the unhurried conversations, the unworldliness, the friendliness of old acquaintances and the politeness of shop clerks. More importantly, my aunts once again accepted me. They fussed over me and laughed at me and generally thought I was their splendid child again. Sometimes I chafed in the role but not enough to stir myself. The irritations remained manageable. I remained manageable.

I had swooped down here and gotten myself stuck. I could twist one way or the other, but I could not take off. Was I really running away from a bad situation when I left Boston for Texas, or was that an excuse for just needing to be home?

Maybe, as Ned suggested in his last phone call, it was a little late to agonize over finding myself. Isn't that what people did at twenty? Just what the fuck had I been doing all these years? he asked. David's question, too, though stated not as bluntly. But I couldn't think of David. Not now. Anyway, he was not dying.

That was absurd. In his inimitable overly dramatic style, he had made the situation sound grimmer than it really was.

My uncles were smiling at me now. I smiled back and envied them their easiness with life. And was that—a sense of acceptance, a sense of place—what I really wanted? Was I always and forever looking for a man like the ones across the table from me?

They were still smiling, and I finally realized they were expecting a response.

"These are the best pies I've ever had," I said and broke off a hefty bite of the pecan just as a balding, round man puffed up to our table, a paper in his hand. "Thought I'd better get this right to you. Looks important," he said to me. Uncomprehending, I stared at him. "It's a fax," he explained to my uncles and me, for the first time acknowledging them with a nod.

"I told you she had a fancy job," Uncle Ben said.

"Hell, we know that, Ben. Probably from the President or somebody like that," Uncle Curtis said.

"I'm Don Anderson, county agent here," the messenger introduced himself. Obviously he knew who I was, but I gave my name and shook hands. "How's your mama?" he asked.

"About the same."

"Called her house, but nobody answered. Then I called Stella's. Nobody there either. Then Bob Gleason dropped by for a cup and he said he'd just seen you in here."

"You should have asked me," Uncle Ben said.

"If I could've found you," Anderson said. He kept standing there. A couple of other men had joined us, too. Finally I realized they were waiting for me to read the important communiqué.

As they watched, I read: *Off Stone case. Need a break. Will be in Rollins tomorrow. Couldn't get a fax through to your machine.*

"A colleague of mine is coming to town on business," I told the expectant audience.

"Don't you worry, honey," Uncle Curtis said. "We'll help entertain him." He patted the tabletop. "Right here."

Hard

News and

Warm

Hands

Ned arrived the next evening while I was at the grocery store. When I returned, he took me in his arms and kissed me on the lips. No man had kissed me on the lips in front of my mother since Keith on our wedding day; however, she didn't seem to mind this display. The two of them couldn't have been chummier.

"He sent you that fax because our machine broke down and he says you never return his messages," my mother said.

"I return his messages. Today he didn't return mine."

"Did you know there are only three fax machines in Rollins and one of them is yours?" Ned asked me.

"He went through Congressman Alan Sack's office in Washington," my mother announced.

"Don't give away my secrets, Sudy," Ned said, obviously delighted with himself.

"What do you mean you went through the Congressman's office?" My curiosity won out over my anger with him for coming down so unexpectedly.

"I called the office and found they used the county agriculture agency because their home office is in Farley, even though this is the county seat. Why is it in Farley?"

"Because Farley is about a hundred times larger than Rollins."

"It used to be just a stop in the road," my mother added, "before it became a part of Dallas."

137

"We were getting worried about you," Ned said, changing the subject. "Your mother told me how absentminded you've become. We thought you had lost your way."

"It's hardly dark," I answered, not sure with which one of them I was more exasperated. "Mother, you should be in bed."

"See?" she said to Ned. "I told you she'd gotten bossy. But if she thinks she's going to tell me what to do, she's got another think coming."

Ned put his arm around her. "That's why I'm here, Sudy, to help get her under control."

"I don't need any help."

"We like to see that spirit of yours come back, Mrs. Reese," the nurse said. "It's a sign you're getting well. But if you don't go to bed, you won't feel like fighting in the morning."

"You shut up," my mother answered. This was vintage Sudy, but I glared at Ned as if it were all his fault. In a way it was: she'd been showing off for him.

"I'd better check into my room," Ned said. "Would it be okay if H.A. shows me the way and buys me a beer?"

"Of course. And you be sure she pays. She makes all that money and won't buy herself any decent clothes. I don't know what she thinks she's saving it for. She and Ruth. Neither one wants to spend a dime."

"She pays for me and I'm not exactly free," the nurse said, determined to be my ally. She didn't know when she was well off. My mother turned to me:

"H.A., you'd better not give this woman a lot of money. She's not worth a damn."

"Do you want me to take them both away?" Ned asked.

"I wish you would," she answered, accepting his good humor. She looked at me. "Ned wants to see that new housing development. Those houses are swankier than any in Boston."

"I'll do it," I lied.

"Make her now. She goes oohing and aahing over those old Victorian things everybody keeps fixing up. They were tacky new and they're tacky now."

Ned had a bottle of bourbon waiting for us in his room. "Since when bourbon?" I asked, my anger less pronounced because of the rush of relief I'd felt on first seeing him. Instead of the easy chair he gestured toward, I chose the straight-back at the desk.

"Since I've come south. Don't Texans drink bourbon and branch?"

"This is not the South."

"It is to me." He leaned over my chair as he handed me a drink and kissed my ear. "I've never had so many people be so nice to me in such a short time in my life. You mustn't spoil the record."

"Tell me about Stone."

"Nothing to tell. He's a bastard. I still don't think he engineered the Cardigan stuff the way you do, but I wouldn't put it past him anymore. Anyway, I'm out of there. I quit. End of story."

"That's it?"

"That's it, and I'm in no mood to talk about him. I've come to talk about us." I should have felt easier, but I didn't quite trust his words.

"As long as you're here, don't I get a capsule version of what happened between you and Stone?"

"Why haven't you told me your mother was older than your father?"

"Did she tell you that?"

"Your aunt Stella whispered it when your mother was out of the room. Seems your mother was always a little embarrassed by it, but you could have told me."

"I'd forgotten. Honestly. But it wasn't more than two or three years."

"Three years, almost four. Stella says I look something like him."

"That's ridiculous. He was tall, slim—"

"Blond? Fair?"

"Aunt Stella is a romantic."

"You hadn't done her justice in your description. She came to have a quick look at me before you got home. I had no idea she was a widow for so long, like your mother."

I gave up. "She wasn't. Her first husband died during World War Two, and she was married within two years."

"She mentioned he died in the war, but she made it sound like she'd been widowed forty years."

I laughed. "It's a wonder my mother let her get away with that. Sudy especially likes to point out that he died in a jeep accident on base. *Not* in combat."

He was still standing in front of me. I gestured him toward the other chair, but he kept standing. Trying again, I said, "Why did you quit? Stone's a horse's ass, but I thought we'd pacified him for the time being."

"I've come here to take you home," he answered, deftly avoiding my questions.

"I have a lot to see about."

"This is nuts, you know that? Everybody else does. Your mother does. Your aunt does. I do. Your other candidates are happy with their substitute care, but Stone is throwing fits to get you back. Pelham is understanding, but you can't blame him for getting frustrated with your absence."

"I've got to settle things here."

"You aren't trying to, though, are you?"

"I'm giving my mother time to get better, if that's what you mean."

"You're kidding yourself. You are drifting, H.A. Your mother is worried about what's to become of you."

"That's nothing new."

He smiled. "I gathered that. I told her she shouldn't worry so much because you are a lot like her—you won't let anyone tell you what to do either. It's easy to see where that stubbornness of yours comes from."

"But we're not alike. Everyone has always said I'm like my father. *She's* the one with the temper."

"Oh? Well . . . she thinks you made your real mistake when you married Keith."

"I always thought she felt the big mistake was leaving him."

He walked to the window. "Did you love him?"

"It was all so long ago, I . . ." My voice trailed off. I was evading. Other than with David, I didn't go into the whys and wherefores of other men, other times.

"So why did you marry him?"

"Probably because I didn't know what else to do."

"Seems to be a hobby with you."

"Fair enough," I acknowledged.

Abruptly Ned stood up. "When you come back, you are going to marry me." He was so calm he could have been giving the weather forecast. His self-certainty infuriated me.

"So your mother and I can get our face-lifts together?" He winced. Too late, I realized the proposal hadn't come easily for him. I tried to soften my reaction. "Look, we were a temporary aberration—a lovely one—but we've got to move on."

He slouched back in the chair and wouldn't speak or look at me. We sat in silence until I couldn't stand it any longer. I picked up my shoulder bag to leave and leaned over to kiss the top of his head.

"I want to strangle you right now," he said without moving.

"Someday you'll thank me."

"Someday, my ass. Where do you get off deciding what's good for me? What makes you think you know so well what I'm about? You don't even know what the hell you're about."

"So I've been told."

He jumped out of his chair and grabbed my shoulders. "I hate your goddamn smugness. I hate it." He shook me hard. When he let go, he stared at his trembling hands as if they belonged to someone else. He sat on the bed, jammed his fists between his legs. "I'm sorry. I promised myself I wouldn't lose my temper with you, whatever you did."

I wanted to go to him, cradle his head, but I stood there, unmoving. "You haven't once said you love me," he went on. "Not

once. You are not respectful of my feelings. You call this an infatuation, as if that explains everything. I know about infatuations. This
is not an infatuation and I am not fourteen. I am a man in love with
a woman. That's all. I am not interested in her age. I am not interested in some glossy package. I care about her. Why is that so hard
for you to accept? Don't you believe you're worth caring about?"

He came over to where I was frozen. "You're not leaving
just yet," he said and gripped my arm.

I thought of the chilly night outside and of my mother, and
of Bev's cows. I set my handbag on the desk. "This does not mean
I'm coming back," I assured him.

"I know exactly what it means," he assured me in return.

"Then will you tell me what happened? You owe me that
much . . . professionally."

"Two sentences, but you have to promise not to press further.
You have to let me handle this my own way." I nodded agreement.

"He fired me. He thinks I leaked the stories. He's in a panic
because he thinks the Hartford *Courant* is ready to run something.
Maybe one of the television stations, too."

"Does Pelham believe you?"

"Yes."

"Why didn't you tell me? Why didn't anyone?"

"What good would it have done?"

"I could have fought for you . . . something."

"You'd better come fight for yourself. Ralph is in no mood
for excuses. He's falling behind."

Ned began to softly knead my shoulders and the back of my
neck. His hands were warm and skillful and I lost my concentra-
tion. "I know about Ralph's campaign needs . . ." I trailed off.

Ned's lips brushed against my throat as his hands moved
under my breasts. There was no more talk of campaigns or age.

I slipped out of his embrace shortly after midnight and headed
back to Sudy's house. I felt the last thing I needed was my mother's
questions and I knew she'd be listening for me until I got home.

✳

Ned left the next morning and I got on the phone with Arthur Pelham, who hadn't much good to say about what had happened with Ned and Stone.

"I don't have to tell you, this could hurt Ned a lot once it gets out. Stone has to be quiet about it now—if he accuses Ned of leaks, then he's admitting Ned had real information—but after the election, it'll be tough shit whether he wins or loses." I agreed and promised to think of something. He thanked me and complimented me on the suggestions and ideas I continued to come up with—under such trying circumstances. Ned had, indeed, done a splendid public-relations job for me. Now it was my turn to help him. Although, whether he'd welcome my help or not remained to be seen. Before he left Rollins, I'd insisted that we had no future as lovers. Within thirty minutes I had booked a late-afternoon flight to Boston.

Making

Amends

Rachel Stone met me at the door. As usual, she was as gracious as she was attractive, and again I marveled at why she had married Ralph Stone. As far as I was concerned, their marriage was all that redeemed him. Could jealousy have been part of Ralph's trouble with Ned? I wondered. Maybe she and Ned really were . . . Ridiculous. I was being paranoid.

"Ralph can hardly wait to see you," she said as she led me to the library.

"Thank God you're here," he said, taking both my hands in his and drawing me closer to kiss my cheek. "Things have turned to shit. I've got a lot to talk to you about—as you know."

The man really did appear relieved to see me, causing a stir of guilt on my part even though I *had* come to place him back on track. This last thought caused a little inner wincing on its own, for helping Ralph meant acquiescing in his undermining of Mary Cardigan. But I could do nothing more to help her, I reminded myself, except at the expense of Ned.

When Rachel left the room, Ralph poured himself a vodka neat and me a glass of Evian water, the strongest drink I dared on this occasion. We sat facing each other in two of the leather chairs bracketing the fireplace.

"So why all the secrecy?" he asked.

"I have a couple of propositions for you, but they stay right here with us."

"Once upon a time I would have made a feeble joke about a tryst, but now . . ." He shrugged his shoulders.

"A little humility is good seasoning."

He brightened for a moment. "Really?" Then, noticing the look on my face, he said, "You're joking."

"Only a little," I said and swirled the ice around in my glass. "A belligerent stance isn't going to do you any good."

"What is?"

"I have a few ideas." I hesitated for effect. "You begin by hiring back Ned Sampson."

He smacked the arm of his chair with the palm of his right hand. "Not on your life. He's a spy. I let you convince me otherwise but no more. He's a conniving bastard. He's ruined me."

"He didn't do it. I happen to know for a fact he didn't."

"Then who in the hell did?"

"We'll get to that in a minute. First, I want you to promise Ned can come back."

He shook his head no. "Even if you could prove he wasn't the one, I can't do it. It's too . . . too . . . embarrassing."

"If he goes, I go."

"You can't go! I'll sue Pelham. I'll sue you. I'll make sure you never get another job. I'll—"

I got up and stood in front of him. "Understand this, Ralph Stone, for these next few weeks you need me more than I need you. I'm the best you're going to get at this late date and under these circumstances." I leaned over and shook a finger in his face. "Don't try to bully me. For once in your life, you're going to shut the hell up when told to—by me. That goes for outside this room as well." I straightened up. "All right?"

He nodded contritely. "Will you talk to him?"

"Yes, but you write a note—nothing elaborate. Say you acted hastily and have now changed your mind. Handwritten; that way not even your secretary has to know what happened. We don't want to give anyone a chance to gossip about anything. Even your other handlers. You and Ned and I plan strategy. Period."

"Can Rachel know?"

Amazed, I stared at him. Within three minutes, I had reduced him to a seven-year-old child. I sat back down. "Of course she can. Unless she's got a best friend other than you."

"She doesn't." He took a final swallow of his drink and got up to replenish our glasses. Movement emboldened him. He handed over my glass and the inevitable question. "If Ned didn't release the names, who did?"

"We've gotten to my second proposition." It was his turn to peer down at me. "This is privileged information I happened on," I said, never breaking eye contact with him. "If you win, it stays that way. If you lose, I tell."

"I don't understand. Nobody knew."

"A few people did. All it took were some rumors and a little investigative work."

"But they've made connections that are almost impossible to make without inside information."

"Ralph, nothing is impossible these days. Don't you watch the news?"

He paced to the door and back a couple of times, then sat on the edge of his chair. "Will you tell me one thing? Just one?"

145

"Depends."

"Would you tell me how you found out?" He paused. I didn't answer. "I'll settle for a clue."

"All right, but no follow-up questions," I said, pretending reluctance. "It behooves you to lay off Cardigan. Call a truce. Now let's move on to what matters right now—getting you elected."

He wanted to argue more, but the enticement of salvation won out. We spent the next hour plotting a press conference to be held before the end of the week. I convinced him that he should take the initiative, should get Stoddard to defend him at the event, cajoled him into working closely with Ned while I worked on position papers and talked to people in Washington.

This last bit was a slight twisting of the truth (but then on this evening, what wasn't?), for I was going to do all my talking to Washington from Rollins. Only someplace as necessary-sounding as Washington would induce Stone to let me stray from him. Capitulation had put him in uncharted waters, and I was the only compass available. Until I closed the door behind me, I managed to keep my hands from shaking.

Not bad, I thought as I climbed into my rented car. David would have loved that performance. As would have my mother. I wasn't sure about the man in the moon.

At an all-night service station I phoned Ned.

"Sorry to wake you. I'm in town for Stone and need to see you tonight. It's important."

✳

Ned had thrown on an old pair of jeans and a rumpled dress shirt but hadn't bothered with shoes. Looking disheveled and stern, he was taking a business-only approach to this meeting. After one last rebuff from me before he left Rollins, his pride wouldn't allow more.

He cleared a stack of magazines and an opened newspaper from his down couch, covered in natural linen and donated by his mother. Most of his furniture were castoffs from various family members and friends. Every surface was covered by newspapers, magazines, C.D.'s, and books, in that order. Having known him as a fastidious dresser with a tidy office desk, I had been delightfully surprised to find this bedlam in his private life.

"Stone wants you back," I said as soon as we sat down. "He knows he made a serious mistake, and he wants to make up. He plans to tell you himself, but I thought we'd better get on with the campaign. I have to go home in the morning."

"This is home."

"One of them," I answered.

"What happened with Stone? Did you make a deal? I don't want some kind of charity."

"Stone is incapable of charity. I pointed out to him why he needs us both. And he does. Have you seen the latest poll? He's trailing by ten points, and the stories haven't even hit the papers yet."

"If he weren't your client, I'd say good riddance."

"Well, he's yours again, too. At least I hope so. I wouldn't blame you for balking, but if he can swallow . . ."

"Okay, you've made your case. This isn't my first campaign, though you act like it is. I've been fired and rehired before. By worse bastards than Stone."

"Honestly, Ned, I'm sorry if I patronize you. I don't mean to. I don't feel that way."

He held up his hand to stop me. "What is it we're supposed to do?" He had become the old stodgy Ned again, and grumpy as well.

"I want him to have a press conference before the end of the week. Does he have that long? Do you have any idea how soon the press will break the story? I want him to preempt the charges."

"I'll find out."

"How fast could you put a nonprofit foundation together? I want all those building suppliers to contribute to an environmental-protection fund, as a show of their goodness and loyalty to our guy. The amount of money isn't nearly as important as the idea behind it." Ned nodded approvingly. I went on: "I also want you to scrape up every piece of information you can on the wetlands. There's been at least one real-estate investment conference, giving the pros and cons. We're especially interested in the cons."

I rummaged in my tote and handed Ned a sheaf of papers. "These come compliments of your friend Don Anderson, the county agriculture agent. He hates all this fuss over the wetlands. Turns out Congress has never passed legislation dealing with the problem. In effect, different governmental agencies make the rules."

"And this gives Stone a chance to run against the bureaucracy and say he's for the environment?" Ned asked. For the first time he was showing some interest in the game.

"That's it. He simply wants to legislate all this responsibly. Get it on the books. But it's all a little more complicated than it seems. Wants to be sure everyone is protected. Do a subtle states'-rights number."

"The environmentalists will see right through him."

"True. The hard core won't buy, but they can't accuse him of being the devil incarnate either. He says all the right things about protecting the environment, not polluting, whatever."

"But we're talking definitions. Just what is best."

"And he, as your trusted Senator, would know."

"God forbid!" He almost smiled. I stood up to leave.

"Do you want to spend the rest of the night here? I can sleep on the couch."

"I'm leaving first thing in the morning, and I haven't been to my own place yet. I need to get out my winter clothes."

"Where can I find you tomorrow?" he asked.

"I'll be in Rollins by noon, but I'll call you as soon as the plane gets to Dallas."

"I think Stone owns a little stretch of wetland himself," Ned said as he walked me to my car.

"Perfect for the press conference! Do you think we can get him to donate it to the state?" I asked.

"He would donate his children if he thought that would help."

He opened my car door and stood there looking stiff and formal. We hadn't touched at all. If he sensed my ambivalence, he was ignoring it. Part of me, I knew, was bargaining with the gods, giving up Ned to save David. But another part had earlier decided in a rational way that as a couple, Ned and I could never work. At this moment, the critical point was to get out quickly before another, more irrational part took over, the part that enjoyed being in Ned's hotel room in Rollins.

"Are you seeing that guy?" he asked as I started the car. We both knew he was talking about David.

"Not the way you mean."

"Then I'm losing you to Rollins. That place is making you crazy," he said as I started the car.

"I'm out of proportion," I explained. "Always have been. Some force is missing that should balance the rest of me. I think I can find it in Rollins. If not, I'm lost." Startled by my own admission, I drove away trying to figure out just exactly what I'd meant. And if I believed it.

Mama

Liked

Babies

Best

"Yep, Mama liked babies best," said Aunt Stella as her cigarette ashes dropped on Sudy's gold nylon carpet. "She wasn't as good with growing girls."

"She was shy," Aunt Clara said. "Also I don't think she saw very well. I'll bet she was nearsighted like H.A." This last was said as if I wasn't present, which, in a way, was true. As soon as

forth. Already she had been through one nurse and one aide. Even if she'd taken a liking to them, she would have had a hard time getting along with them on a daily basis. She had lived alone too long and, as much as she might complain about loneliness, she needed her privacy and solitude. To have someone in constant attendance left her a prisoner. Neither of us wanted to face the loss of her independence.

Nor could I face the loss of mine, and that was what moving back to Rollins or Dallas felt like—the alternative I most often confronted with persistence and dismay.

To all this turmoil had been added visits to David in the hospital. What had begun as a routine check-in for additional tests had turned into an extended stay and an extended nightmare for me— one I was not sure would end if he died. All the love for him that I had relegated to labels of lust, obsession, anger, or hate now surfaced. But why should love belong only to the vocabulary of sentimentalists?

Whenever possible, I visited him, sometimes for no longer than thirty minutes. I had come to dread that drive back and forth between Rollins and Dallas. At those times my mind chewed itself up with details of the immediate hours before me: What to fix my mother for supper? What amusing story to tell David next time? Had my mother raised her left leg higher than yesterday? Were her spirits better? Were his? Any question would do so long as it kept me from thinking about anything other than the immediate. I had no desire for a life that could not be counted in coffee spoons. Feelings were an unaffordable luxury; tears, an affront in this battle.

"I think I'm brain-dead," I said out loud, unintentionally.

My aunts and mother stopped arguing and looked at me. Finally my mother spoke: "I think you'd better go back to work."

"She'll go back to work when she feels like it," Aunt Stella said.

"I never thought a daughter of mine would turn out just like Stella." My mother started crying.

"I should have married Bob Watson," Aunt Stella said to no one in particular. "He was going to be a Methodist minister. I would have made a good minister's wife."

"Ha!" my mother said but continued to cry.

"If Dad and Mama hadn't been so dead-set against Methodists! Nowadays you can hardly tell the difference between them and us, but then you would have thought I was marrying a Catholic."

"Stella," my mother said, frustrated, "you've told us this a hundred times."

"H.A. has a good job, makes good money, and is devoted to you. I don't know what else you can expect from her," Aunt Ruth lectured my mother. I looked down at the ground.

"I will never have grandchildren." My mother, body heaving, shook her head from side to side.

"Sudy, hush, stop crying like this," Aunt Ruth said.

"At least you have a daughter, Sudy," Aunt Stella said. "I won't have anybody to look after me when I get old, so stop feeling sorry for yourself."

My mother blew her nose. "You are older than I am, Stella."

Aunt Stella, ignoring the last comment, continued talking.

"H.A., don't say you're brain-dead, because if you are, what about the rest of us?"

"Lord, isn't that the truth," Aunt Ruth joined in.

They all laughed and bound up our emotions and reassured themselves that I could still tap into their humor, their strength. I had never sensed more strongly the firmness of their bonds. For all their squabbles, they were there to heal one another's wounds, conceal one another's losses. And always with laughter.

"You've got to keep yourself in good shape, H.A., because one day you're going to have a lot of dotty old women on your hands," Aunt Ruth said.

"You never could have been a preacher's wife," my mother told Aunt Stella.

"Have you seen Dr. Jimmy lately?" Aunt Ruth asked. "His hair has gone white. I can't get over it."

"Of course I've seen him," my mother said. Dr. Jimmy, now in his late sixties, had semiretired for reasons of health, but the family still considered him their doctor.

"He looks older than I do," Aunt Stella commented.

"The next time I see him I'm going to turn that white hair black again," my mother said in anger. We all looked to her for explanation. "He said my contrariness would get me back on my feet. And look at me! I can't do a damn thing."

"Don't worry, Sudy," Aunt Ruth said, "you'll be up and at 'em in no time."

"I'm not up and I'm not at 'em."

This was her first admission—out loud, at any rate—that she wasn't getting better. To have her concede it frightened me and made me ashamed of my impatience and anger with her for not coming to grips with the enormity of her problem, for letting me wrestle alone with our dilemma.

"Do you want a Coke, Sudy?" Aunt Ruth asked.

"I hate Cokes."

"Do you remember old lady Cranston, who lived down the street from us?" Aunt Ruth asked. "She drank six Cokes a day. We thought she was so old." She sighed. "She probably wasn't much older than H.A."

"No, she was the same age as the Old Bad Woman," Aunt Stella said.

"How do you know?"

"I know because Jake Johnson told me. He was a friend of the Cranstons and he knew the Old Bad Woman and her husband before they moved into Dad's tenant house."

"The Old Bad Woman isn't exactly ancient."

"How long did she and her husband live there?" I asked, curious about what they might say.

"Until she ran away with Dad," Aunt Ruth volunteered.

"She tricked him," Aunt Stella said. "I don't care what she says to defend herself." I looked to my mother, who was looking down at her hands and not saying anything, although I was pretty sure she hadn't faded out of this conversation.

"He was a fool," Sudy finally said, refusing to defend him, also making her pronouncement in such a way as to preclude any further conversation on this subject.

"Was Papa Bear shy, too?" I asked.

"No, he wasn't shy. He was too mean for that."

"He could be shy," Aunt Ruth said.

"I always thought of him as being a little like Santa Claus," I put in. Nobody said anything.

Finally Aunt Stella spoke up: "He teased us a lot. Got us to fighting with each other or him, then we'd get the spanking."

"He was always teasing me for being little," Aunt Ruth said, pulling out another cigarette. (Why weren't they all dead of lung cancer? I wondered.) "I was so small that hand-me-downs swallowed me. I looked awful. When we got older, you made me a new dress every season, Sudy. Remember?" But my mother had closed her eyes and did not rouse herself.

They were silent for minutes, but then Sudy stirred and said, "He had a temper, and he was strict. I guess that's what we all remember most."

A father who did not satisfy—was that worse than none at all? Even so, they had found men who gave them the recognition and appreciation they must have longed for. Those men still teased them, but this time out of love.

"He was as sloppy with his children as he was with his cars," Aunt Ruth said.

"But not his grandchildren," I amended, tucking my legs under me.

"You touched his heart."

"We never did," Aunt Stella said sadly.

"He had a sister who got pregnant before she married. He never got over the shame. Mama told us that was why he was so strict," Aunt Stella added.

"He did tell us we'd better love each other, else someday we'd be sorry," Aunt Ruth said.

"He could be a son of a bitch," my mother said.

155

"Sudy!" both aunts responded at the same time.

So were all the sons of bitches I could find now paying for those long-ago days?

As my aunts left the house, I hugged and laughed with each of them.

Travels

With

My Mother

The summer after graduation my mother and I traveled together through Texas, Oklahoma, Louisiana, and New Mexico as she embarked on her new job as an account auditor for Western Auto. Since we'd taken to the road, I had been in a permanent torpor. The heat, the sameness of the towns, the stale-smoke feeling of the motel rooms, paralyzed me. By contrast, my mother was thriving. She had escaped Rollins.

She loved eating steak dinners on an expense account and walking into a store and shaping it up. Besides discovering daytime television, I had come to know which credit managers were "jackasses" and which were just "saps." None were competent. It was a wonder they ever operated a profitable store before my mother came in. From what I'd seen, she was probably right, but I was in no mood to share her victories. I was in no mood for much of anything except figuring out my own escape.

* * *

On this summer day we drove slowly along a wide treeless street in a dusty south Texas town looking for a certain rooming house where we would make a bill collection and retrieve a suitcase for a battered woman.

"This town's hot enough to fry," I told her. "I don't want to get killed in a town this hot."

"Before you interrupted me, I was about to say you are too young to get married. A year or two on your own will be good for you. We'll make an adventure out of it."

I cringed. On my own with my mother? What kind of "on my own" was that? I cursed my indecisiveness for getting me in this fix. I didn't know what kind of job I wanted. I didn't know if I wanted to go to graduate school. I didn't know if I wanted to pursue philosophy, math, or economics. I didn't know if I wanted to pursue Keith, a boy I had known and dated since high school.

Only two things I knew: one, David was out of my life; two, my mother was about to be. I just needed the nerve to tell her that I wouldn't be living with her in the fall as she had planned.

She continued her lecture: "It's stupid to think you're in love with Keith when you haven't been out of love with David more than a month. You're just fickle. Sometimes I don't think you have any common sense. Working in the real world will be good for you, a lot better than going back to school. You need to learn something about taking care of yourself and stop thinking in such highfalutin terms."

I sat there in silence, not about to argue with her about Keith. Since he still had another year of law school, he was not pushing marriage, anyway. Over the years, he had put up with my moodiness, my doubts, my posturing, and David. I depended on his calmness. A few minutes earlier I had remarked that Keith would make somebody a good husband someday, a remark that led to this conversation.

"That one down there, I'll bet," she said. "It's the only two-story house around." She looked over at me. "I've got the air conditioner on. Stop pouting." She stopped the car. "Now, why don't you take a walk while I see this man. And pull your shoulders back."

"I'm going with you," I said, "because you shouldn't be here at all. The man is dangerous."

"Somebody has to show these people how to get things done. This store has too many uncollected accounts. When Mr. Buddy Giles sees I don't mean maybe, he'll pay up."

Although bill collecting was by no means part of her job, she had done it occasionally and appeared to like it. Usually she got the money. But I knew she had come today for reasons other than saving Western Auto.

Since we had always taken in stray women, even families, in trouble, it should have come as no surprise to me when she showed up yesterday afternoon with a Mrs. Giles. She had a "no-good" husband, my mother informed me, and would sleep on a cot in our room until she could get to a brother's house in Arkansas.

The woman had come in to explain why they were so late in their payments. Mother, noticing her bruises and swollen eye, asked her to lunch. Now we were in the process of effecting a rescue.

"I'm not nearly as worried that this guy is a deadbeat as I am that he's a wife-beater," I said. "This is for the police to handle, not you."

She took one more drag of her cigarette before saying, "You can't rely on the police in these small towns, not where some man's wife is concerned. Besides, he's an ignorant, superstitious man. He won't be a bit hard to handle." She got out of the car, and I followed her up the walk.

Although it was four o'clock in the afternoon, the sun was unrelenting. In this neighborhood, no one had bothered to plant flowers or to water the grass. Even the weeds were brown. Not a living creature stirred on that light-drenched street. Only we were crazy enough to be out.

She turned toward me. "Now, go on. Shoo! You're not too big to spank."

"You are not going by yourself, and this time *I* don't mean maybe," I said.

She glared at me. I stood there, arms crossed over my chest. Then she shrugged. "Well, at least comb your hair."

Buddy Giles stood in the doorway in his undershirt and rumpled pants. My mother treated him with all the formality she reserved for ministers and Northern accents as she maneuvered us into his living room by some fast footwork without asking his permission.

Oversized rattan furniture and scattered newspapers crowded the room. A ceiling fan pushed around hot air and years-old cigar smoke. The shades were drawn and in a corner a small television set flickered without sound.

My mother sat down on the sofa, again without asking or receiving permission, and I followed suit. Mr. Giles reluctantly sat in what he probably considered his easy chair, though springs were touching the floor and stuffing was coming out the back. He looked perplexed but not surprised, not unlike the way I felt, as if this delicate-boned, curly-haired woman might have answers beyond any either of us had come up with for ourselves.

But her concerns were always of the here and now—most specifically in this case, how Mr. Giles planned to pay for his purchases, to be followed by how she was going to get his wife's clothes out of here.

Though that's not how she started, of course.

"That your son?" she asked, indicating a photograph on top of the TV and almost as large.

"My wife's."

"When did he pass away?"

He looked puzzled, but answered, "Three years in March."

"It's hard, isn't it? We don't ever get used to losing a loved one." He gave a noncommittal grunt. "He's a handsome boy," she went on. "Looks like he could be yours."

"Never cared much for him," he said.

A fly was buzzing from one wall to another, and the cigar

smoke was making my nose itch. We were with a vicious drunk and she was acting as if we'd come for tea. I picked up a news-paper to fan myself.

"Children can be a worry," she said and frowned at me.

"He gave his mama grief," the man said.

"I don't think he's the only one." For an instant his eyes became alert, but again he grunted.

"I can tell you're a decent man, Mr. Giles, the way you've kept your stepson's picture in deference to your wife's feelings. But you've made a few mistakes I know you are ready to correct. You don't want to be a poor credit risk."

He gave my mother what could only be described as a men-acing look, but she didn't blink.

"Your drinking has caused you enough problems already, but there's no sense in using it as an excuse to let the rest of your life get out of control."

"Why don't you mind your own business, lady?"

"Right now, Mr. Giles, you are my business—mine and Western Auto's. You're a grown man and we expect you to act like one."

He stood up. "You'd better leave now."

"There's no need to be rude, Mr. Giles. I plan to leave when I have a down payment on what you owe."

"You'll be here a long time because I'm broke."

"No, you aren't. You've got money for whiskey. You've got money for cigars and money for newspapers, and you don't look like you've missed many meals lately. You've got the money."

"You go tell Western Auto to—"

Standing up, she wagged her finger at Giles. "Don't talk to me like that. Fool with me and I'll have the police here so fast it'll make your head spin. If you don't find some of that money, then you're going to land in jail and there, sir, you will not get any liquor at all."

"You can't put a man in jail because he's broke."

"I have my ways," she answered ominously.

They looked ready to kill each other. I scouted the room for a phone and a blunt instrument with which to bam Mr. Giles over the head. A prison term on manslaughter charges would certainly solve all my immediate problems, I thought in the middle of my fright. I was going to become a woman of action after all. I thrilled to the idea.

But Buddy Giles was no match for my mother. "I can give you ten dollars," he said.

"Fifteen. And thirty more on Friday. That's when your disability payment comes in."

He started to protest, sighed instead, and left the room. My mother took out a cigarette and I walked to the front door. The place had become more oppressive by the minute, but outside was no better. Even the trees drooped under the weight of the heat. Our red Plymouth looked like an oven.

My mother, obviously pleased, came over to whisper, "Now, this is where it gets a little tricky. . . ." She broke off when he came back in the room, and drew herself up in an attempt to give the impression that she towered above him.

"One more matter, Mr. Giles, and I'll be gone," she said as she stuck the money in her purse. "I have also come for your wife's belongings. She does not want to come back, so if you would step aside, I will take her clothes with me."

"Like hell you will, you bitch."

"Witch, Mr. Giles. I'm a witch."

This last remark visibly disconcerted Mr. Giles. He backed away. "You loony or something?" I was beginning to wonder the same thing.

"I happen to know you've had some experience with ghosts yourself. Why would you not think I have access to the spirit world?"

"My wife tell you this?"

"No. One of your ghosts did."

By now I remembered Mrs. Giles saying that her husband saw ghosts when he was drunk. In fact, he swore they sometimes were the cause of his beating her.

Just then my mother announced that by the time he turned to look out the window, she would have started her car coming in this direction. He turned; I turned. Sure enough, the car was rolling downhill. The next thing I knew she was bounding down the steps, losing a shoe in the process. I chased after her and watched as she grabbed the wheel and steered it toward the curb.

Her hand on her heart, face flushed, she panted heavily. My stomach clutched. "Are you all right?" I asked.

She nodded reassurance, tried to smile, and started back toward the house. "Mama, let's get out of here," I said, having called her nothing but "mother" for years. Stopping only long enough to put on her shoe, she paid me no attention.

Mr. Giles meekly stepped aside as she came through the door. "Sometimes I am not able to stop those things I set in motion," she told him as she put the photograph of Mrs. Giles's son under her arm. "That's why it's particularly dangerous to fool around with me—or your wife, who now has my protection whether or not I'm with her."

She proceeded to the bedroom; I followed and helped pack a few cheap dresses and some other photographs. Far better than I, she had understood the need of securing Mrs. Giles's possessions, or wresting them, and the power, from Buddy Giles.

As she began talking loudly about the terrible heat, with one deft motion she opened the top bureau drawer and pocketed the money she found underneath the Kleenex box. Giles was nowhere to be seen as we left.

On the way back to the motel, she turned to me: "Call Keith if you like and tell him we're coming in this weekend. We can leave as soon as I put Mrs. Giles on the bus. Did you know that old so-and-so had over a hundred dollars in that dresser drawer? She didn't think there would be that much. I have another week here, but it's not so far we couldn't spend the weekend with Stella. And next week, I think we'll try that motel we saw on our way into town. The people in the store say it's a little better."

"You were something back there," I said to her with admiration. "But the car?"

She grinned at me. "Just as I said, I'm a witch."

"A lucky one."

"It's all in the reflexes."

If I told her she had to let me run my own life, maybe living with her next year wouldn't be so bad.

"Anyway," she continued, as much to herself as to me, "you can't let the S.O.B.'s win. Not when you can help it."

Stopping

in

Phoenix

I lay in the motel bathtub reading *Middlemarch* for the first time since the seventh grade. These days, when I wasn't watching the television, I had taken to reading all those great books that had worked before—the ones with strong, smart, independent women. Always I had found strength in my heroines or, when necessary, in heroes, transforming them into heroines. In the past, I had also used math problems as a kind of therapy, especially useful when I couldn't sleep or needed to calm myself. Now nothing worked; even my mother's own dynamism did not inspire me.

Tonight, when she had turned out the light in our room, I had taken to the bathroom, determined to read whether I wanted to or not. Better to read than sleep my life away in a stupor. All summer I'd been telling myself I was resting up from a lifetime of school, but over these last few days I had decided to return to Austin in September. I was relieved to have made a decision— any decision—I just hadn't told my mother yet.

"H.A., why don't you come to bed now? It's almost midnight," my mother called from the bedroom.

"As soon as I finish this chapter." I didn't look up, but I heard her sit down on the closed toilet seat. I knew perfectly well my mother was not one to be ignored, but I went back to my book.

Over the years we had a ritual that worked for the most part. When she came in a room where I sprawled, she signaled her readiness to talk by making some comment on my position: I was reading in the dark, or holding the book too close, or ruining my posture, or getting too old to have my feet over my head. More often than not, I would agree and ask her what she'd been up to. Tonight, out of perverseness, I kept reading. She endured my inattention for five pages, about three more than usual.

"Aren't I good enough for you?" she asked, and before I looked up, I knew it was too late for any question from me.

"Don't say things like that," I answered.

She squashed a large red ant with her toe. I lay there hoping she would let matters drop, but knowing how hard it was for her to stop herself once roused. I also knew I hadn't been very good-humored lately, especially since I'd made the decision to stay with her.

"I'm not living with you anymore," she said. The way she said it—so matter-of-factly, not with anger or self-pity or recrimination—made me sick to my stomach. And scared. We were two adults talking now. "You can have all our things for your apartment. I'll be happier by myself in an efficiency. I can't stand this." I felt relief sweep over me. With these last words, she had gone too far. She was only playing with my sympathy. We were back on familiar territory. I might not like it but I understood it. And I was the child again. I turned around in the tub. "What have I done? I'm just reading."

"I'm through arguing with you. You go on about your life. I'm just an old woman, holding you back."

In more mature phases, I might have joked that all old women should look like her—no wrinkles and terrific legs. I might have mentioned her great new job. I might have tried to raise the level of discussion. Instead I told her to quit feeling sorry for herself.

She jumped up and shook her fist in my face. "Shut up!" she said, turning to leave the room, then pivoting toward me again. "I hate your high-and-mighty attitude. I want you to leave."

"I don't want that, but I don't want to feel smothered either." Now I was also standing, water rushing down my body. "Don't you see? After these years away, I'm used to a little more independence—just like you."

"I never get in your way."

"I know you don't mean to, but sometimes—"

She interrupted. "Our living together is a mistake. You should live your own life."

I nodded my agreement. I was too choked to speak. "I have to." I finally got the words out of my mouth and felt, in that confession, something in me come back to life. "I need to live in another city. I want to strike out on my own. I want to feel grown-up." I didn't know where the words were coming from, but even the look on her face didn't stop me. "This has nothing to do with you, Mama. I just want to be on my own. I want to see what it's like to be strong in myself, the way you are." I was crying now. "Please understand."

I had cried so seldom in front of her that she fell silent. She started back to her bed, and I followed. We lay silently in our twin beds, the space of a night table creating chasms between us.

After a while, I asked, "Do you remember when you surprised me with a new jacket and then took me and Laura and Bev and Jane to Dallas to eat so I could show it off?"

"No."

"The bright pink one? On our way to the table Jane kept

his firm had ever had, while I devoted myself to my research project, promising political candidates, civil rights issues, and the Vietnam protest.

✳

We generated lots of motion and hummed along our separate courses until the night of the moon walk.

Peggy Barnett and her husband, Don, asked us over to watch the event on television with them. My mother, in town for a visit, reluctantly agreed to come along. She thought Peggy "snooty" and Don dull and, correctly, figured them both to be Republicans. I had hoped she wouldn't join us because she could perfectly well decide to "put them in their place."

The evening began early. Peggy and Don had a pool, and I swam slowly through the last sheaths of sun, content to watch the play of green and gold crinkles in my small waves. Afterward I took a sauna, though the outside air was sauna enough. Keith and Peggy raced each other in the pool, and I noted Peggy's ability to bring off a bikini with the aplomb of an eighteen-year-old. Don, always the correct host, engaged Sudy in conversation about the operation of Western Auto stores. Sudy stayed on her good, if loquacious, behavior. I felt grateful to them both for entertaining each other. Even without Sudy around to worry about, social occasions these days exhausted me.

Once again Keith was urging me to quit work and devote my full time to getting pregnant, and, for a change, I agreed with him. If I wanted a baby, I needed to concentrate on having one. Sudy, always ready with advice, had remained silent on this issue, partly from ambivalence. She wanted a grandchild—so much so that I had spared her the disappointment of my last miscarriage— but she also took great pride in my career. That's how she referred to my employment: "H.A.'s career."

I had not told her that my "career" had taken a downturn. My long-term report recommended that the financial community diversify its holdings, not depend so much on oil. I predicted economic disaster within twenty years. Hard as my arguments were to refute, no one agreed with me. I received an institutional pat on the head. Whether my colleagues were simply obtuse or prejudiced against women, the experience soured me on my profession. This job, so beloved by my mother, had already seen its best day before I even turned thirty.

The blow hit both professionally and personally. Until this experience I had not realized how dependent I was on the illusions of others. Now I discovered an unsettling truth: when nobody else thought I was wonderful, my image of myself collapsed. Not only was my occupation a sham, but so was I, my suspicions proving true after all.

Suddenly I went from having energy to rival my mother's to feeling worn down most of the time. To hide out from life by staying home had a great deal to recommend it. Still, I also knew myself well enough to know that living without a superimposed structure could drive me into permanent mindlessness.

Peggy in her bikini, a towel wrapped around her tanned, eighteen-inch waist, came over to sit with my mother. "Mrs. Reese, I hope it's not too hot for you out here tonight."

"I've seen hotter."

"Of course," Peggy laughed, "why should I apologize to another Texan about the weather?" My mother flicked the ash of her cigarette onto the weedless grass and stared at her hostess. Peggy laughed again. Then she launched into clothes: "That's a snappy pantsuit you're wearing. I looked all over Neiman's last week for something in that red for my mother but couldn't find it."

"Try Sears," my mother replied, blowing cigarette smoke close to Peggy's nose.

"Red is a good color on you, Mother," I said.

My mother's dark eyes shot around to me. "Don't *you* patronize me," she said, "and hold yourself up." I felt she was referring to more than just my posture.

Keith, also dressed in a towel, walked over. Both Peggy and I looked at him expectantly, but he had no idea he was to extricate us from Sudy. Then Peggy's face lit up.

"Oh, H.A., I forgot to tell you, I ran into your aunt Clara

at the airport last week." Peggy looked delighted to have another conversation gambit, and so was I. "She's your spitting image, Mrs. Reese. That's how I recognized her."

"First time she's ever been stuck with that," Sudy answered.

"I looked a mess myself. My nails were plain tacky. I'd gone out there to meet my sister and never dreamed I'd run into anybody I knew. I started to do my nails before I left, but my goodness, if you can't let down before your sister, who can you?" She looked to my mother and me for a response. My mother set her mouth and searched the sky for the spaceship. I marshaled my resources for a smile—a calming smile, one to shut her up. Having my mother around made it impossible not to notice idiocies.

"Well, I think I'll see what else Gladys has fixed up for us in the kitchen," Peggy said.

"I'll help," Keith volunteered. He alone appeared to believe Peggy's nails deserved rapt attention.

By the time the moon shot started, we had eaten and drank and swam for days, it seemed. Keith and Peggy kept laughing at each other's jokes, showing off for each other. Keith was strutting about the way he used to after a particularly satisfying bout in bed. Sudy gave both Peggy and Keith clipped answers—a sure sign she was disapproving. I wondered if they were having an affair, but in the next moment dismissed the notion as absurd.

I turned to Don. "I'm excited about this moon walk," I said and realized how true it was. Having done a prodigious amount of homework for the occasion, Don began a discourse on the moon. He talked about its composition and its meaning in Buddhist thought: how the moon embodies the idea of sacrifice through its embrace of night, of death, in order to be renewed. He talked about the enormity of our galaxy and of the myriad of others like it.

Once Keith rolled his eyes at me and Sudy's head nodded a couple of times as Don droned on but I wasn't bothered by our host, only by what he was talking about. Science might take away mystery, but the idea of boundlessness, limitlessness, remained intact, throwing back in my face that old nemesis *eternity*.

I watched Neil Armstrong hit the ground and clapped with everyone else. Tears came to my eyes—the courage, the exuberance, the pluck. The tears turned to another kind when I considered the implications of my life. What did I propose for *my* moon walk? And were they having an affair? More important, why did thinking about the possibility make me feel as light as those white suits bouncing around on the moon?

Watching Keith offer Peggy his beer, I thought about leaving, bouncing out of the life I had made. The exertion of entertaining and worrying about my mother, Keith, Keith's parents, my aunts, was enough to occupy anyone. But when would Peggy ever have the time for an affair? Between sorority sister get-togethers and Junior League and church work, she kept a full schedule, as full as Keith's. There was also Keith's heavy sense of duty. No, probably the only affair going on here was very much confined to their fantasies, if either of them bothered with such things.

Neil Armstrong walked about and planted the American flag. How did one become conditioned to floating? To giving up fears of an ancient kind? The flag waved. Peggy and Keith cheered.

With amazing clarity I realized my marriage was a hoax. I had felt unloved without knowing it. Unbearable to know it. Unbearable to have the void of man once more in my life. Out of my despair I had constructed small edifices of activity. My mind was handling it all right, but somewhere in there my spirit had checked out.

If Keith was screwing Peggy, I wouldn't have to have a baby. I wouldn't have to ask Keith about his day or go to dinner with his family or spend weekends with Peggy and Don. I wouldn't have to feel guilty with my own disaffection with our marriage. I wouldn't have to feel guilty about my longing for a more passionate man, a more passionate life. Keith could be happy without me, happier than now.

Until that moment, I think I saw myself as being as indispensable to Keith as I was to my mother. No matter how he felt about me, he still needed me, could not manage without me. To imagine that I had misjudged his strength filled me with a kind of peace, for the only thing more unbearable than to think he could survive without me was to think he couldn't. If my leaving wouldn't kill him, then there was a chance for me to test myself, to see how I would do alone. Not alone forever, but for a while; for some while.

"H.A.," Keith said, his voice brusque, "Don just asked you if you'd like to travel in space?"

"Leave her to her dreams," Don said, but for the first time in weeks I felt like talking.

"Space terrifies me," I answered. "All that floating, the disconnection. Then, of course, it points up our insignificance—our aloneness and insignificance. But the boldness of stepping into an orbit not already known overwhelms me. The courage to do—"

"I didn't bring her up to have such wild thoughts," Sudy said to Don.

"Your mother has a point, H.A.," Keith added. "Don't turn this into a metaphysical discussion. Just answer the question before you. I'm curious."

I rejected the impulse to slap him. "I have long been a space traveler, Keith. I thought you'd noticed."

Filled with angry resolve, I decided no amount of good causes and civic responsibilities and private duties were going to keep me in this bind. Space might be dangerous, but it beat suffocation all to hell.

Until now I had been responsible in all the ordinary ways. I played the good girl to the hilt. I saw obligations even when they didn't exist. But I could not stay earthbound any longer. Something in me could surely retrieve the promise of the moon of my childhood, the moon that controlled deep currents in the conduct of the world. But I couldn't renew by clinging. Once my father had tried to tell me as much. I had to let go a little, only a little, my need to construct a perfect world, a perfect life, and a perfect self.

Within six months I had taken a job as a political consultant in Atlanta. I caught the eye of one of Georgia's finest who asked me to give him a call if I was ever interested in joining his firm. I called, and my mother helped me pack but refused to take me to the airport. I left behind everything I didn't need, including Keith.

A

Stone's

Throw

Adversity helped Stone's appearance. The makeup woman had left traces of his dark circles, to remind people he was human. Some candidates just needed a little rumpling up. Nobody likes perfect. He had gotten the hang of a humble look, thanks to Ned's coaching.

Also, thanks to Ned's coaching, he should ace this press conference. Sunny and crisp, the weather had cooperated also. We had scheduled it to be held on a plot of land Stone owned not far from Hartford—close enough to be an easy trek for reporters, far enough to be considered country. Ned convinced Stone to donate the land and announce the environmental foundation at the same time. Stone threw in an old house for the foundation's headquarters. So long as nobody went to look at it, we were all right.

Fortunately, we had a good representation of city and state

reporters. Stone usually did especially well in front of the television cameras, for he was a quicker study than we had realized and he retained his facts. With a little luck, he could come out of this a lot better than he went in. Not such a difficult accomplishment, really, since his ratings in the polls continued to drop and his contributions had dried up—the negative stuff had not come out yet, but the press had nothing good to say about him anymore. Until now the opposition had been calling him a friend of the developers, especially of Jack Stoddard, but they weren't ready to spring any hard evidence. Not that the evidence was all that hard. A lot of it was circumstantial, too circumstantial for the press to use. They were waiting for the campaigns to present it first, then they'd report it.

A quietness had descended on Stone's campaign. Were the vultures circling? Were they readying for the attack? Was it imminent? As it turned out, so imminent that we had moved the press conference to Thursday instead of Friday. The opposition planned to hit the Sunday papers with the revelations that Stone had known full well what Stoddard was up to when Stone invested in the Stoddard enterprise. Someone in Stoddard's office had come up with the documents to prove that Stone had signed on after the environmental-impact report had appeared in the papers.

With a backdrop of autumn leaves, cattails, and a field of thrushes, Stone got up to confront the charges directly. His voice echoed beautifully through the marsh. We couldn't have come up with a more effective setting, I complimented myself.

"Of course I knew," Stone was saying. "But I had Jack Stoddard's word that anything detrimental to the environment would be removed from the plans. Unfortunately, he and I have different ideas about what is detrimental. That was an honest misunderstanding on both our parts. I doubt there is one of you who hasn't taken a friend at his or her word only to find later the two of you saw the problem differently.

"You could say I should have followed the situation more closely. You'd be right. I got busy with my own campaign, my own business. I learned a long time ago to delegate. To be an effective leader, you have to. But mistakes got made on my watch and I have no one to blame but myself. For whatever it's worth— and I hope it's worth a lot—I think I've learned a valuable lesson.

"Every citizen in this state will have a long wait before seeing me trip up again like this. And for everyone in this state who cares about the environment around us, and I believe that is every one of us, this situation has made me even more sensitive to the need to stay vigilant.

"Did you know that in the next twenty-five years we will cause the loss of a greater number of species than all the extinctions of the past combined? If you compressed all existence into one year, this would happen in only one-eighth of a second on that timetable."

These last words—my words—made me cringe. I had tried to put out of my mind the seriousness of the environmental charges against him.

"That is why I want to be elected. I don't want to leave these problems to the bureaucrats in Washington. I want Congress to legislate guidelines that keep this kind of mix-up from happening in the first place. Do you know we have no federal legislation? Regulation is subject to the whims of a bureaucracy with tunnel vision. What do they know about the balance between jobs and environment, decent housing and environment? These issues are all of a piece, and we can't have one without the other.

"That, ladies and gentlemen, is why I am here today: to see to it that our environment is sound. Our economy is sound. Our living conditions are humane. A large order, but with your help I'll try my best to see it happens.

"Questions?" Stone finally asked.

A reporter in the front, the one Ned knew had stuff on Stone, raised her hand. Per instruction, Stone called on her.

"What about the charge that the building trades and construction companies have financed your campaign in order to ensure their interests are represented in Congress, especially those that are diametrically opposed to those of environmentalists?"

177

This gave Stone the opportunity to announce his environ-
mental-goodie package, including a $65,000 fund to buy up and
protect wetlands. That it was being given by the sharks to be run
by the sharks was incidental. We had even snagged a few environmental types to be on hand to express appreciation. Maybe
they hadn't figured it out yet.

Nobody asked a follow-up question. I could hardly believe
our luck. Nobody had heard of the Gary Boatwright incident, the
one matter that could unravel our whole strategy. Only my sense
of timing, not caution, had prevented me from leaking Stoddard's
letter to Stone about the rigging of Boatwright's removal. I had
saved it for the time when it would do the most damage: three
days before the election. Without it, Boatwright himself couldn't
prove anything.

All, in fact, anybody knew was that Boatwright's job with
Stoddard had been made less interesting, and he'd been offered
a better job in Florida with a firm that did a hell of a lot of
business with both Stoddard and Stone. Nobody had made the
connection.

Stone and I had not discussed this tie-in, though I now had
open access to his contributors' list, where I had found the orig-
inal note. The copy of the letter had been removed from the file,
and I wasn't supposed to know that Gary Boatwright existed.

Even more important, nobody had a clue that Ralph, through
Stoddard, had access to a huge investigative apparatus. My own
contacts in the security community had confirmed that. Once I
considered distributing that information but ended up scratching
the idea as too hard to get at, to prove.

I smiled at Ned. The hard part was over. No matter how
tough the questions were on the environment, Stone had sound
bite after reassuring sound bite on his commitment to it. Clean
air, clean water, clean jobs, clean houses. We loved clean as much
as we loved mother and country. How could he reconcile the
commitments? Well, trust him, he could. He had statistics and
studies to prove it.

The same old bullshit, but coming from such a vigorous,

attractive package. The press knew it, too, of course, but their seduction had started. A long time between genuine heroes, we were willing to accept just about anyone who could make us believe.

"Lord, we are willing, Christ to receive," went the old hymn. What Christs we settled for these days.

But Ned's reputation would be restored and the attacks on Mary Cardigan halted. The country had survived worse asses than Ralph. We could survive one more.

An

Old, Old

Helpless

Longing

David's daughter had needlepointed *W*'s on his bedroom slippers, a long-ago birthday present. Now a sophomore at Tulane, she made only brief duty-stops at home during major holidays and vacation breaks. She had never gotten along with her mother, and David, because of his frequent absences and preoccupations, had become irrelevant to her life early on, or so she said. Now she was too angry to allow him to atone, and he accepted her decision.

Neither she nor her brother understood how sick he was. I wasn't sure he did himself, yet by his own account the doctors painted a bleak picture. Their prognosis of six months to live hadn't changed, he informed me. In the next breath, he made plans for our future. He was sure the operation would cure him, although his doctors now actively discouraged it.

Today he sat in a straight chair, his legs crossed, light blue pajamas starched, navy wool robe pulled tightly about him. While I was there, he refused to stay in bed and insisted I take the easy chair. I had learned not to argue with him, or, for that matter, even talk a lot. A repository for dreams and hopes needs to remain ungarnished.

"Where do you want to live?" he asked. "Someplace new to both of us, maybe?"

"What about a ranch?"

Little-boy pleasure spread across his lined, drawn face, already the color of cold breath, and the contrast overwhelmed me. I wished he could dress for my visits. Pajamas were too revealing of his bony frame, sucked free of health. "Would you give up your career? For us? I somehow never thought you would."

"For all intents and purposes, it appears I already have."

"Two months. You've been off two months. Believe me, that's nothing." He began coughing, a new occurrence; and unsettling.

"Can I get you anything? Water? A nurse?" He shook his head no, the question itself annoying him. As soon as the cough stopped, he began talking again, his throat scratchy.

"But will you really come away with me?" he asked. "Do you mean it? It is so important that we make a life together. I know that now. I made such a mistake."

"Don't be too sorry. You've had years of me as fantasy. After the real thing for a while, you may wish I were fantasy again."

"I'm willing to trade," he said, "but I'm worried you can't give up your freedom, or what you think of as your freedom."

"And I'm willing to revise my definition. I've spent a long time equating freedom with indulgence. I've played to my weaknesses and limited my choices. Does that make sense?" I asked. He nodded his head but didn't speak.

"I'm not sure I ever really wanted freedom, since it forces one to be even more responsible for oneself and the rest of the world. Pretty soon you start to feel even more guilty about the quality of life in our times and what you have and haven't done for your friends."

David smiled and pulled his robe more tightly around him. "Would you hand me that blanket?" He pointed to the foot of the bed, and I jumped up.

"Why not get back in bed?" I suggested. "I've always liked you there." But he was too irritated with himself to accept the humor, and he refused to let me help him wrap up.

"I am coming to believe," he said as soon as he caught his breath, "that the power of Christianity has as much to do with the need for forgiveness as it does the need for transcendence."

"And my urgent sifts through all those philosophers—another way to get myself off the hook?" I asked.

He nodded agreement and shut his eyes. "I was jealous of all those fellows. You were so clearly trying to find something or someone you could rely on. I wanted it to be me."

I laughed. "Well, I discounted contemporary minds. I wanted people who wrestled mythically with good and evil. You can't be forgiven your trespasses if nobody acknowledges there's anything to forgive. Everything just gets explained away." He kept his eyes closed, but through nods and smiles he let me know he was listening.

"Your insistence on mercilessly questioning everything inspired me but also intimidated me," he said slowly. "I never understood how you kept it up."

"If you already have a familiar sense of terror, it's not so hard to be rigorous. Much as you wish otherwise, you don't have many illusions to part with." He opened his eyes, ready to pursue this new tack, but I retreated to the earlier one. "That stubborn, old-fashioned part of me won't give up evil, won't even give up sin, though my definition of it slides around a lot." I smiled.

"Forgiving yourself isn't nearly as easily done or as effective as having another do it for you."

shaking as it stroked my breast. This time I pulled away and stepped back.

"You know perfectly well a nurse is liable to walk in."

"As soon as I get out of here . . ."

"You'll have to fight me off," I said with all the conviction I could muster.

"We have nine lives together. You do remember that?"

"How could I forget?"

"I need one of those resurrections now," he said. "Touch me."

Walking down the corridor, I wondered what I was going to do when he got out of the hospital. I couldn't avoid making love then, but the thought brought on a kind of hysteria, a violent shudder deep within. Having lost the fantasy altogether, I mourned my loss and cursed my cowardice.

A nurse whose face I'd come to recognize nodded to me. She worked day shifts, and from her sympathetic glances, I sometimes wondered if she mistook me for David's wife. His family should be here more. Even if he had been a lousy husband and father, he'd loved them and stayed with them. That should count for something. They had a real man in the house. And a decent, kind man at that. "He shouldn't be left alone so much," I mumbled out loud as I unlocked my car door.

Once inside the car, and without warning, the spoken words released some secret torrent of grief in me; the bleached-out emotions of the last few weeks gave way to spasms of pain. "God damn you, David!" I screamed. "God damn you! God damn you!" I pounded the seat and cried and buried my head in my arms.

When the heaves stopped, I curled into a ball, not to still myself but to make plans. If I made plans, forced tough decisions, we could all survive. My life had been on hold long enough.

My mind began to work—a little frenzied, but that was expected, necessary. My mother would have to go into a rehabilitation center; it was her only hope of getting better. This limbo I had allowed us to fall into was defeating her.

Until I settled my mother, I would spend the days with David and the nights with her. She woke up a lot. I'd stay awake and keep her company. She would be with me almost as much as now. That way both of them would be cared for. Sudy would be on the path to recovery and I could give David enough love to get him out of there. He believed I could, and I would.

The only hitch was Ralph, but Ned was capable of taking care of him for the time being. Right now Ralph Stone was willing to accept me on any terms, but if worse came to worst, I could do a turnaround commute a couple of times a week.

Plans worked for me. They created order and they comforted. Plans were my magic. I headed for Rollins to announce my first one.

Caretaking

On my return from the hospital, my mother and Aunt Stella sat waiting for me, but they had already been to the fish buffet at the Holiday Inn. "Your mother didn't want me to cook," Aunt Stella said, and I silently blessed my mother.

"We thought you'd be back sooner. We were starving," my mother scolded. "You got all these phone calls, but we didn't know what to tell people."

"We told them she'd call back, Sudy." My aunt turned toward me. "Ned called. Bev called. Laura called. She sounds like she always did. When you girls were growing up, she was one of my favorites."

Since my mother's illness, Laura, now a lawyer in New Orleans, had been dutifully calling.

"And a David Wright also called," my aunt continued.

"Don't I know David Wright?" my mother asked.

I nodded, unable to get words out of my mouth. For David to call . . . I wouldn't let myself finish the thought. And where was his idiot wife? Why wasn't she seeing to him instead of leaving him to rot alone? Well, he wouldn't. I wasn't going to let him.

"Where are you going?" Sudy asked.

"To your bedroom to make my calls."

"This phone works better."

"The other one's fine."

"You'd better call Ned. It's awful the way you treat him."

Over the phone, David's voice sounded strangled, and I lapsed into my Pollyanna chirp and began poking a cigarette burn in the bedspread until he quickly did away with niceties. "The doctors were just here and they told me they're not going to operate. It's pointless."

"Of course it's not pointless. They are plain wrong. We'll get you better doctors. That's all." By now I had made the cigarette hole larger, but I didn't stop prodding.

"It's over, H.A. I'm—" Here his voice broke off.

"No!" I screamed. "Those assholes don't know what they're talking about. Fucking assholes!" I made myself take a breath, calm down. "We'll go to another country if we have to. Do you want me to come back tonight? I can try to make some arrangement here. Have you told your wife?"

"She's coming in a while. I'll tell her then."

"Do you want me to come later? Spend the night?"

"By the time she leaves, they'll have knocked me out. Just try to come tomorrow. Please."

"First I'm going to find out about other doctors. That may take a while. Then I'll be there."

"All right."

"David? David?"

"Oh, baby . . ." But he was crying and hung up.

I sat there staring at the white Princess phone. So unlike my mother to get a white Princess phone. The idea of my mother selecting one, inventing a slightly altered Sudy to go with it, made me want to cry. I concentrated on the names of doctors I might tap for new leads and decided against telling my mother tonight about my new plans. A few more days made no difference.

With great deliberation I began writing down the names of doctors, research institutions, teaching hospitals. As I wrote, I became more determined to carry out my new resolves, the magic formula to get me through all this. I began the litany to myself: I would settle my mother. I would forget about Ned, shut him off for good in my heart and my mind. I would get back to work. Engage myself in it, stop flitting around as David accused me of doing.

Then I counted the syllables in the agenda: set-tle-Moth-er, four syllables; shut-off-Ned, three syllables; get-to-work—that depended on where David ended up. But Boston had the best doctors in the country. Unless we had to go to Europe. Had she always wanted a Princess phone? Settle Mother, I began again. Shut off Ned. Get to work. And to this: cure David.

I walked back into the living room dry-eyed and dry-mouthed.

"I have never heard you use the kind of language you were using on the phone, young lady," my mother said.

"I'm sorry. I'm upset."

"That's no excuse."

"Sudy, you've been known to say a few words yourself," Aunt Stella said.

"Not those."

"Ones just as bad."

"Like what? Name them."

"After I have a drink," I said.

"What?" she asked.

"Let her relax a minute, Sudy."

A rainstorm had come up and the water thundered against the roof of our house. "Reminds me of driving in west Texas on those few occasions when it rained," my mother said, evidently cheered by the thought. "The water couldn't run off quickly enough, so you never knew when you were going to land in a flood instead of a storm. No houses and no cars. Nothing but sweeps and sweeps of wind. I'd just burn that rubber and pray for a town."

The rain continued to slam down as I watched my mother hobble to the bathroom. Once more I questioned my resolve to get her situated in a center. She had made progress—not enough, but at least she could get out now. And tonight her mind was working better than mine.

If even I questioned whether this was necessary, how was I ever going to make her understand? *Burn that rubber*—such an unusual expression for her. I wasn't aware of the fact that she used it or, more to the point, colored herself as someone "burning rubber." Secret selves. And why shouldn't she have them? Thousands of hours alone, of course she had other selves.

"I've been thinking about you," Aunt Stella said to me. "Do you remember how you used to love to hear about your great-grandmother?"

"Oh, Stella, don't start that story," my mother said. "I hate this dwelling in the past. There's no sense in getting that old," she added with scorn.

"If it's not *our* pasts, it's okay," Aunt Stella said and laughed.

I dreaded her reaction. Along with everything else, I realized I'd put off the decision about Sudy because I didn't want my aunts angry with me. Or disapproving. Or disappointed.

On my occasional visits home, I could always serve up for a few days the sweet, wholesome, happy niece they expected. My gift was to allow this illusion, and now I was about to take it away. From their standpoint I would be betraying family. That was the long and short of it for them. Nothing else much mattered but family.

"Maybe I could come by for coffee in the morning," I whispered to Aunt Ruth, who had called to make sure we were all fine. I hoped to avoid taking Mother and Aunt Stella with me. Aunt Stella did like to "gad about," as she herself put it, and staying with my mother was cramping her style. She welcomed any outing. Well, I would take them all to Dallas for a meal the day after tomorrow. Tomorrow itself was spoken for. Tomorrow was for David.

Set-tle-Moth-er, I said to myself, but before I could begin, the phone rang again. It was Ned, telling me that the early, informal polls showed that things had turned around for Stone. The stories in the papers and on TV had, on the whole, been favorable. He thanked me for getting him involved again. "I owe you a lot," he said, warmly.

"Then we're almost even. Look at how much I owe you. How could I have been here and kept my job without you." For a few minutes we discussed strategy. I could tell he was excited by the developments, and I tried to match his enthusiasm. He didn't ask when I was coming back, and he didn't say anything of a personal nature until the end, when he said, "When this is over, I'm going to marry you."

"I told you a long time ago I don't intend to marry again."

"So we'll live together."

"Let it go, Ned. Please." I hung up and called Bev before he could call back, but she wasn't in.

Overcome with weariness, I lay across the bed, my arm over my eyes. Set-tle-Moth-er, shut-off-Ned—one job done, in as graceless and tactless a way as possible. I had no hopes of doing any better with the next one either.

To postpone thoughts of how difficult that effort was going to be, I called Laura. After the briefest of preliminaries, I blurted out, "I'm putting my mother in a rehabilitation home."

"You have to. You don't really have a choice."

"I could take care of her. She would do that for me."

"You can't give up your life. Sudy is too proud ever to let you. Besides, it's only temporary."

"To her it won't be. And what if it depresses her beyond . . ." I let my voice and thought trail off.

"She'll understand. *You* are the one I worry about. Your voice has taken on a . . . on a . . . a strange quality—like you're not in it."

"Could you do this to *your* mother?" Laura was silent. "Could you?" I asked again.

"If I had to . . . I don't know," she answered.

We talked only a little longer. She would come if I wanted, and I promised to spend a few days with her—after I had taken care of my mother. An unfortunate choice of words, those last.

Aunt Stella came to the door and asked, "Did your mother come in here? I smell a cigarette burning but can't find it. She swears she hasn't been smoking, but I don't know if I believe her." Together we searched the house, as discreetly as possible, for my mother was furious that we didn't accept her word.

"Your daddy and I always had a rule not to smoke in bed," she said as Aunt Stella and I checked under the bed, in the closet. Sudy walked away as we looked.

"She used to talk about your daddy all the time," Aunt Stella said in a low voice as she looked in the chest of drawers. "He's all she could talk about when they were dating, and here she always made fun of me for liking boys."

"Did my father drink a lot?" I asked the question as if it were the most natural in the world and had only occurred to me that minute.

Aunt Stella straightened up, brushed lint off her skirt. "Not any more than anybody else around here during Prohibition. Everybody liked to have a good time back then." She started out of the room. "I'm going to take one more look under the sofa cushions."

I checked the bathroom again. So I had asked. Finally asked and knew no more now than before. But I must have known that would be the case. If Aunt Stella had to choose her loyalties, my mother would always win, hands down. My mother and the family image.

But what if she were right? I asked myself, rifling through the wastebasket, What if my father's death that day had nothing to do with me. All these years I could have been distorting and exaggerating and twisting the details to fit preconceived images that never happened. "Aunt Stella," I called loudly, "I've found it."

As it turned out, the smoke happened to be coming from one of Aunt Stella's brand, and, indeed, Aunt Stella's cigarette, as she sheepishly admitted. My mother felt vindicated enough to resume speaking to her sister. Again I stretched out on the bed, too weary to plan any more for now.

Occasionally a car passed, disturbing my urgent listening to the silence. The people in the car didn't know what was going on in this house, in this room, in this mind. Why should they? Most of Rollins didn't know. A house-to-house poll would prove that, for the town was not so small as I had thought it was.

On my night drives in from Dallas, I could now see the aura of lights hovering like fine mist over the houses, not just those individual pinpricks huddled to the right of the water tower. "I see the water tower, I see the water tower," Joey used to say long before it was in sight in order to win the game. I would argue with him the rest of the way home, but I couldn't prove that he hadn't actually seen it. A chronic agitation for proofs set in somewhere along in there, for instance my fascination with math. And whatever happened to that old love? I wondered, turning over on my side and putting the pillow over my ears.

But sleep didn't come. I thought about trying Bev again. Did she know David was dying? I should say it aloud. She wouldn't question my knowing. *David Wright is dying. David Wright is dying.* And I am about to sentence my mother, Sudy, the solace of our childhoods, the companion of our youth, my tormentor, and the only steady, loving witness of my life; I am about to give her over to purgatory. Or worse.

How to

Make It Work

in This

World

"Who is it?" my aunt called in the same suspicious voice my mother used, even when she knew to expect me.

"H.A.," I replied, stifling familiar irritation. She also knew to expect me. This lunch was Aunt Stella's idea. She had a bad cold, but she wanted a visit, probably to shore me up. So far, I had neither saved David nor told Sudy my plans, and the strain was showing.

At first the door opened only a crack, as if she suspected that some impostor lurked on the porch, but when she saw me, she opened it all the way, I went to hug her, and although she held out her arms, she turned her head away.

"Don't get too close. You'll catch my germs," she said as she began spraying the air with a container of Lysol while leading me into the house. I took a good look at her for the first time since I'd come back, even though she spent the better part of every day at my mother's house. At the age of eighty-two her hair was still the same soft auburn it had always been dyed; her eyes, the same clear blue; her skin that of a much younger woman. But her housecoat, missing snaps, opened to reveal a stouter figure and a soiled slip. Although she made a bigger effort most days, this was not the Aunt Stella who had always managed to look glamorous even covered with body cream under her chenille robe.

She led me to a red plastic–covered kitchen chair and sprayed

Lysol around our heads. "Sit here and talk to me while I get dinner on the table. I've fixed all your favorites." These included fried chicken, mashed potatoes and gravy, fresh green beans, fresh black-eyed peas, creamed corn, hot rolls with real butter, and a chocolate pie—all saturated in grease, for Aunt Stella believed lard to be an indispensable seasoning, heart attacks notwithstanding. My stomach turned.

"What a treat!" I said. She directed me to sit down, planning to serve me, much as she did the men in our family, my protests notwithstanding. I wasn't sure if acquiring male status was an upgrading or a demotion.

"You can't get decent hens anymore," she said. "They don't taste the way they used to when we kept our own. Every Sunday Mama would send me out back to kill two. I don't know why she chose me. Thought I was the only one mean enough, I guess, and I was. I could wring their necks without blinking an eye. The others couldn't do it. Sudy included."

To keep away the peeping Toms, the shades were drawn—also the better not to see the floors, which, by the looks of them, hadn't been vacuumed since the house was painted. Cleanliness and neatness, never among Aunt Stella's strong points, had been given up entirely.

In the kitchen and dining area the overhead bulbs were out, and no replacements could be found for me to change them. Food smells from many past meals layered the room, and every time she coughed she squirted the air around us with Lysol. I moved my food around my plate, but there was no faking it. She monitored too carefully.

"How do you keep those stockings up?" I asked, admiring the way hers stayed rolled precisely below the knee.

"Garters, of course."

"You're right in fashion. Real stockings are the 'in' thing."

"Rosemary Jackson's mother died and left boxes of these stockings, never taken out of the package. You can have some if you want. I've probably got garters, too."

She handed me a piece of pie, which was just as I remem-

bered chocolate pie should be. I hardly noticed the thin layer of
Lysol that had settled on the fork. With one brief exception, we
hadn't mentioned my mother, but now she began an indirect approach:

"Someday you'll be all alone, like me, only you won't have
the sisters or nieces and nephews. At least I have you and Will
and Joey. I used to ache I wanted a baby so much. Your mother
should have had another child." The remark was meant as a dis-
paragement of my mother, but upon remembering the present
circumstances, she corrected herself. "Well, she did the best she
could."

I knew she felt sorry for me. Children were doted on, discussed endlessly and loved. Children provided them another base,
a way to come together, a mending after their feuds. Children
created a collective energy.

"Did you ever consider adopting?" I asked.

"With my husbands? Hah!"

"But what about Uncle Dick?" Uncle Dick was the first, the
made-over war hero.

"Oh, well, yes, Dick. We were so young we never thought
about it. Didn't have enough money, and just as well. I would
have been left a widow with a child same as Sudy."

With the introduction of the subject of husbands, she ap-
praised me, then said: "You look good for someone getting close
to fifty."

"Don't rush me, Aunt Stella. That's six years away."

"Four."

"Five! *You* lopped off ten." Twelve years ago she had a serious heart attack but refused to go to the hospital in Dallas where
she had worked, since everyone there thought she was sixty instead of seventy. Interestingly enough, the staff hadn't believed
she was as old as the sixty she alleged. Sick as she was, she was
not about to let them find out the truth—not for the best medical
care in the world.

"One extra year isn't worth lying about, especially if you've
already got a good-looking younger man snapping at your heels."

I had pretty much kept Aunt Stella on my side through both my marriages—one fewer than she, after all—but when I began to settle for boyfriends instead of husbands, I lost her support. She herself had never had much use for male companions unless marriage was in the offing.

She started clearing the table, motioning for me to keep my seat. "Fact is, I wouldn't have been a good mother." She laughed. "I'm too mean. Mama was right."

"That's not true."

"Yes, it is. When you don't feel loved yourself, you just make everyone around you pay for it. Dad and Mama weren't good at it." She stopped clearing dishes to come sit by me. "I knew Mama loved us, but she didn't know how to show it. I'm not saying anything bad about her. She just wasn't any good at showing affection. Neither are her children. Look at us. None of us touch much or say sweet things easily. We're fine at talking baby talk to babies, but we don't do so well after that."

"Your banter suits me fine," I said, recalling the hours she had spent giving me manicures and facials, especially during my college years, when the shock of my departure from our cozy entanglement hit us both. "I wish you'd wear a sun hat," she would say, peering down at my face as she lathered her latest concoction on my forehead. "If you did, you could get rid of all those freckles."

Now she jumped up to exchange my iced-tea glass for coffee, then leaned on her chair, continuing in a less confidential tone. "When we were young, Dad never let us talk at the table. I guess he wanted peace and quiet." She laughed. "All those women."

As she spoke, her chin resting in her palm, she stared into space, apparently neither expecting nor wanting comment. I listened with only sympathetic murmurs from time to time and wondered if these recollections were why I'd been summoned. "He and your mother never got along. Mama used to say they were just alike—hardheaded. The hardheadedest man I've ever seen in my life, and she's just like him." We waited for a coughing spell to pass, I dodged the Lysol, and she sat back down.

"He and I got along well, so I helped him with his books and all. I thought that was great, but he never paid me for it. And I didn't have enough sense to mind." She searched her pockets for a cigarette while she continued: "Hard to believe about Sudy, isn't it? So frail and ... forgetful ..." She halted, began again. "Such a shame ... she's the one with the mind." She began crying. "I need her," she confessed between sobs.

I rose and went to her, awkwardly patted her shoulder in an effort to comfort. Her shoulder, such a vulnerable, knobby shoulder, sagged under the weight of my hand and her grief. How strange to find her body not a fairy godmother's at all, but only another easily hurt.

Even in the hospital with her heart attack, she'd appeared unconquerable propped on her pillows, makeup in place, sneaking a cigarette. She had laughed at her own stupidity for not recognizing what was happening to her. After all, she had worked in a hospital. She knew as well as any doctor the symptoms involved. One of her husbands had suffered years with angina. Now her shoulder, hardly larger than a child's, revealed another myth of my making.

As suddenly as she broke down, my aunt collected herself. "You know, pretty as she was, she never really considered remarrying."

"In spite of all my best efforts."

Aunt Stella laughed. "You were always scheming in that direction."

Without looking at Aunt Stella, I said, "Things never quite worked out as they were supposed to for her."

"Don't say that. She has friends who love her. A loyal family. A wonderful daughter."

"But I refused to see her as she was. I could never face the pain of her life." Even now, I thought.

"Maybe she didn't want you to, H.A. She's a proud woman." She hesitated, evidently considering something, then continued in a quieter voice. "Remember the stories of her lambasting that banker in Kentucky?"

"I remember. Thinking of what my mother did then has given me backbone in more than a few situations." I smiled and added, "And made me ashamed in others."

"The real event has another ending. She had them, all right—the bank and the lawyer and the judge. But just before the money came through, her lawyer tacked on fifty thousand dollars to her fee and withheld it from her final payment. The bastards didn't get everything, but they came damn close."

"I never knew."

She folded her hand over mine. "It's hard enough being a woman. She wanted you to know the value of a good fight."

"That she taught me. She once convinced a man she was a witch." We both laughed.

"All that work to make life suit her," I said, "but not once anything easy."

"We're not about easy, H.A. We're about trying. You, too."

I wanted to assure her that I was setting my affairs in order, though exactly what order, I didn't dare say. Didn't quite know myself just yet. But whatever it was, it had to count for both our lives, Sudy's and mine.

Later, as I was getting into my car, she called out, "Honey, I've got some good body cream. Why don't I give you some? After all, if he's younger . . ."

Broken

Promises

Sudy stared at me in disbelief: her only child banishing her to an empty life, exiling her from the living. All the devotion lavished on me had not saved her from my betrayal. We were cursed, and she let me know it.

If this didn't work, I would come back, I promised. We would make other arrangements. "I don't want your goddamn other arrangements," she yelled. "I want to be left alone to do this my way. I'm not ready to turn my life over to you or anybody else." Just for a while, I kept assuring her. Just until we get you better again. But a home could not make her better, she screamed. Maybe nothing could.

She wept. She raged at me. She wept again. All night she got up and down and up and down and cursed and wept. Neither I nor Aunt Stella nor Aunt Ruth, who appeared around midnight at Stella's urgent pleading, could calm her. With morning I called the doctor, who came by the house to give her a shot, although sedation cheated her out of rightful mourning—another betrayal.

My aunts left together, each of them kissing me as we parted at the front door. They had supported and soothed me in the face of Sudy's wrath, but now their own fear and guilt drove them to cling to each other. Not to me. I wasn't old. My predicaments had solutions; theirs claimed none.

Sudy—the smartest, the strongest, the toughest of survivors—had turned her back on them. Left them to witness her disintegration with the certain knowledge that theirs was to follow, and soon. Their sister would die, and their perfect niece did not exist. I could find no way to comfort them.

Before I lay down to rest, I arranged for a nurse to come in the afternoon since my mother would be too groggy to know what was going on. I also made a new list of people to call about rehabilitation homes. Then I crawled into my old bed and lay staring at the wall, reciting my mantra—set-tle-Moth-er, shut-off-Ned, get-to-work, cure-David. I would do all this and she would get better. Much better. She shouldn't have said nothing would help her. She was wrong.

My failure to satisfy my mother was now complete. Not that I hadn't tried to be a good and attentive daughter. She had taken vacations with me. She had helped set up my houses and apartments. She had felt free to give advice. She had shared my career successes. Paltry as they were, they were enough for her to enjoy and brag about to friends.

But what I had withheld was the only thing she could not ask for: that inarticulated need for an intimacy I refused to share with her. We talked of clothes and politics and gossiped about relatives and friends, but I shut her out of my soul. And its entry became our lifelong wrestling place.

Until now, she had only made two direct requests of me: to give her grandchildren and to keep her out of an "old folks' home." On both counts I'd failed her, the one person who would defend me and love me without regard. I was selfish enough to survive, but the shame of it all.

I watched a band of sun expand itself on the white wall—as much of daylight as I could take, that one strip bulging out, revealing the smudges and uneven spackling job of the dingy surface. Last year I should have had the house painted as a birthday present. Freshly painted rooms always pleased her.

But who was I kidding? I had flung thousands of futile gestures at her to make up for not saving my father. The memory of my last day with him never goes away. Not that she blamed me. Not that I blamed me—except where it counts: too deep inside to touch.

✳

Over the phone Bev sounded half-kidding and half-miffed. "Where are you keeping yourself these days? You're mysteriously out when I call, but I'm the only friend you have around."

"What's up?" I quickly asked, not up to explanations.

"Did I wake you?" she said, apology in her voice.

"Not at all," I lied. I didn't know how long I'd slept. I raised up and listened for my mother, but no noise came from her side of the wall. The medication was still doing its work.

"If this isn't a good time . . ."

"Bev, what's going on?"

"Nothing much, but I thought you'd want to know David Wright is in the hospital. They say he's very sick. Maybe you'll call? H.A.? You okay?"

"I'm okay."

"I've been thinking about how ill-prepared we all were for what's happened to our lives. I had a story I thought might entertain you, but I don't think I've picked the best time."

A fine time, I assured her and hated it that she was so needy. Maybe I would tell her about David, how sick, but not that he was dying because, of course, he wasn't.

"I had this awful thing happen a couple of months after Jack and I separated," Bev started. "I mean, it was awful then, funny now. But it's probably boring to you."

"Bev, stop it."

"Well, not long after I moved to Dallas I went to a party given by one of the young teachers. I met a man there, overweight but nice enough looking—I think he dyed his hair. That was okay, too, because it meant he was older than me and insecure and maybe even a little tired of keeping up with a younger crowd. I think I got him pretty right, for he asked me out. The first time to dinner, the next to a movie. It was cheap of him not to take me to a movie *and* dinner, but he was nice enough.

"After the movie, we went back to his apartment, which looked just like my idea of a bachelor pad—all that heavy Spanish furniture and orange shag carpet and black leather throw pillows and brassy-looking stuff on the walls passing for art. Just walking into the place made me nervous. He fixed me a drink, but it turned my stomach funny.

"I was afraid this man thought I was more experienced than I was—I mean, H.A., when Jack and I married, neither one of us had much experience—so I told this guy I was a little new at all this. He said he had already guessed. Next he asked if I'd like a little grass to relax me. I told him the girls might be up when I got in, and besides, I hadn't ever smoked pot. He said he wasn't surprised about that either." She stopped for a second, then said, "H.A.?"

"Yes?"

"Just wondering if you're there."

"I'm right here."

"Anyhow, finally we made it to the bedroom. Before we'd even kissed! I kept telling myself, You've got to start sometime, but when I saw the room, I almost backed out. All one wall was mirrors—just like Las Vegas, where Jack made me turn out the lights because he said we'd ruin the mystery if we looked. Now here I am with a playboy! Well, I thought, at least you'll get some real experience."

As she talked, I held the image of Bev when she was twelve years old. Back then, in the same hushed drawl, she recounted movie dates with boys and whether or not she let them hold her hand.

"The next part was romantic enough. He dimmed the light, and while we stood there, he undressed me slowly like in my fantasies and looked me all over. I think he approved. Without his glasses, he probably couldn't see the cellulite. Then he undressed himself. I helped a little with his shirt buttons, but that was all I could make myself do. So we stood there looking at each other and I knew I had to ask: 'Do you have any communicable diseases?'

"He looked taken aback. Then he went limp. Maybe my timing was a little off, but it was a perfectly logical question. Don't you always ask?"

"Mmmmm," I said.

She continued: "We got in the bed, limpness and all. He said, 'I want to eat you.' H.A., I thought he meant I looked good enough to eat. But that wasn't what he meant. Honestly, Jack never in his life . . ."

She is still twelve years old, I thought and felt torn between laughing and throwing up. I wanted to hide Bev where no one would hurt her again. "Well, did he make it?"

"Oh, yeah. That's why it's funny and not sad. The ending was happy enough."

"Does that mean you still see him?"

"Every so often. But nothing is going to come of it. He's found a thousand ways to tell me he never plans to remarry—just in case I haven't gotten the point. Who cares? I don't even want him. The first time he was just showing off."

"I see." And the seeing made me want to crawl under the covers and not come out, so much misery for so little return.

"No. What I want you to see is why I took up with four married men. They're easier." She waited but before I could think of a response, she said, "You haven't laughed."

"I smiled, Bev. But stop worrying about my approval."

"I want your understanding."

"I understand. I do. I'm coming to see you as a beguiling courtesan."

"H.A.? I'm getting retribution at last."

"How's that?"

"My ex-husband did you one better. Seems his live-in is in her twenties."

"Don't . . ." I began but she cut me off.

"Anyway, seems he can't get it up enough to please her, so he's gone and gotten himself an implant. Has himself a half hard-on all the time. The young one finds this acceptable." We both burst out laughing.

"Are you putting me on?" So much misery. So much desperation.

"I swear." We started laughing again. "If anybody had something coming to him . . ." But her voice cracked, close to tears now. "That big broken bull— Oh, H.A., what's becoming of us? I mean, the men, too.

"Did you ever notice how easily these Texas men get caught in a bind? A lot of them have their own strong mothers to deal with so they find strong women attractive. They're challenged by them, but they rebel, too. A no-win deal for us and them."

"I was never any good at answers. My luck with men has never been anything to brag about."

"I didn't mean to upset you. I only wanted to tell you funny stories. Did that news about David Wright depress you? I'm sorry, but I thought you'd want to know."

"I'm tired. That's all." And David Wright is dying and my mother . . .

"Have you decided what you're going to do about things? I'm enjoying having you here, but I know you can't just hang around forever."

"I'm staying," I announced to both of us at the same time.

There was a pause on the other end of the line. Then: "That's great . . . if it's really what you want."

I considered only a second and blurted out: "I've lost my nerve. I'm sick of fighting out there. I'm sick of trying to make a life. I've done a lousy job of it. You choose married men. I'm choosing Rollins."

"I thought you had a wonderful life. I'm so envious." She hesitated a second. "But I've always been envious, especially of you and Aunt Sudy. I always wished my mother paid as much attention to me as Aunt Sudy did to you. She made you . . . *bold*."

"I run a good show, Bev. That's all it is."

"Are you sure you're not just tired? Maybe you shouldn't make any decisions right now."

"This is the first time I've had any peace in weeks. I can't stand not having peace any longer."

A

Phone Call

and a

Letter

I had made the decision to open a branch of Pelham and Jackson in Dallas if Pelham would go along with it, and at this point he was interested. A Boston-Austin political connection had remained strong since the years of Kennedy and Johnson. I had almost convinced him that Dallas would do as well as Austin, a natural linkup. Besides, I had already lined up one Senator and the Governor, both up for reelection in two years, and one of whom might be presidential material. Along with this new resolve, I swore to myself to stay out of trouble. From now on I would screen candidates more closely before taking them on, and the ground rules would be crystal clear at the outset.

Having several bigwigs in the same state could be tricky (all claiming "great respect" for the others but staking out territories at one another's expense when possible), but the list was impressive. From Texas I could work the whole Southwest—a selling point to the region's candidates.

At first, I would have to do a lot of commuting, dividing my time between Boston and Dallas. During the week Sudy would stay in the rehabilitation home but on weekends Aunt Stella and I would have her with us. This was the basic outline, but I had variations of the scheme to play with when she began voicing objections. My plans had barely gelled when I got a call from Ralph.

"You've done it!" Stone said, hardly giving me time to get out a "hello." "I'm fifteen points ahead, and we only have a week to go."

"That's what my sources tell me."

"Ned you mean?"

"Yes."

"You were right about him, H.A. I'm glad you made me see the light. Stoddard is impressed with him, too. Thinks he might be good material for his company. I told him he could have Sampson, but you I'm keeping for myself. You've got to come to Washington with me."

"Let's get you there first, Ralph."

"But once I'm there, I'm going to turn that place upside down. Get myself on all the right committees. I can change this country, H.A., I know I can. In no time at all we'll have me ready to run for President." Even he laughed at himself on that one. "When will you be back? I know it's crazy, but I feel better when you're on the property. You're my good-luck charm."

"I'll be there day after tomorrow. But you don't need me. You're in high cotton now."

"If I say I need you, I do." A pause. "Did I sound like a bully? I don't mean to."

"I didn't take it that way. Besides, that part of the deal is almost over."

"Not if I want to keep you around. I'm not the complete dolt you think I am." On the last, he had a point. Touché, Mr. Stone.

"By the way, the nightly news has the story that I let Sally Cummings go. Had to. Everyone was saying I had spread the rumors about Cardigan. Not the image I want to create, but that bitch Cardigan keeps yelling I've played dirty pool. I say where there's smoke there's fire. Anyway, she was going to lose. A poor sport. Too bad about her. Really."

"Sally didn't do anything! You can't just fire people like that."

"I had to. The woman's dangerous, besides she's fucking

everything in sight, maybe even Mary Cardigan. This time you've got to go along with me, H.A. Trust me."

He hung up, victory singing across the phone lines.

I put my head in my hands. The son of a bitch was living proof of what could be gotten away with. He had just enough smarts to pull off his plans. Not as soon as he'd like, but someday. And we'll all live happily ever after on a landfill of excrement.

Ned's letter arrived in the next morning's mail.

> Dearest Colleague,
>
> I understand from Arthur Pelham that you plan to divide your time between Boston and Dallas. When did you come to this decision and why couldn't you talk to me about it? I wouldn't try to stop you. I'm not keen on a long-distance marriage, but we can make it work. Maybe Texas and I will adopt each other quicker than you think.
>
> I can already see you forming one last reply to me in your head, but by now you should have learned I am not easily discouraged. In fact, I can't be discouraged at all. I need you too much. I know your next argument: I need you because I don't have you. I need you because my ego doesn't like to lose. Men are hunters, you say, and I haven't yet won the hunt. The game isn't complete.
>
> Well, okay, I'm a hunter, and it's my hunting instinct that keeps me persistent. But if you would ever stop to look at me, you would know I'm a lot more.
>
> "Yeah, stuffy, too, and bad-tempered," I hear you answer, and I admit it. But my stuffiness—and my temper—covers over a timidity I would just as soon not own up to. "I am a timid man" is not a very sexy statement, but one that happens to be true. I am timid with people, timid with life.
>
> I don't have an easy time of it with most people, and that's made for more loneliness than I care to go into. After I met

you, one day I realized I wasn't lonely anymore. By then we had known each other two or three months, and I was so pleased with my discovery—this gift from you—I wanted to tell you. I didn't because I didn't want you to have the gloom-and-doom image of me I sometimes have of myself. You know how to encompass and envelop and would have no patience with someone who hasn't learned to give as much or as well.

Believe me, I've asked myself a thousand times why I should miss anyone as much as I do you. Lots of reasons come to mind, but you'll be as surprised as I was at what I miss most, for you, I'm sure, see it as a liability. I'm talking about your discontent. I'm convinced it drives your restlessness, your sense of adventure, even your contrariness. And I need all those things—your life force—to energize me. Since I've met you, I've used them for my own.

I know this confession does not flatter me, and I only make it out of desperation. You have to understand what you are for me—I know that's a lot to ask, because you haven't a clue about your worth to anybody. If I can't make you see how much you mean to me, you'll never get beyond our ages.

There. I've written the dread word *age*. If we are lucky, someday it will kill us, but it won't kill our love; more precisely, my love for you. What I love in you has nothing to do with age—I've told you that in as many ways as I can think of, but you won't let yourself hear it because you don't think it's possible that there is anything inside that attractive, vivacious exterior worth loving. You think of yourself as all show, which is the least of you.

Now that I've exposed myself, I may have destroyed the possibility of your ever loving me. I don't know about that. I do know I am dependent on you in ways I never dreamed possible. This scares me. But the opening up makes me happier than anything I've ever known. I'm not sure you even understand exactly what I mean, for I'm not sure you've ever let yourself experience this much letting go.

And I can once again hear you: "The arrogance of such a statement!" Maybe so, but it wouldn't hurt you to 'fess up to some things in yourself. If you did, you might find you'd like us both more. In the meantime, know I am devising new plans daily and one of them will get you. A threat and a promise!

And, as always,

your Ned

Twice I reread the letter on my late-afternoon walk before tucking it back into the pocket of my blue sweater. But it's too late, I told myself. Ned, you're too late, a lifetime too late. David will die. Stone will win. I will suffocate. I've waited too late to fix my life. I've waited too late to fix our supper. I hurried back toward the house. But Stone didn't have to win. If I acted immediately, getting Stone was still possible.

Sinking

Stone

Gary Boatwright and I lounged side by side on his blue-stone terrace in two heavy wooden chaises, made soft by beige duck pillows. Thick white clouds covered the sky, but the Florida air warmed us without benefit of the sun. The green shrubs and hibiscus and orange trees effectively created walls to shield us from any cool breezes. We faced the pool, the surface of the water marbled blue with the reflection of the clouds. To one side a cabana protected a large television and three more chairs like ours.

The setup was not so different from the one twenty-three years ago where I had watched the first moon walk and decided to leave Keith. Though never admitting to an affair with Peggy Barnett, he had been, after the first shock, as eager as I was to get out of the marriage. The last I heard he had three children, three short of what we used to say we wanted.

"This is a beautiful place you have," I said to my host. Stone may have gotten him removed from Stoddard Development, but Boatwright had certainly benefited in other ways.

"Yes," he acknowledged, "my family and I still can't quite believe it. My wife and I were both brought up in Baltimore row houses. We hardly know what to do with ourselves here."

Boatwright had suggested I come to his home, certainly pleasant but not especially conducive to a clandestine meeting. Lying back in a chaise longue didn't help to convey urgency either. Maybe that was just as well.

Yesterday on the phone he had hesitated before inviting me to visit. Understandable, since I had hesitated long enough before calling him, had almost given up the idea altogether only minutes before I picked up the phone.

Without knowing quite when it happened, I had lost the stomach for going around breaking people, even major jackass people. But I wasn't sure I could, in good conscience, wash my hands of Stone. I could also hear my mother saying, "Don't let those sons of bitches get away with anything." With those words clanging in my head, I had braced to make the call to Boatwright and extract an invitation.

Now I was eager to find out his reaction to my proposition. The election was five days away, and I was running out of time. I handed him the copy of the note I'd taken from Stone's files months before. He read it once, then again.

"Ralph Stone was behind my move? But why?"

"Stone, through a Delaware holding company, owned almost

half of Stoddard. Careful as you were to work within the Stoddard organization, you were too effective an environmentalist. They all knew you would never agree to filling in the wetlands, even if they tried to create new ones. You were too questioning of that process. It was your reputation as a man of integrity that scared them off."

"So they got someone else to offer me a fabulous salary about the same time they threatened to transfer me to Detroit to work on another project. I thought it was something like that. What do you have in mind?"

"First, let me make clear this is your call. I've messed up enough lives already, but I'll tell you what I would like to do. I would like for us to take this letter and present it to Mr. Ralph Stone for purposes of facilitating a career change. I would like to suggest to him that he withdraw from the race in return for this note. If he goes forward, his reputation will be ruined, for I've also got enough evidence from his contributors' files to prove that the campaign donations from a lot of the builders were essentially kickbacks. This last charge is more circumstantial, but that one coupled with this letter should do him in."

"I thought you said you worked for him."

I shrugged.

"But why now?" he pressed.

"I guess I'm sick of watching bastards get away with the kind of filth that sells out the environment and destroys reputations."

"Sally told me." He shook his head. "Still, blackmail is serious business."

"I know that. But if he doesn't resign, I have to consider releasing this to the press—with your permission. That's why I'm here: to make my case to you. I'm not sure I have the right to go ahead with my plan without your consent"—or with it, I thought, but I kept that reservation to myself. "After all, it's your life that will be affected. You'll be a public man, in the news, whether you want to be or not. Whistle-blowers get to be heroes of the moment, but once the hullabaloo dies down, they can run into a lot of brick walls and nobody gives a damn."

"What will all this do to you?"

I grinned. "I expect to be looking for another line of work soon."

A little boy of about eight wandered toward us. "Daddy, when is this lady leaving so we can go swimming?"

"Don't be smart," his father said sharply.

I laughed and stood up. "He's a good reminder that there's more to this world than political intrigue."

Boatwright rose also. "And if I agree to this, what happens next?"

"We'll confront Stone right away—provided I remain convinced I can make it work," I said, leaving my options open as usual. "I'm sorry I didn't get to you sooner, but it's taken me a while to sort through my priorities."

"What made you call?"

"Hearing Stone sound like a victor. Hearing him talk about making a bid for the White House. The trashing of Cardigan. The firing of Sally. The spying. The lying. It just got to be too much. I decided we'd better take this business seriously."

What I said was true enough. I believed every word of it. But I had known what Stone was like for months now. How to explain to an amiable stranger about the complications of beliefs and fears?

Boatwright's wife came out then and looked to him for a clue as to whether to extend a dinner invitation. I accepted. Better to give him more opportunity to observe me, to help him make up his mind to trust me. Our timetable didn't allow for a lot of deliberation.

"They robbed me of my purpose," he said. "I think I can't forgive that more than anything else."

I had sense enough to realize that it was not necessary for me to say another thing. I had him. I had him for his reasons. I had my own reasons.

"Do you have children?" his wife asked as I took the hand offered me by a little girl named Melissa.

"None. Or nieces or nephews. My cousins don't either," I answered, telling her more than she could possibly care to know. "We got so busy with the generation before us, seems we didn't give much thought to who was coming after."

Halloween

"This is preposterous. How dare you!"

Ralph Stone was not reacting well to our proposition. He paced back and forth across the long stretch of his library. For thirty minutes now neither Gary Boatwright nor I had spoken more than a few words. The two of us watched Stone, watched each other, watched the well-made fire but remained silent while Stone ranted and made up his mind. Occasionally he pleaded, but most of the time he shouted and threatened and paced.

Since my last visit a plaster bust of our host had been added to the fireplace mantel. I half-expected an American flag to be planted on his desk. In the past, these affectations would only have confirmed my sense of his colossal arrogance. Today they spoke more of human frailty and vulnerability than smugness. Indeed, who could be smugger than I with my judgmental zeal to rearrange lives? Sickened by the whole enterprise, I vowed to give up vigilante pursuits. But that is for the future, I told myself. This one is for Sudy. After this, you can quit, but you do this one for Sudy.

"And what do you get out of it?" he asked me for the tenth time.

I wanted to answer, "Nothing," and head for the front door.

Instead I kept staring at him, wondering how I could explain about Sudy.

"Satisfaction," I responded, breaking my silence.

"But what's so *wrong* with me?"

"I don't trust you. You lied about Mary Cardigan."

"I did not! It's true about her!"

"You can't prove it. You lie about a lot of things."

"You're a fine one to talk about trust. You . . . you . . .scheming bitch."

"Mr. Stone, this is the last warning. Stop calling her names," Gary Boatwright said. Stone was larger than Boatwright but without the control, a point which Stone must also have taken into consideration because he changed tactics again.

"This is blackmail. You ought to go to jail for this," he said.

"I might go to jail," I said, "but you lose the election *and* have a lawsuit on your hands. We might throw in discrimination, too." I didn't look at Gary Boatwright as I said this last, because I hadn't discussed the issue with him. I doubted he would approve. I didn't approve myself, found exploiting race in any way reprehensible. I was bluffing. I hoped I was, at any rate.

"We might also throw in a phone tap charge," I added, fishing.

This last threat stopped him, literally, in his tracks. "So I withdraw? Just like that?"

"Your children need you. You came home and found your son crying and saying he would never see you again. You realized how small and vulnerable he is, and how right. When they are older, you might reconsider. But for now . . ." I pulled a large index card from my blazer pocket. "I've put a few words together. I'll arrange the rest."

Boatwright and I prepared to leave, but Stone remained seated. As we started out the library door, he asked, "How do you know I would have been such a bad legislator? What gives you the right to play God?"

I wondered the same thing myself, but I responded, "Not God. Only the wicked witch."

Unconditional

Love

Dressed in her beige pleated skirt and starched white cotton blouse, she sat in her living room, ready to do battle with me once again. She had on her panty hose, which she insisted on wearing every day, and her high-heeled shoes, which she could no longer manage. I had not argued about the shoes because she was going nowhere. She had taken to bouts of uncontrollable weeping and now refused to go out, afraid one would occur in public. And there was almost no plan I could bring up that she didn't object to.

"Stella and I would kill each other. She couldn't take me. I couldn't take her." On my own arrangement: "You would try to tell me what to do all the time." Or in another mood: "You have your own life."

She sat with her hands folded primly in her lap to keep them from shaking. "Do you know how long you've been on vacation?" she asked as soon I joined her on the sofa.

"Three months?" Until her question, I had not once considered this a vacation.

"Since I can't afford to support you for long, I think you had better get back to work," she said.

Given my latest shenanigans with Stone, the advice, unfortunately, might not be so easy to act on; but I wasn't about to tell her so—possibly because I wasn't yet ready to address the problem myself. Instead I reminded her that I had a good enough income to accommodate this "vacation," even if I wasn't being paid.

"I know you do, and I'm glad I've lived to see the day women make as much as the damn lazy men around them." She looked ready to say more about this but brought herself back to the first subject: "You have made something of yourself, and I hate to see you throwing it away."

"I'm only rearranging a little. I've told you that."

"And I'm telling you: I did what I wanted. Now you do what you want." She looked determined to be reasonable. "Sometimes I think you are a little selfish. . . ." She searched for words. "Too hardheaded where men are concerned. Part of that is my fault."

"You always said never let a man tell you what to do," I teased her, astounded to hear this particular lecture on men.

"I know I did, but you have to be willing to give in more. Your daddy would have taught you that." Her eyes lighted as they always did whenever she spoke of my father. My unromantic, practical, tough mother had the passion, not me. Unless John Reese counted for both of us.

And, as if she'd read my mind, she continued: "I tried to be both father and mother, and that was a mistake. Though I didn't think so at the time, you'd have been better off if I had remarried. I never could make it up to you—your father's death.

"Sometimes I think you make new losses for yourself just so you can keep the feeling going. You know? Lots of little losses because you never dealt with the one big one that mattered." The veins on her high forehead bulged.

"That's so long ago." I wanted to change the subject, calm her down, but she wasn't about to stop.

"Do you remember when your daddy died? How you wouldn't go to the cemetery when we got back to Texas? How you didn't want to tell him good-bye in Kentucky when we closed the casket? You fought me, tried to run away. I finally made you kiss him. Thought you'd regret it later if you didn't. As soon as I told you he was dead, you started acting like nothing had happened. I thought if I could get you to see for yourself, you could better accept his death. But you didn't. You never really accepted it." She paused for a moment, but her body remained tensed.

"When we got to Texas you refused to go to the graveside service, and by then I was afraid to make you. Maybe I'd been wrong to force you before . . . your hurt ended up so deep inside you that it will never see the light of day."

"I had you as my anchor. That's no small gift."

"You won't always have me. I can't do any more for you. You've got to get your own life together now. Don't you see? Marry Ned. You aren't too old to have children. Women your age have them all the time—I heard on television the other day. This family needs children. You need children."

"Let's not get started on children again. I know how you feel. I understand, and I'm sorry."

"The point is you don't know how *you* feel. Is your father behind that decision, too? You stay a little girl for him?"

"A question of commitment, Mama."

"Same difference. Another version of Peter Pan. At least Mary Martin *sang* about it. So far as I've ever been able to tell, you haven't sung a lot. Now you have a chance to make a real life with a young man who isn't all caught up in himself." She put her head in her hands. "If your father had lived, you would understand there's no such thing as a perfect man. I made a mistake letting you think he was."

"I knew better than that," I assured her, though I did and I didn't. I knew he made her cry. That made him—men—dangerous. But I could split off that living man from the dead one. And the dead one got to be perfect, while the living ones who seemed most dangerous—the Ralph Stones of the world—got strung up and quartered. A true and just punishment for making women and children cry. "I've never had a lot of illusions."

She brought her fist down hard on the sofa arm. "That's *all* you have, but you've got to get hold of yourself!"

"But that's what I'm trying to do. For a change, I'm making myself face the consequences of my acts."

"And somehow you'll end up one more time without any responsibilities. Honey, you think you're a free spirit, but you're the same scared little girl who was afraid to go to sleep by herself. You never let yourself enjoy anyone or anything too much because you think you'll lose whoever or whatever it is. After your daddy died, you stopped asking for presents. You were afraid to get what you really wanted, because then something bad might happen.

"I've watched you do the same thing with men," she continued. "As soon as you think you're going to lose someone, you are off like a shot. Even faster when you think they might die on you."

"I've never left someone sick, let alone dying."

"You come up with other reasons, but you don't leave until you notice they're mortal."

"That's not true. David—"

"David is not your lover, is he?" I shook my head no. She had guessed correctly.

"Check the record, H.A. You left your second husband as soon as you could after he recovered from hepatitis. The next man smoked two packs a day and had a brother who died of lung cancer."

"How do you know?"

"You told me." She went back to her argument. "Even David when you were both young. No disease, but a test pilot doesn't look good on the insurance charts."

"Keith doesn't fit your theory."

"He wanted children more than anything and you didn't want to risk another miscarriage. Don't you think I've known that? Besides, with babies you risk a lot of pain: you can't run away from them—your answer to life. You've played a hoax on yourself. Look at your career. You refuse to pay dues. You never commit yourself to your jobs, no matter how good or interesting. By now you should be a walloping success, but you never stay put long enough to make your mark. From what I can tell, you're getting ready to do the same thing all over again."

She looked at me, tears in her eyes, hands still neatly folded. "I don't mean to be so hard on you; I know sometimes I am. I couldn't ask for a better daughter. I am proud of you. I have been a lucky woman."

I am proud of you. She had never said those exact words before. I had waited a lifetime for a completion of that process of praise begun and promised so easily by my father, only to have it rejected as debilitating by my mother. For her, strength did not come from praise; strength came from "showing people." Strength came from scrapping and working hard and laughing at the world and relying on no one. Now her words brought us both a sense of closure.

She was crying now, and so was I. I stooped by her chair, my arms around her. She patted my head and in a choked voice said, "Just don't be so afraid. Don't keep fighting all the time. Like I did. I am proud of you," she said again. Then she took my face in her hands. "What matters most is that you feel free. Not happy, but free. You've got to get rid of the ghosts, including mine. You're not a little girl with a sad young mama to look after. I got fixed up a long time ago, and you need to do the same."

"I'll try," I said.

"Promise?" She seemed relieved.

"Promise."

"Then let's celebrate with peach ice cream," she answered.

"Ice cream?"

"You've always liked peach ice cream. So did your daddy."

"But you're not big on any kind of ice cream."

"Must be my condition, because I've got a real hankering for it now."

"A quart of peach?" the young girl behind the ice cream counter repeated to me.

"Ice cream, anybody?" Bennie asks. "No, because I am going blind," I say. "You and my daddy mustn't drink. My mama doesn't want you to," I want to say. The monkey he got drunk and fell on the elephant's trunk . . .

"Peach," I confirmed.

"A lapful of butterflies, is that what you want?" my father asks. *"Yes," I answer. Yes, yes to you always, even at the risk of my mother's anger.*

The girl handed me the ice cream. *"You've caught my blindness," I tell him and roll up the window. And roll down the window.* The girl behind the counter and I smiled at each other as I left. *Such a price to pay for that loving complicity.* Shifting the bag from one hand to the other, I walked slowly back toward my mother's.

✳

I knew she was driving even before I saw her erect, determined head as she backed her old red Plymouth out of the garage. This can't be, I reasoned, because there's no way she could get to the car by herself. She's moving too fast, I said to myself and started running.

Straight and sure she steered, but when she reached the street, she didn't slow down or make the turn. Now I was close enough to see the set of her jaw, the tight grip of her hands on the wheel.

The car, as if on a course of its own devising, continued directly backward toward the house across the street, gathering speed as it went. I screamed, "Mama, don't!" but it was too late. She smashed through the hedge, a brick wall, a dining-room table.

I leaped over the rubble to get to the still-erect figure wedged behind the wheel. Afraid to move her, I took hold of her hand. "Did I hurt anyone?" she asked.

"No," I answered as we heard a dog barking.

"That's good," she said as she lay her head on the wheel. I thought she had passed out, but she raised up again. "Have I hurt the car?"

"A little."

"And the Hills' house?"

"A little."

She closed her eyes.

"Talk to me!" I yelled.

Neighbors began to arrive. Sirens screamed. A fireman approached. "You're too late!" I shouted to the fireman.

"Let go her hand, lady. I can't do anything until you let go of her hand."

Settling

the Books

Smoke from my aunts' cigarettes filled my mother's living room, as did our family. "But why did she have to die? I mean, where did she think she was going?" Aunt Clara asked for the fourth time in an hour.

"Clara, she was running away," Aunt Stella snapped. "How many times do I have to tell you?"

"But to where?" Aunt Clara asked again.

"She didn't want to be a burden on us," Aunt Ruth said.

"She couldn't stand being dependent," Aunt Stella added.

"It was an accident," Will said. "Her foot got stuck."

"Of course it was an accident," Aunt Stella repeated angrily.

"What did the doctors say, H.A.?"

"Ruth, she's already told you what the doctors said."

"I don't care. I want to hear it again."

"The doctors said . . ." I began.

"Ruth, you'd better go see about poor Ben," Aunt Stella said.

"Ben is asleep."

"Why don't you all go now? I'll stay with H.A. a little longer," Will suggested.

"She's our *sister*," Aunt Clara told him.

"Sudy would know what to do," Aunt Ruth said as she began crying.

"Will is right. It's time for us to go," Uncle Curtis said.

"*I* am staying with H.A. Sudy would want me to," Aunt Stella said, asserting the prerogative of the oldest.

Neither my aunt nor I wanted to go to bed, so we sat on the couch, holding hands, our eyes closed. Sometimes she would mention a funeral arrangement, and I would make a note. Because we had not yet reached Joey, who lived in Wyoming, we decided to delay the funeral for a few days. Then conversation stopped altogether until Aunt Stella asked: "What do you do now, honey?"

I shook my head and confessed, "I don't know what to do. She's set me free . . . I . . ."

"Can you handle the responsibility?"

"I owe it to her to try."

"You owe it to yourself."

"That, too," I replied. And maybe, I thought, just maybe that means facing up to myself and my fears and my messes. I patted Aunt Stella's hand and stood up. "I have to call Ned," I told her.

"Tell him someone will pick him up at the airport."

"This is about unfinished business. I can't tell him about . . . about . . . Mother tonight."

"Then what if you wait till morning? You're so tired. You're not quite yourself tonight, you know?"

"I doubt if I've ever been more myself, Aunt Stella."

The phone call to Ned went as badly as expected. How could I have leaked Ralph's list of contributors? Of course he remembered the night I stayed late at Stone's office. Yes, it had crossed his mind that I had access to the files then. He had dismissed the possibility. Felt guilty for having that kind of thought in the first place. How could I? Without waiting for an explanation, he hung up. My behavior defied all his codes and I hadn't even told him about the blackmail. I hoped he knew what the confession cost me, especially now, especially when it guaranteed I would be even more alone.

In the living room, I sat back down near my aunt. "It's scary, being free," I said.

"I know." Though she had wisely kept her own counsel all these years, she knew better than anyone what went on between Sudy and me. For my mother had colored all the spaces in a room, and I was satisfied that it be so. What I asked and never received was permission to leave that room when I wanted. Until now.

Atonement

In the hospital parking lot I applied eyeliner. Three times I applied it—did I really think kohl eyes distracted from the bags and crinkled edges? Daylight spared nothing.

Before I buried my mother, I had to say good-bye to David. He had reluctantly agreed to hospice care in his home, which would preclude my seeing him. I had slipped out of Rollins to be with him one final time at the hospital. Sudy had charged me to free myself, an impossibility so long as David remained the father who dies and is resurrected, without end. But he couldn't change for me until I faced my own fears about him.

In the corridor I nodded to the nurse who had come to recognize me. "He's been looking for you," she said and smiled.

In the room he waited, his hair wet, combed back, wearing my favorite pajamas and a robe I didn't recognize. He had positioned himself in the straight-back chair.

Now I was sorry I hadn't had a drink. I was sorry I hadn't put on more eyeliner or bought a new dress or lightened my hair. I was sorry I hadn't slept. I leaned down to kiss him on the lips, to pretend as long as possible that this was no final meeting.

He would not go along with me. This time he knew the doctors were right, and we both had to accept the gravity of the situation. He actually said "gravity of the situation," and when he did, I wanted to cry because I knew I could no longer tell him he sounded like a pompous ass.

Instead I tried to lighten the tone. "We're not quitters, you and I. Look at us now, all decked out for each other." I put my arms around his head. He stroked my bottom. Stopped. Looked up at me and quickly put his hands under my dress.

"Oh, sweetheart." He grinned. "You didn't . . . you remembered."

"Try the top," I whispered and leaned my breasts into his face. He took his time with each one. They sagged more now than when he first held them. They had lost tone, as had my bottom, as had my stomach.

He lifted my skirt to kiss me and murmured, "You're fantastic." He meant it. Nobody else ever would, but he did. He filtered this body through the lens of our youth. For the last time in my life, dimples and flab and soft thighs meant nothing. This one time.

I found the opening in his pajamas and reached inside. "Any locks around here?"

"They won't bother us in the bathroom," he said, making an effort to get up by himself.

"Do you mind if they know?"

"I doubt they think you're my sister."

The bathroom was too cramped for us to lie down; even sitting took some doing. For all kinds of reasons we needed to get this over as quickly as possible. I just wasn't sure how possible that was. I brought the pillows from the bed to prop against his back and hoped I wasn't making a mistake, hoped he wouldn't die and I wouldn't break down.

Husbanding his strength, he closed his eyes. He had so little color. Only his mouth had life; his greedy, searching mouth I knew so well. His breathing became labored, his clasp weakened.

"We could wait until tomorrow," I said, trying to keep the fear out of my voice. He terrified me. I felt an unreasonable rage building and wanted to run away. I stood up.

"Down here," he said, his voice husky with emotion.

As I knelt, he opened his eyes in surprise. "Take off that dress." The words belonged to the old David.

"That's not such a good idea, is it? The nurses . . ."

"Come on, take off your dress."

While he watched I slipped it off and he looked happy. I untied his robe, unbuttoned his pajama top, but we both knew he would be too cold without them. Together we pulled down his bottoms. His groin area had turned an eerie blue and his pelvic bone protruded unmercifully from his body.

Crouching over him, I was afraid he couldn't take my weight. And if he died in me—this male rod I'd worshiped; the staff of life, I'd convinced myself—what would I do? And would I ever want another?

I took him in my hands as if to receive Communion, steadily massaging him, closing my lips around him. While I worked, I felt the cold toilet touching my hair and smelled the disinfectant coming from the floors and the dankness from the shower.

"Now," he said.

I crawled on top and spread my legs. With the first thrust, he went limp. I urged him back to bed, promised we would try another time, but he pleaded, "Give me time."

I lay myself across his lap and we fondled each other. To keep from screaming, I counted the tiles on the wall and the drips from the shower nozzle. Why didn't a nurse stop this?

Count-the-tiles. Anemic tiles, white and cracked. I put my face in his stomach and prayed for strength. Better to have the smell of death, the taste of death, than the evasions. I was finished with evasions. They strangled my life. If I had to fuck death, so be it.

I made my body a shroud; raised myself to kiss his eyes, his mouth, his neck. I wanted to scream. When my father died, I wanted to scream. I refused to cry. The scream stuck in my throat. I took each of David's fingers, his toes, then moved back to his cock. "Try again," he whispered.

He smiled as I mounted him, then bit his lower lip and began again. How careful did you have to be with death? I wondered. I stared at David's hollowed face. I had kissed such a face once before, my father's. A kiss. And then misery. Such misery.

Dripping sweat, I moved my body away from David's. Mustn't let him get hot. Mustn't let him perspire. But, of course, he was. Such costly effort. We rolled and swayed to death's beat until my fury took us over. But so intent was I on every line, every grimace, every sign of rapture, that twice he had to repeat his request.

Only as he tried to change position did I understand. Somehow we managed to get my back on the floor with him between my legs, but not before I saw the look on his face mirror my own panic. Wedged, I could do little to help.

I continued to watch his face and worry about his prick. And how many kinds had I obsessed on? How round? How long? How full? Sometimes only balls mattered. Not with David. What mattered with David? I couldn't remember anymore. Ned's were compact. Compact balls. Compact mind. Was this ever going to be over?

Let it end before I go mad. Let it end before David dies, I prayed to our bodies. Our bodies so valiant and pitiful in their making of spasms. Such extraordinary effort for an ordinary act. And what ordinary words we say. New bodies; same old words. Endearments from a first love passed on and on and on. Worn-out words of love from worn-out lovers. But David called them first. Called them and called them while I called "Anybody there?" and got only echoes and sweet swellings.

And sweet swelling now. We would have my come if not his.

"That's it. That's a good girl." His eyes widened in readiness, just as they always had. Then I gave myself over to the unexpected gift.

He got back into bed without bothering with his pajama bottoms. Fearing we may have done him harm, I opened the door to his room in hopes that someone would check on him, and I pulled a chair over to the bed with my foot. He made some joke about our position in the bathroom being impossible.

"Our most intricate yet," I agreed. Then we laughed and marveled that he hadn't ruined his knees and that we had forgotten to make use of the pillows.

"I was afraid it would be terrible for you," he said, "but I wanted you so much I didn't care. I was completely selfish . . . what I put you through."

"Don't," I protested.

He touched my hair. "I've been worried about you because I can't be here to . . . oh, to give you unconditional love, I guess. That's how it's always felt to me, and that my giving made you dependent on me. The constant man in an inconstant way."

"You don't have to worry. I'll make it now." I stroked his forehead, but he was right about my dependency: most of my adult life he'd gotten to play a version of my father.

Over and over he had provided me with opportunities to lose him and romanticize him and keep the illusion of unstinting love in the background—all the while railing against him. This morning, having reached beyond myself, I'd got beyond old dreams as well.

"You don't need me anymore," he said, anticipating my thoughts. He sounded relieved.

I began. "My mother . . ."

He nodded absently and took my hand. "Stay now." We sat in silence. A nurse came in. He opened his eyes and smiled at her but didn't let go of my hand. I moved away only long enough for him to have his pulse taken and receive an injection. Later, he held on tight even in his sleep.

I lay my face on his bed while he dozed and for a small, blessed while felt beyond grief. Only once did he rouse himself and ask with a grin: "What if we do have nine lives?"

In early afternoon I left. And as I walked for the last time through the hospital parking lot on a sun-crisp November day, I knew I would survive these nightmares, would come to treasure this day, for I had freed myself of all my Davids, my fantasy Davids. Though this wrenching was not the same at all as missing my constant, inconstant friend.

Sudy

We buried my mother under a gentle sun. In the church Joey and Will read Scripture. A minister I did not know spoke words and sentiments that had no meaning to Sudy's life. Aunt Stella said he had been a little intimidated by Sudy Reese. I liked knowing that. By the graveside we sang "Amazing Grace." A second minister whom I did not know said a prayer I did not know.

Out of an old, protective instinct, my aunts and uncles took turns standing by me as they tried to comfort me with their presence, but my comfort came in believing that Sudy would be pleased with me from now on.

More often than not, I had felt the unfolding of my life filled my mother with disappointment. She saw through my trappings—used them as it suited her but refused to be taken in herself. She expected more from me. With my opportunities, she would have dreamed herself a larger world than mine. She understood about courses taken, and she understood about costs. She had never been sure whether I did, and I had had no way of telling her. Our personal vocabulary did not allow for such explanations.

Sorting through my life these last few days, looking for meaning, searching for clues, I had turned to face the signifying of my life through my mother. Running away had served to heighten the guilt, exacerbate the fear, provoke the anger. It also disguised the pain of our separations—and the sure knowledge that she would one day die. Better to leave first. Leave over and over. As I did with everyone. But this time I was the one left behind.

As the minister prayed, the sun fell across me and across my mother's coffin. For a moment we are back on a train—my mother and I—watching two men handle my father's casket.

"That's your daddy," she says, and I wonder where they are taking him. Where do you go in a box? And will he be afraid, all alone in there? How will he know where to go? And how can I ever find him?

Once more that old terror on the train filled me. "What if she's afraid?" I sobbed out loud.

Will put his arm around my shoulder and I became a woman again, composed and filled with mere longing.

After the service I asked the undertaker to open the casket another time. I kissed my mother good-bye and knew I would never understand the mystery of partings. But as I closed the casket, I closed the lid on the pain of my past. Later I stood and watched the undertakers bury her until the earth seemed to expand with her love.

Reckonings

Honey light from the street lamp poured over the rolltop desk as I opened my apartment door, and smoke from a neighboring chimney wavered across the window pane. A rush of regret swept over me, gathered me into itself. I would have to give up this nest of mine, along with my current job, my hard-fought career, my mother, David, Ned.

Stone had withdrawn, right had prevailed, but the implications of my actions had forced themselves upon me. Enough rumors had leaked out to make me *persona non grata* at Pelham and Jackson. Possibly I could still make it in the Southwest, on the local level, but the big leagues were over. I had put Stone in his place, but Pelham and Jackson would put me in mine. During the past few weeks of turmoil, I'd ignored the consequences of my actions, for, much as I moaned at times about my profession, I didn't want to give it up.

Over the years, I had tried to imagine myself in another line of work, but I never came up with anything else I wanted to do. The intrigue, the puzzles, the intensity, the immediacy and maneuvering, suited me. I liked having a hundred problems to think about. I also didn't mind the unsavory nearly as much as I should have. My saboteuring aside, I enjoyed the mischief-making, the sheer aggressiveness of the exercise.

At my desk, with its multiple pigeonholes jammed with keepsakes, notes, and stray objects, I leafed through a stack of bills and letters I hadn't bothered to open on my last two visits here. It was a wonder I still had heat and electricity. These few months I had lived as if a hefty, steady income was an ensured right, almost as if someone else were taking care of me. I hadn't even bothered to look at my bank statement lately. I couldn't afford to think about what I couldn't afford.

White paper napkins were stuffed in a cubbyhole. Why did

229

to accept and I acted badly. Apologizing isn't enough. My mother and David—"

"No, no. Not so fast. Not so fast. Don't change the subject. I want you to know that what you have done is so reprehensible, the word probably hasn't been invented yet that properly describes it. Except maybe—terrorist? Terrorist. Yeah. Maybe that's it. You're a terrorist. A goddamn moral terrorist. No different than some fanatic with a ski mask over his face threatening to blow up a TWA 747. He decides who lives or dies. You decide who lives or dies. You decide whether Mary Cardigan has put the make on that goddamn secretary. And then you decide whether the people of the State of Connecticut will know about it. There is only one God, H.A., only one. The arrogance of your—"

"I am guilty as charged and I know it. I am not trying to defend myself. I admit I was wrong."

"This isn't a Catholic church and I am not your goddamn priest, lady."

"Lady? I hate that."

"I don't give a shit what you hate. I only give a shit that you get it. That you get that rifling through other people's drawers and secrets, violating every conceivable trust that exists in our business, makes you worse than Stone. Do you get it?"

"I get it."

"Bullshit."

I really did get it. But I also realized that it was possible, maybe even a certainty, that I would never convince Ned of that.

"I'm sorry about your mother," he said suddenly.

"Thank you."

"But about that guy . . . As I remember it, he meant nothing to you."

I cringed at his youthful cruelty. He was making it so easy on me. "I lied. He meant a great deal to me."

Ned stood up, jerked his arm in an impatient gesture. "I don't give a rat's ass about ol' David, whoever in the hell he was."

"Stop acting like an asshole and listen."

"You call *me* an asshole? I wish I was quick enough to come up with something clever, the asshole's equivalent of calling the kettle black."

"Try not to make me feel worse than I do."

"Try not to make me worry about some goddamn knight who has your soul while you allow me the use of your body. No thanks."

I plunged on, hoping his pride would make a scant defense against the more outrageous forces in us. I told him about David. Enough, anyway, so the truth wasn't hurtful but wasn't obscured either. I told him how my father's death had started coming back to me.

"The important part," I explained, "was to hold on and not go crazy . . . see it through . . . remember it . . . feel it." I slowed my words before going on. "Through the memories I began to understand how responsible I felt for so much that had gone wrong in Sudy's and my lives, a guilt neither of us had caught on to. I think for a long time my mother was so busy working out her own salvation she had taken mine for granted.

"Then one day she figured out that I was locked in a misery she'd failed to remedy. So she set about making it right for me. And that's why I'm here now. To finish making sense of all this. I hope for both of us."

Before he could respond, I put my fingers to his lips. "I need you, Ned. I've given up those ghosts that kept me from loving you, and I wanted you to know." I stood up and allowed myself to touch his hand. "Whatever you decide, you should respect us both enough to know I would never have come here if you were just a warm body for me."

He stood motionless. I quickly let myself out. In the car I forced my eyes straight ahead. For now, I had said what mattered, and I had Sudy to thank.

Something's

Burning

It took Ned five days and one and a half hours to arrive on my doorstep in Rollins. As I wiped my hands on Sudy's old apron and tried to take in his coming, he stood there shivering, his arms clasped across his chest. The season's first "norther" was blowing in, and to mark that occasion I was preparing an apple strudel and an old-fashioned sauerkraut dish I hadn't made in twenty years.

"Do you want some supper?" I asked, still fussing with the sticky flour on my fingers.

"Don't go to any trouble." The cold air blasted in, but we seemed frozen to the open door. Finally, he unlocked his gaze, releasing mine, and surveyed the scene inside, as if to reassure himself that he had come to the right place and, possibly, found the right woman. Evidently assured, he strode in, headed for the couch, stopped short, and began to straighten the picture of the horses hanging over it.

"This was crooked the last time I was here. I knew you'd never get around to fixing it."

"Thank you for going to this much trouble. I mean if you had faxed me instructions, I could have saved you a trip."

He gave me a wicked look and blew on his hands, red from the cold. Stepping back from the picture he said, "Not bad. It kind of grows on you."

"Kind of." I choked on the words.

"Something's burning," he said, sniffing.

Indeed, the onions for my dish had turned black, and smoke rapidly filled the kitchen area as I belatedly turned on the exhaust fan and ran cold water over the skillet.

"What is this gunk?" he asked. Dabs of dough were strewn over the counter space, with a few bits scattered on the wall.

"Happens every time I make apple strudel."

"I mean this stuff," he explained, pointing to my casserole. "It's not nouvelle cuisine, I feel fairly certain."

"My kraut specialty," I said proudly and began to stir the concoction with a large spoon. "That's sausage," I pointed out, "and that's veal. And the onions were going in here, too." We were standing shoulder to shoulder—as if this were a normal oc-currence, an everyday habit, not some miraculous happening. "The beer, too. Of course, the beer still has to go in, but I don't have any more . . ."

We both stared at the six-pack of empty bottles stashed next to the back door.

"I've talked to Rachel," he said quietly. "She says you had him right. She figured I saw through him, too. I didn't." He went over to the sink. "Where're the Brillo pads?"

"I don't use Brillo on my skillets."

"I bet Sudy did," he said, opening the cabinet and retrieving one from a pail pushed into a corner. He turned on the faucet and began scrubbing. "The day after you left town, Rachel called to tell me she'd left Ralph. She decided it just wasn't worth it anymore. Too many lies. Too much heartache. Apparently there were other women.

"She says I didn't know because I didn't want to know. A lot of people are that way about him. As she pointed out, you don't have to be too swift to pick up on his 'white lies.' Of course, she's right; they ought to have told me something."

Why was he talking about Rachel? Had he come all this way to tell me that he and Rachel were now an item? My stomach did not react well to this bit of speculation.

"Early on you tried to warn me he was a charlatan, and I wouldn't listen." He turned the skillet over and scrubbed its bot-tom even more furiously. We had not looked directly at each other since I met him at the door.

"Over the last few days, I've had to come to grips with what

235

a chicken-shit I am. I'm not saying what you did to Ralph was right; but, at least you did something and you're paying for it with your career. And don't think I don't know how much our foolish way of life means to you. I've seen the look of satisfaction that comes over you in the heat of battle. You love it. I used to wish I could make you look that way." Ned, in a mist of steam from the hot water, attacked the front of the skillet again. Never would it be the same. Neither would I if he didn't hurry and get to the point.

"You sure found a screwed-up way to act on principle, but I wouldn't even acknowledge there was a principle at stake. All week I've been wrestling with my conscience—a little late, but I'm trying; and, honest to God, I don't know what I should have done. After all, the man was worse than your run-of-the-mill bastard; he was a crook."

He dripped the clean skillet across the floor to the stove where he lit a gas burner to dry it. From there he faced me, his eyes finally meeting mine.

"I want you to come back with me. I'm well aware that you don't need my help or anyone else's to pick up the pieces of your life, but I don't do so well without you."

My mouth felt stiff from holding back so much, but I managed to say, "I do need you; I told you."

"After I got over being angry, I realized how hard that admission was for you. Frankly, I didn't think you were capable of reaching out like that."

I could only nod in agreement.

"Do you still mean it now that you know I'll take you up on it?" he asked.

This time I nodded vigorously, but he knew me too well: that part of me is forever wanting to cut and run. At the possibility of real commitment, real love, that devil restlessness started creeping up. But I *had* changed, and I did love Ned.

"I mean it," I finally said, feeling I was taking first-time marriage vows.

With great formality he came toward me and took my hand.

As the space between us closed like magic, he licked my palm and said, "I like unbaked cookie dough."

I licked his chin. "I like day-old stubble."

He pushed my hair back and licked behind my ear. "A fool here for perfume."

"I'm not wearing any," I said before I ran my tongue over his teeth.

He lifted my arm out of the sweater I was wearing and nuzzled that crevice. "Such a nice deodorant," he murmured.

"Rock crystal," I corrected. "I use a rock crystal. But I am unemployed, you know that?"

"I can support you," he said, removing my sweater altogether.

I pulled away to explain: "That's not what I mean. In fact, Sudy left me a lot more money than I ever expected. She was so damn frugal . . . she . . ."

But I couldn't talk about Sudy. I took a breath and continued. "The money will come in handy while I look for a new line of work and get myself back together. The problem is I'll just be hanging around the house a lot . . ."—Ned had unzipped my jeans and was in the process of pulling them down, but I felt he should know the perils of living with me—". . . and that makes me grumpy." I pulled up my foot to untie my sneaker, so my jeans would come off. "I'm not great without structure. I can be hard to get along with, but I'd like to take my time in sorting through where my life is heading. I . . ." I caught myself and smiled. "Do you think I'll ever stop agonizing over what I'm going to do when I grow up?"

"I didn't want to say anything," he said, running his hands down my sides.

"The fact remains I can be mighty hard to get along with, especially when I'm not gainfully employed." Since he was trying to unsnap my teddy, I was no longer sure I was expressing myself coherently.

"You can be hard to get along with under any circumstance. If I weren't crazy about you, I wouldn't stay around for a minute.

You are, if I may say so, one of the most stubborn people I've ever known." I could not get the damn snaps loose. Why did I wear such a thing? I wondered. Maybe I *wanted* a chastity belt. Maybe that was my problem. "Have the women in your family always been so stubborn?"

"Determined. Call us determined," I answered, as the offending garment came undone.

Legacy

"We're getting too old for picnics," Aunt Clara murmurs as she spreads a pallet on the ground for Will's infant boy.

"Hush, Clara!" Aunt Stella scolds. "You're no older than you feel."

"Then I'm a hundred and twenty-two," Uncle Ben says in earnest.

"Stella has a boyfriend," Uncle Curtis teases in a singsong. Because of Aunt Stella, we are indebted to a Mr. Currans, a widower, for the tomatoes and bell peppers in our salad this late June afternoon.

"I'm too old for boyfriends," Aunt Stella answers, not meaning it for one minute.

"Why aren't we having this inside where it's air-conditioned?" Aunt Clara wants to know.

"Clara, if you do any more complaining, you can go home," Aunt Ruth says. "The rest of us are having a good time. What will Beverly and Ned think?"

"I, for one, am honored and grateful to be included in your

family gathering," Bev says. She looks more relaxed and content than she did our first evening eighteen months ago.

"And my only concern is that *you* like me," Ned adds. "It's no secret that H.A. will throw me out if this family stops approving of me."

"No, she won't," Uncle Ben says. "I'll box her ears." Everybody but Uncle Ben laughs.

I put my head on his shoulder. Over the winter his condition has deteriorated; but, since my mother's death, he has taken to fretting about me. Aunt Ruth says he sometimes thinks I'm a little girl again. He has always worried about you, she tells me. In these last few days he has grown fond of Ned and wants him around, too.

Aunt Ruth shoos flies from Aunt Stella's fried chicken. "Did anyone bring bug spray?" she asks.

"Of course we did," Aunt Clara says.

"I don't know why we couldn't have gone to the roadside park outside of town," Uncle Curtis grumbles. "Get more breeze there."

"Stella hates driving on the highway. That's why," Aunt Clara explains.

"I like the city park best," Aunt Ruth puts in. "This is where we've always come. Children especially like it here."

Will is holding his baby, who cries a lot. Will's wife is working this Saturday afternoon and can't come. The marriage was sudden and already it isn't going well. "To be honest," he'd said, "I'm no great shakes as a husband. But I'd hate to lose her. She's the only woman who has ever taken me seriously. Doesn't pat me on the head; doesn't just give lip service to whatever virtues I might have as a man."

"Here, Will," Aunt Clara says. "Let's put the baby on the quilt so we can all watch him."

"Remember those great watermelons you used to get, Uncle Ben?" Will asks and hands over the baby.

"They don't make 'em so good anymore," Uncle Ben answers. "Haven't found a good one in years."

"Oh, Ben, you haven't *tried* to buy one in years," Aunt Ruth corrects.

"You don't know so much," Uncle Ben snaps back. He is getting almost as short-tempered with Aunt Ruth as she is with him.

"Yours used to be great, Dad," Joey soothes. He's home on a visit. Graying now, he looks tired and worries about both Aunt Ruth and Uncle Ben.

Uncle Ben turns to me. "You want some duck and oysters?" he asks. We all laugh as if it is the first time the joke has ever been made. Will tries to explain it to Ned.

"I like this June heat," I say, stretching. "Makes me feel secure."

"H.A. always did talk funny," Aunt Ruth says to Ned in a confidential voice.

"H.A., Ned, you two put on chigger chaser?" Aunt Clara asks.

"Do people still use it?" My tone conveys my disbelief.

"Young lady, Sudy would spank me good if you didn't put this on," Aunt Stella says.

"Her bark was worse than her bite," Uncle Curtis adds.

"My landlord is trying to make me pay the sewer repair," Aunt Stella tells us. "Wouldn't Sudy give him what-for if she knew?"

"Sudy loved picnics," Aunt Ruth says.

I nod in agreement and try to enter their banter. Though I still have a hard time speaking of her, I have changed. I no longer cling as tightly to surfaces. Even so, my mother unaccountably has taken the place of the man in the moon. It is she I most often long for now.

After we have eaten, Ned tosses a softball with my cousins while the rest of us watch and my aunts enjoy their cigarettes. I am grateful and amazed that they are not all dead of lung cancer.

"Look at this evening sky," Aunt Ruth says with the awe of someone discovering sunsets for the first time. "Just look, everybody." The vividness of the reds and purples and blues surrounds us. Holding on to the moment as long as we can, we listen to the lull and whack of a ball from one glove to another. I finger the scarf round my neck covered with small white horses, a gift from Ned, and close my eyes long enough to pull in the magic, not ready to give up such notions altogether.

"I think the mosquitoes are getting worse," Aunt Clara says.

"Don't complain," Aunt Ruth scolds. The baby begins crying. "See what you did, Clara."

"I did not."

Bev picks up Will's fussy baby, and she and I stroll with him away from the group. "So how do you feel about Seattle *really*?" she asks as soon as we're out of earshot.

"Seattle is great. Really. My job? Not so," I answer, flicking my palm up and down. "Corporate accounts just aren't as much fun as politicians, but I'm lucky to stay in any part of the business. And I'm a hero with the environmentalists' groups out there."

"At least, some good word gets around, too," she says, smiling.

"And the good word on you? I can't remember how many of those four lovers you have left now. I never have kept them straight."

"I couldn't either and that was a problem. Now they're all gone. None of them were free on weekends, anyway. I was still stuck feeling lonely, especially after the girls left." We turn back toward the picnic, and Bev hands the baby over to me but continues talking: "But my life has been transformed. Nowadays I'm not worrying about men. While I don't chase them away, I've stopped breaking my heart over them."

"Good for you."

"Good for my poodles! I now have two small ones, the champagne-colored kind I always made fun of. They're at home with me at night. They're always glad to see me. They're good for middle-of-the-night cuddles. Jane thinks they're such a good idea, she's going to get one."

I nudge her with my elbow. "Maybe we should promote this

on a national scale. Cut the loneliness factor overnight."

"Which brings me to how you and Ned are working out."

"Really?"

She shrugs. "As much as you'll tell. I personally do not understand coast-to-coast commutes."

"At first, Ned didn't either. He thought I was looking for an excuse to leave him. But, after a few weeks of having no luck in the job market, I knew I couldn't hang around Boston any longer, no matter how much I loved Ned—and I do love him in a big way. There just wasn't a firm there that would touch me."

"My daughters think you're weird to take a chance on losing a good man like that, and I'm inclined to agree with them."

"The truth is, we are both loners, and this arrangement suits us well. He has taken on a couple of clients out my way now, and I get back for long weekends and sometimes we meet here in the middle. We know every frequent-flier gimmick in the books. We probably average two weeks out of every month together, and that's enough time to spend with someone else—for both of us."

"Do you think you two will marry?"

"Maybe. Maybe soon. We both needed to be sure this arrangement would work."

"I don't think I could marry again," she confided in almost a whisper. "I can't imagine giving up whatever it is I've gained, and I can't imagine a marriage without the giving up. To think otherwise is to kid myself."

"It's complicated," I agree without elaborating on just how complicated the situation sometimes seems. For I still don't always know if I'm doing the right thing. In some early-morning hours I congratulate myself for not running away, for accepting limitations and possibilities as they are, neither enhanced nor discredited. At other times I wonder if I'm not giving in to my old needs and fears, repeating my pattern, however much its guise changes.

As I put the sleeping baby down, Ned comes up behind me and begins massaging my shoulders. At his touch, a rush of joy spreads through me. Lightly with my fingertips I brush the back of his hand. I have taken him at his word and grown easy around him. I trust his acceptance of me, and the trusting has opened worlds that nothing else ever has.

Mostly, I believe my choice comes out of strength.

We are leaving the next morning and with every leaving I grow sad. I need the reassurance of these people, the familiarity of their love; but I've learned to claim the energy I find here and lay hold those values that nourish me even while I'm away. For this place is Sudy, it's David, it's the source of my strength.

"Will, you need to lose some weight," Aunt Stella says to him as he walks toward us. He leans over her chair. "You're sounding more like your sister Sudy every day."

Sudy flows through us all—her pluck, her spirit, her irascibleness. I once thought of us as working on each other like bumper cars hitting and getting hit and no gentle nudging—all without much success at control. Now I see us as more fluid forces, a pouring back and forth, an interweaving of everything, and the violent ruptures gradually wearing down.

"Come on, dear heart," Aunt Ruth says, patting Uncle Ben's hand.

"Where're we going, honey?" Uncle Ben asks, grabbing hold those small, dark fingers extended to him.

"Oh, I don't know," she says and smiles, staring at the first stars. "Maybe downtown."

Kate Lehrer is the author of *Best Intentions*. A Texas native, she lives in Washington, D.C., with her husband.